FORTRESS

THE ROGUE STATE SERIES: BOOK 2

DC ALDEN

ABOVE AND BEYOND

I would like to thank the following for helping me to flesh out my depiction of one of the most mysterious and heavily-defended diplomatic missions in the world.

Ian Hearne (Consilium Risk Strategies)
The Diplomatic Security Service
USMC Embassy Security Group (*In Every Clime and Place*)

And the real Tom Bosco.

Thank you one and all.

"I am concerned for the security of our great nation; not so much because of any threat from without, but because of the insidious forces working from within."

Douglas MacArthur

PROLOGUE

I AM IN HELL.

It was Vann Jackson's immediate thought, as consciousness returned and his eyes opened. A distant memory flickered like a silent movie, his childhood Sunday school in Cheyenne, the preacher's warnings of eternal damnation, of fires, serpents and pitchforks, and the screams of the damned. The cursed were silent, but he could feel the stifling heat, could hear the scampering of rodents in the darkness. And there were bodies.

Lots of them.

He lay somewhere in the middle of the pile, crushed beneath its weight, a slippery mess of fluids leaking across his body. His head was twisted at an angle, the matted hair of another corpse brushing against his mouth. He felt no pain, no fear or revulsion, just the urge to be somewhere else other than entombed by the dead.

He began to move, inch by inch, squirming like a pale, sightless worm, freeing one arm, then another. He clawed and bit, feeling the squelch of putrid flesh beneath his fingernails, between his teeth, as he burrowed and gnawed his way out of the rotting heap. He slipped out onto the concrete floor, given new life by the festering womb behind him, drenched in the afterbirth of purification. He slapped a wet hand against the wall and clambered to his feet. He swayed in the darkness like a newborn foal. He was alive; he knew that much, but his consciousness extended no further. He could feel and taste, could see, smell and hear, but whoever he'd been, whatever he'd known, was lost.

Hell had a door.

He found the handle and shouldered it open, staggering along a dark corridor. Ahead, a square of bright light cut through the shadows. He headed towards it. Glass crunched under his bare feet. He looked up through the broken window. Blinding sunlight burned his eyes, and he hissed, scampering back into the shadows. He heard a cackle behind him, saw something shift in the pile of corpses. They mocked him, his fear, the way he cowered from the light like a frightened child. He snarled and reached up for the window ledge. Glass teeth chewed his fingers as he pulled himself up and out into a new world.

Overhead the sun was hot, prickling his skin. He was struck by the familiarity of the colours and shapes that surrounded him, the clay-coloured buildings, the grey concrete walls, the yellow sand that drifted across the black tarmac roads. He knew this place, but his memories of it were fleeting, nothing more than sparks of recollection that faded as quickly as they appeared. He squatted on his haunches as he emptied his bowels. He watched the road, breath rattling in his lungs.

He saw a figure, then another, entering a building across the street. They wore patterned clothing, and once again the silent reel flickered in his mind. He remembered a struggle, the crack of gunfire, the stabbing pain. He stood up and twisted around, using a filthy fingernail to explore the rip in the flesh of his buttock. The nail dug deep, but instead of pain he felt something else, something rushing to escape. He doubled over, spewing a gush of fluid onto the dirt, a mixture of blood and yellow pus. He reached out and steadied himself against the wall. The world swam before his eyes. His body was failing, instinct told him that much. It needed repair.

A noise penetrated the blood and crust in his ears, a low whine that grew louder, and then it hummed into view, a small vehicle, stopping outside the opposite building. His eyes narrowed. There was something about that structure that called to him, something that promised to heal his wounds. It would numb the pain behind his eyes and give him the strength he craved, a strength that would lend itself to the fury building in his chest, a rage that ground his teeth and tightened every muscle in his body until it ached. A rage that screamed for release.

He headed towards the building, staying out of the sun, keeping to the shadows. Others drifted towards its doors, creatures pale and dark, many of them clothed in that familiar pattern, their voices piercing his head, forcing him to crouch in the shadows, to chew his tongue and stifle the scream of rage, to beat his fists against the dirt until they were caked and bloodied. He panted in the wake of his efforts, reminded again of the urgent need for food. Images flickered through his mind, a montage of dead flesh and wriggling worms, of rotting fruit and animal carcasses. His empty stomach moaned, and a silvery rope of hunger dangled from his jaw.

He clambered to his feet, saw that the path to the building was now clear. He stepped out of the shadows and onto the burning tarmac, feet slapping as he scampered towards the door. Cool air washed over him, and the sensation energised him, his bare legs driving him forward. He moved along the hallway, quickly now, the smells that bombarded his nostrils filling him with both hunger and revulsion.

He turned a corner and stopped in front of a set of double doors. Beyond them he could hear the noises made by the creatures inside and an uncontrollable rage replaced the hunger. He cuffed saliva from his mouth, his fists bunching and flexing, the fury, the adrenaline, flooding his body.

He heard whistling behind him, the squeak of rubber on the floor, the footfalls approaching fast.

His breathing quickened.

He put his hand on the door and entered the creatures' nest.

CHAPTER 1
VANN THE WILD MAN

The girl across the aisle looked at him and smiled.

Doug Walker's cup froze halfway to his mouth. He turned away, sipped his coffee and then turned back. The girl was still smiling, a cute blonde, decked out in combat pants and a green T-shirt. She was young, mid-twenties maybe, her hair cut short, like a model. And just as pretty too.

Is she smiling at me? Doug glanced to his right; the guy chowing down a couple of seats away probably weighed about two-fifty, most of it blubber. He turned back. Now the girl was grinning. He offered a polite smile and refocused on his eggs. Flattered as he was, the girl was a sudden and painful reminder of Holly; same age, same mischievous grin. That youthful promise would have left her by now.

He turned his attention to the giant TV screen on the wall. Back at home, things were messy. The President had been impeached, and dozens of politicians, military chiefs and establishment figures were now languishing in jail. Details were still sketchy, and according to the media, they were all involved in some giant Wall Street scandal. The political fallout continued to ripple around the globe.

The well-groomed news anchor was speculating about

Presidential succession and the stable of current contenders. Doug imagined the political dance going on in DC right now would be—

The ear-splitting screech behind him was so loud, so primal, that Doug thought a wild animal was loose inside the commissary. His body spasmed as if he'd been shocked.

A woman screamed.

Everything moved in slow motion.

His head snapped left. He saw a naked guy scrambling over a table across the aisle, falling on top of the blonde girl, both crashing to the floor in an avalanche of crockery, breakfast trays and cutlery. He watched the man mount her, his face twisted in fury, neck veins bulging, his fists thudding into her face like pistons—

Doug's world spun back up to real time. He lurched to his feet, just as the attacker disappeared beneath a wave of bodies. The crowd pinned the man's thrashing limbs to the ground as he continued to spit and scream, his head coming off the tiled floor, eyes bulging, teeth snapping, the sound from his throat barely human. Doug felt the hair rising on his neck.

Everyone in the commissary was on their feet. Diplomats in shirts and ties, maintenance crews in coveralls, Marines from the Embassy Security Group. Even the cooks had spilled out from the kitchen, a gaggle of chefs' whites crowding the hotplates.

"Medic!" a chorus of voices hollered.

Doug moved a little closer, saw a couple of uniforms administering first aid to the victim. Her attacker lay close by, his thick dark hair caked with dirt, his beard crusted with blood and saliva. He looked and sounded like a wild man, almost primordial. Then he vomited, spraying his captors with yellow bile. Doug took several steps back. The wild man bucked and heaved, his head thrashing left and right. The guys pinning him down were struggling to keep him there. Doug winced.

Two Marines backed up the onlookers and the uniformed females helped the girl into a chair. Her hands shook, flapping like beached fish in her lap. He heard someone call her *Walsh*. Her good eye fluttered open, moist, bloodshot. The other remained closed, the side of her face already horribly swollen and flecked with bloody saliva. A broken cheekbone, maybe an eye socket too, Doug guessed. When she spoke, her throat rattled.

"I didn't do anything. I swear to God—"

She threw up all over the woman kneeling in front of her. Doug cringed and looked away. Must be the shock kicking in. He had a sudden vision of Holly being beaten in a filthy alleyway and his stomach lurched.

"Make a hole!"

Gurney-wheeling medics sliced through the onlookers. They worked on Walsh for several minutes, then loaded her onto the gurney and wheeled her out of the room. It took a little longer to restrain and stabilise her attacker, then he got evacuated too. The commissary doors swung shut and a buzz filled the room.

People huddled together and traded viewpoints. Doug looked down. The floor was smeared with food, blood and vomit. Med wrappers lay scattered across the linoleum like confetti after a bizarre and violent union. Maybe they were lovers, Doug speculated. Maybe Walsh had screwed the guy over. Still, no one deserved that.

"Stand fast!"

A phalanx of suits and uniforms filed into the commissary. They were led by Tom Bosco, the embassy's Regional Security Officer. Doug had met him only once when he'd first arrived in-country. Bosco had issued Doug with his Special Access Program credentials and the man had seemed pretty bad-tempered. Doug figured that anyone responsible for security at an embassy located deep in hostile territory might not be a barrel of laughs, but as he watched the glowering Bosco listening to witness accounts, he decided that pissed off was the man's natural disposition.

The sandy-haired RSO stood with his legs apart, fists bunched on his hips, an ID lanyard dangling over a sweat-stained white shirt, a dark tie tugged from his neck. He was a few inches shorter than the heavy-set Marine he was talking to, but in terms of authority, he was the tallest man in the room. Bosco was flanked by two of his own Diplomatic Security team and a grizzly looking Non-Com.

"Show's over," Bosco barked across the commissary. "Enlisted personnel, leave your names at the door." He had a mid-west accent, and Doug thought he might be from Minnesota, or one of the Dakotas.

"You heard the man. Move it!" the Non-Com growled. He cocked his shaven head towards the commissary doors, now flanked by two of Bosco's staff armed with clipboards and pens. The uniforms complied without question, forming an obedient line towards the exit. Bosco turned to the remaining onlookers.

"The rest of you grab a seat. I'll need statements."

Doug righted his chair and sat down, the food on his breakfast tray no longer appetising. He pushed it aside and checked his watch. A little after eight. He thought about Walsh and hoped she was okay.

He toyed with his coffee cup, his heart still beating fast inside his chest. More people entered the commissary, clerical types in shirts and slacks, weaving between tables and handing out yellow legal pads and pencils. Doug took one of each and wrote his name at the top. Across the room, Bosco was still growling instructions.

"Make them concise and to the point, people. Just what you saw and heard. Let's go." He punctuated his words with several sharp handclaps. Doug put pen to paper.

"Jesus Christ, did you see that shit?"

Freddie Cruz flopped into the seat opposite Doug. The thirty-something power plant engineer was a native of New Mexico. His normally neat black hair was all messed up, his face puffy and red. He wore tan-coloured maintenance coveralls over a white T-shirt, the sleeves bunched at the elbows. He scribbled his name on a legal pad, then tapped the pencil on the table in a nervous tattoo. "You hear that dude scream?"

"You're bleeding," Doug told him, pointing to his hand.

"Damn." Freddie cuffed the blood on the leg of his coveralls, revealing an angry-looking crescent of puncture wounds below his pinkie. "Fucking guy bit me."

"What?"

"For real." Freddie winced as he dabbed at the wound with a napkin. "I saw him outside, running across the road like a goddam ape, all dirty an' shit. I thought the guy was fooling around. Next thing I know he's in here, going loco. I grabbed hold of an arm and hung on. That's when he bit me. Creeped me out, dude." He pulled a gold crucifix from under his T-shirt and kissed it, tucking it back beneath the sweat-stained collar.

"At least he didn't barf on you."

Freddie shook his head. "That was fucking disgusting, bro. That shit stank."

Doug tapped Freddie's pad with his pencil. "Write it all down."

Freddie was shaken up. So was Doug, but he was doing a better job of hiding it.

It didn't take him long to finish his statement and hand it off to a passing pen-pusher. He'd kept it brief, and besides, there wasn't that much to say. A scream, a vicious assault, that was pretty much it. He tried not to think about Walsh's flapping hands.

Two men strode into the room and everyone stopped to watch.

"D-Boys," Freddie whispered.

Delta's presence at the embassy wasn't a secret anymore. Doug frowned as he tried to recall the big guy's name. *Roth*, that was it. He'd seen him in the Chancery a few days ago, heard Bosco call his name.

The Delta commander stopped right by their table. He was tall, wide-shouldered and square-jawed, with unkempt blond hair and a beard to match. Like a Viking quarterback, Doug thought. He ran a hand through his own dark hair, across the stubble of his face, the skin on his arms that had burned brown beneath the hot Iraqi sun. Freddie often joked that Doug was turning native.

The man alongside Roth was shorter, a tough looking Italian-American who sported a thick, drooping moustache. Roth's number two, Doug guessed. They resembled the Special Forces guys he'd often seen portrayed in movies; unkempt hair and beards, dressed in an insubordinate mix of military and civilian clothes. They were lean and hard muscled, not gym-pumped like some of the Marines, and they walked with the confidence of guys at the top of their game. Through no fault of their own, SEALS had gone Hollywood; Delta were still ghosts. He watched Roth wrinkle his nose at the mess on the floor, then beckon Bosco outside. The doors closed behind them and the buzz of conversation returned to the room.

Doug recalled the moment Delta had flown in, almost a week ago. He'd woken from a nightmare about Holly, so he'd left his room an hour before dawn and went for a run around the vast, deserted embassy. That's when he'd heard approaching rotors, had watched the black Chinook barrel right over him and set down on one of the compound's helipads. Curiosity had got the better of him, and Doug had moved closer, creeping between the cars in the adjacent parking lot.

He watched from the shadows as the helicopter disgorged

a belly full of soldiers before lifting off and banking out over the Tigris. The troops had double-timed across Main Street and filed into a huge tent set up on one of the chow-hall basketball courts. He'd heard the high-pressure hoses, had glimpsed the line of semi-naked men carrying their kit and weapons into the adjacent building. It had been a bizarre sight, and a troubling one too. Doug knew what a decontamination team looked and sounded like. By the time the sun had risen, the tent had gone and the embassy headcount had increased by another forty guys.

"So, what do you think?"

Doug shifted his focus back to Freddie. "About what?"

"About all the crazy shit that's happening."

"It was probably some kinda domestic."

"I mean the President being busted, everyone leaving the embassy. Word is the other embassies have cleared out too. Then Delta arrives in the dead of night and no one knows why. That's the shit I'm talking about."

"You thinking twice about staying?" Doug asked.

Freddie shrugged. "I wasn't prepared for the scale of the problems out here, man. This place is seriously fucked up." Then he leaned in close and winked, the familiar smile returning, his teeth whiter than driven snow. "Truth is, they're paying me double time plus bonus just to keep the lights on. You think I'm giving that up, you're crazier than that hairy dude."

Doug smiled. "Only double? They bought you cheap."

"They bought my Navigator, man, fully loaded." The Latino's smile faded, his fingers toying with the cross around his neck. "I won't be sorry to leave this place. It's kinda creepy, all deserted an' shit. Feels like there's something in the wind, you know?"

Doug heard the scrape of a bucket, the slap of wet mops on the floor. Kitchen orderlies were straightening chairs and cleaning up the mess. Beyond the hotplates, the cookhouse crew had disappeared into the kitchen. Doug finished his coffee and stood.

"You should get that bite looked at."

"It's just a scratch, man."

"Technically it's a workplace injury. You should log it, cover your ass."

"Sure."

"I'll catch you later."

Doug left the commissary to find a hungry and curious crowd gathered behind a ribbon of security tape. The sun was climbing into the sky, its heat tempered by a rare breeze. He slapped a once-white Patriots cap on his head and flipped his Oakley's down. That's what the desert did, Doug had learned. The heat was an oppressive hammer and sweat a permanent fixture. And it was still only May. He wasn't looking forward to high summer when temperatures could reach a hundred and twenty degrees. Still, he was grateful for that breeze.

His State Department buggy was parked in the adjacent lot, and he twisted the key and stamped his sneaker on the pedal, leaving the commissary behind him. He turned onto Main Street and headed west, the tarmac shimmering in the building heat.

He drove past the State Department accommodation blocks, his eye drawn to the single Black Hawk helicopter that squatted on its pad, its drooping rotor blades tied down, its engine intakes plugged with dust covers, the cockpit screened off from the burning sun. Every day the crew fired up the engines and every day they shut them right back down again. Poor guys must be bored stiff, Doug thought.

Dozens of vehicles were scattered across the adjacent parking lot, their tyres and windshields gathering sand. There was nowhere for them to go and no one to drive them. The embassy was closed, period.

He passed the Consulate on his right, also closed for business. The Chancery building lay dead ahead, the administrative heart of the United States embassy in Baghdad, the Stars and Stripes on the pole outside fluttering in the breeze.

The building itself was four storeys tall and protected by thick walls, ballistic glass and crowned with black anti-mortar screens on the roof. Doug swung the buggy around the back of the building and parked in the shade of a blast wall. The main doors were heavy, reinforced with steel and Kevlar, and strong enough to withstand a mob armed with sledgehammers and crowbars, someone had told him. If things ever got that bad, Doug didn't give much for his or anyone else's chances.

He yanked one open and stepped inside the security lobby. To his right was a steel and glass booth staffed by three Marines. Doug passed his bag through an x-ray machine as the Marines bid him good morning. He strolled past the booth and swiped through the inner doors, into the diplomatic heart of the embassy.

A heart that had pretty much stopped beating.

The atrium was an impressive chamber of glass walls that climbed up to the top level. Doug crossed the marbled floor and circumnavigated the Great Seal of the United States inlaid into one of the huge tiles. It was disrespectful not to, in Doug's opinion. There were few people around, either walking the atrium or in the offices above. Since the evacuation, the embassy was barely ticking over.

He swiped into Service Corridor A and walked twenty-five meters to another security door. His Special Access Programs card made short work of the security. From this point on he was in highly restricted territory.

The concrete stairwell beyond took him down into the most sensitive area of the whole installation. He paused in the gloom of Sub-Level One, waiting for the proximity sensors to trip the lights of the access corridor. He glanced over the handrail. The stairs led down to another level, one submerged in darkness, and Doug wondered if that was the Safe Haven, the final defensive position should the embassy be overrun. It was a frightening thought, trapped deep below ground, no way out, the enemy running amok above.

He shook off the thought as he stopped outside The Hub. He thumbed the biometric reader, blinked for the iris scan and swiped his access pass, a three-phase security process designed to keep almost everyone out of the room he was about to enter. The door hummed and clicked.

Doug shouldered it open. The Hub was a communications network centre crammed with high-tech servers, routers and switches that connected the facility to the outside world. He sat down at an empty desk and unpacked his laptop. He opened the automated email he received every morning, the one that listed the various fault conditions of all the systems that fell under his jurisdiction. The list wasn't huge, and he saw that most of the fault conditions were informational only. Today would be an easy day.

He punched a few commands and checked his watch. It was a little after nine am. Maybe he would hit the pool later, or run the perimeter. Either way, he would try to keep himself busy, bank another day's pay, and try not to think about the lives he'd destroyed back home.

CHAPTER 2
THE CANDIDATE

The cell phone rumbled across the nightstand, insistent.

US Secretary of State Amy Coffman rolled over and snatched at the instrument that had interrupted a particularly thrilling dream. She'd been the focus of attention in an opulent ballroom, well-wishers in chic evening wear pressing in to congratulate her for something she couldn't quite remember. She'd grasped hands and kissed cheeks, and flash-bulbs lit up a sea of smiling, expectant faces. Someone had gushed, *Madam President...*

She snapped the bedside lamp on and fumbled with her glasses. It was Erik, and it was damned early.

"Please tell me this is of vital national importance, Erik."

"I'm on my way over," her Chief of Staff replied.

Coffman's eyes flicked to the bedside clock. "Now?"

"I'm fifteen minutes out."

"Raymond will show you up."

She kicked back the covers and climbed out of bed. It took two minutes to shower, another ten to fix her hair and apply face creams and body lotions and the lightest of makeup touches. She studied her reflection in the mirror. She looked good for fifty-two, considering the unrelenting treadmill of politics. Her dark brown hair showed little grey, the skin around her eyes and neck still tight and smooth. There were some lines of course, but a good diet, a little exercise and some very expensive skin care products helped keep the ravages of middle-age at bay. Her wardrobe was an asset too, the designer labels tailored to her lean frame.

She chose one such outfit from her walk-in wardrobe, white Fendi sweatpants and matching roll-neck top, the kind of high-end clothing that would never see the inside of a health club. She slipped white sandals on her feet, an Oyster Rolex over her wrist, then headed downstairs.

Erik Mulholland waited for her in the drawing room. Her Chief of Staff was dressed in sneakers, jeans and a dark coat, his thick grey hair bed-messy, a masculine shadow around his strong jaw. Scruffy-chic suited him, Coffman decided. Such a pity he was gay.

"Morning, ma'am."

Coffman waved him onto a sofa and snatched at the wall phone. "Coffee please, Raymond." She held a hand over the mouthpiece. "You want English muffins?" Mulholland shook his head. "And English muffins." She hung up the phone. "You should eat," she told him, settling into an elegant wing-backed chair. Of all the rooms in her luxury Georgetown mansion, the drawing room was by far her favourite. It was warm and intimate and decorated with traditional furniture. Coffman loved the details, the delicate sweep of dark woods, the smoothness of silk coverings, the hues and shades of imported rugs and period art. It made her feel important, regal almost. She'd always had a taste for finery, something that went hand in glove with her other obsession in life: power.

A white-coated African-American steward arrived, resting a breakfast tray on the table between them. Coffman dismissed him and poured two coffees into delicate china cups. She scraped a wedge of butter onto a well-toasted muffin and leaned back in her chair.

"So, what's the emergency?" she asked, taking a bite and savouring the taste of warm butter in her mouth.

Mulholland tapped the cell phone in his hand. "We have a problem at the embassy."

Coffman took a moment to process the information. As Secretary of State, she was responsible for every United States diplomatic facility across the globe. And it was still very early.

"Be specific, Erik."

"Baghdad."

Coffman's muffin froze halfway to her mouth. She set it back on the china plate and waited. Mulholland took his cue.

"A naked man entered the commissary and launched an unprovoked attack against a female military specialist. She was badly injured."

Coffman raised an eyebrow. "You woke me for a domestic dispute?"

"The assailant's name is Vann Jackson. He's Delta." He handed her his cell phone. "Take a look."

At first, it was difficult to see what she was looking at; a room cast in shadow, a bed, a figure squirming beneath a sheet. Then someone threw a light switch.

The figure in the bed bucked violently, straining and thrashing as much as the heavy restraints that secured his limbs would allow. The sheet slipped off his body and Coffman saw it was a man, bearded, his dark hair wild and matted, the sounds that leaked through the mask over his mouth inhuman, animalistic. His eyes bulged and his skin appeared translucent, the veins beneath clearly visible. The medical gown he wore was spattered with blood. On either side of him, a couple of soldiers in grey protective suits and Perspex face shields were trying to administer a hypodermic shot without success. The footage ended abruptly.

Coffman swallowed. "What the hell's wrong with him?'

"Undetermined viral brain infection, according to Doctor Veronica Hays. She's the Chief Medical Officer in Baghdad." He dropped a large brown envelope on the table between them. "That's a hard copy of the report Bill Jacobs cabled to your Inbox an hour ago. It includes supplemental statements from the Delta commander and Captain Young."

"Remind me who Young is."

"She heads up the Twenty-First Chemical Company. The decontamination team that went out with the advance party."

Coffman stared at the envelope as if it contained anthrax. "Does it make any recommendations?"

Mulholland nodded. "An immediate deployment of USAMRIID's bio-containment team to Iraq. CDC's outbreak response team too."

"For one patient?"

"It's not just Jackson. The woman he attacked, Walsh, is also infected. Hays has got them squirrelled away in a secure warehouse, along with a dozen other personnel who came into direct contact. She believes there are more. The cover story is viral meningitis."

"Are you telling me that Delta brought this back from *Messina*?"

"Correct. Seems Jackson went off-mission, got himself wounded and kept his mouth shut. Whatever he caught down in those labs has turned him into some kind of homicidal maniac."

"Jesus Christ."

"Hays has sealed off the Chancery as a precaution. She's also recommending a facility-wide lockdown and Jacobs is supporting that decision. He's briefing Ashcroft and key personnel on *Messina* too. It's all in the report."

"Jacobs doesn't have the authority."

"Ashcroft and his leadership team will need to know. That can't be avoided."

"Who else has seen this report?"

"Jacobs sent it straight to Crisis Management. Karen's sitting on it until she hears from you."

Coffman settled back into her chair, relieved. Karen Baranski was one of her favoured disciples. A decade of slavish devotion to the Coffman cause had earned Baranski the Crisis Management lead at the State Department's Operations Centre, the global communications hub that linked Coffman with every US diplomatic mission in the world. Baranski was a junkyard dog, fierce, loyal, more so now that her boss was a strong favourite to win the White House.

"This isn't Angola," Mulholland warned, "it's something else, something they missed at *Messina*. This could have serious global implications." Mulholland paused for a moment. When he spoke again he softened his tone. "They'll expect you to manage this, Amy. It'll mean ruling yourself out of the presidential race—"

"No."

Coffman wanted to hurl the phone at Mulholland's chiselled face, but instead she re-ran the video several times, pausing, rewinding, freeze-framing. It was grotesque, like something from a particularly disturbing horror movie. Jackson was barely contained, the force of his exertions jolting the bed off the floor. And his skin, the veins and sinews, muscles bulging and contracting in a way she'd never seen before. Blood from the man's mouth soaked his mask.

"And Hays thinks this thing has spread?"

"Yes."

"The embassy is still operating under a communications blackout, correct?"

Her Chief of Staff nodded. "Essential diplomatic, military and logistical traffic only. Baghdad is a black hole."

Coffman handed the phone back to Mulholland.

"Then we have an opportunity."

Mulholland tapped the report on the table. "Amy, the only

play we have is to kick this thing up to the Congressional Committee and the Pentagon. You've seen the video; whatever Jackson is infected with it's a whole different ball game. We have responsibilities here." He leaned back in his chair. "Four years isn't such a long time. We can build something special from the ground up. I know a great campaign manager who's about to jump ship from—"

"Stop talking, Erik."

Coffman got to her feet and wandered over to the window. Normally she enjoyed quiet moments like these, the stillness of the world outside, the promise of a new day. And more often than not, new opportunities. Her breath fogged the glass.

"The American people are growing increasingly uneasy about the empty chair in the Oval Office. They see the Crisis Committee and the Pentagon holding the reins of power and fear they might not let go. The people need a restoration of faith in the Office of the President. In democracy." She paused for a moment, then said, "What they need is a leader."

"And in less than a month they'll have one, but you can't ignore this thing in Baghdad. If you continue campaigning, your opponents will destroy you for putting personal ambition over duty of office, and the public will agree. Your numbers will fall through the floor."

Coffman watched a bird swoop through the air and settle on the lawn below. It stabbed its yellow beak into the earth, head swivelling for predators, before taking off and disappearing into the trees. She turned to face her Chief of Staff, her arms folded across her chest.

"What are my chances, Erik?"

"Ma'am, I think we should focus on—"

"Humour me," she ordered.

Mulholland considered the question as he took a careful sip of coffee. "Well, the reality is you should be thanking our former President. His involvement in the Angola conspiracy has handed you State and cleared the line of succession. The VP's in jail, along with the Speaker, and the Senate President and Sec State both ate a bullet. The Attorney General has ruled himself out on health grounds and Sec Def's stroke has ended his career. You and Warner finished top of the party nomination ballot and both your hats are still in the ring."

"Keep going," Coffman urged.

"Smart money says you've got the edge. Lew and Burwell are pretty solid as far as Republicans go. Both have good records in state government and public service, but they don't have your experience and they're weak on foreign policy. Warner may be a party grandee but he's too stale and old school; our polling is telling us that voters aren't connecting with him. Thankfully you didn't belong to the Presidents' inner circle so that can't hurt you, and the conspirators were mostly men, which plays well for you because you're the only woman in the race. Right now, I'd put your chances at seventy percent. If you're on your game, seventy-five, maybe eighty. There's a buzz building around you, Amy. It's a real shame."

Coffman turned back to the window. She was so close now, and never had the presidential field of play been so level. All that stood between her and the White House were three national televised debates. There would be no corporate or personal endorsements, no multi-million-dollar advertising campaigns, no primaries or caucuses, just the TV cameras, a studio audience and four lecterns. The candidates, two Democrats and two Republicans, would then have the opportunity to prove their suitability for office and share their personal vision for America with the rest of the country.

The first of those debates would take place in ten days' time, the last, three weeks after that. The nation would then go to the polls and the Electoral College would announce the results shortly afterwards. The Twelfth Amendment had been duly revised, the election timeline crunched, so that the next

President of the United States could take office quickly and lay a steady hand on America's tiller. A hand that was urgently needed.

Coffman glanced at the office door. It was solid mahogany, beautifully engraved—and soundproof.

"How long do you think it'll be before someone talks, Erik? Before the world discovers that the financial scandal story is bullshit?"

Mulholland shrugged. "Not much longer, I guess."

"Exactly. And when Americans discover that their beloved President and half the Executive branch were conspiring to unleash a modern-day Holocaust on their own people, they will be angry and terrified. Their trust in government—*any* form of government—will vanish overnight. Law and order will crumble, and waiting in the wings will be General Moody and his shiny new North American Command Group, ready to park his tanks on the White House lawn and his boots under the Resolute desk. That will be the day the Constitution dies."

Coffman saw the look on her Chief of Staff's face and smiled. "Relax, Erik. I'm not about to start beating a drum or waving a flag. If we have to gush about the Bill of Rights in front of the TV cameras, then so be it, but if the truth does come out and the country spirals out of control, democracy will be obsolete and you and I will be reduced to mere spectators."

Coffman turned back to the window. The sun was rising now, filtered by the surrounding trees, throwing smoky bars of yellow light across the grass. This dawn had indeed brought with it another opportunity, another test of her political dexterity. Her foresight had proved accurate, a clear validation of her suitability for high office, but it was her next move that would decide her fate.

Coffman felt a momentary shiver. She was so close to the top, the summit in sight, but a storm had blown in all the way from Baghdad, threatening to paralyse her advance. She had two choices; hunker down and ride it out, or push on.

"The infection must be allowed to spread."

"What?"

"You heard me, Erik."

Mulholland sprang to his feet and joined Coffman at the window. "You can't do that," he whispered. "People might die. That'll be on your head."

"Not true. In fact, we're the victims here."

Mulholland raised an eyebrow. "How d'you figure that?"

Coffman gave him a hard stare. "Think about it—why order Delta to Baghdad at all? Why not fly them straight back to Kuwait after they took out the Messina labs?"

"Moody wanted the team to remain in-country, remember? Some kind of Quick Reaction Force, in case they were needed to mop up elsewhere."

"I do remember, and I didn't believe it then, either."

She turned back to the window. She also remembered the meeting in the conference room, deep below the Pentagon. She remembered the uniforms around the table, their urgent insistence that she evacuate her embassy in preparation for the *Messina* operation and its aftermath. She remembered the patronising looks, the whispered conversations behind blue-veined hands, the class-rings that winked beneath the bright overheads. It all made sense now.

"They knew something might go wrong," she said. "Yes, they had solid intelligence, and yes, everyone was inoculated for Angola, but did they really *know* what they were cooking up in that lab? I doubt it. So, they took out a little insurance, just in case. And where better to dump any potential problems than the Baghdad embassy? A self-contained fortress located deep in the heart of what those assholes would call a *hostile environment*."

"C'mon, Amy, that's just speculation."

"Really? They couldn't drop a fucking bomb?" Coffman

snapped. "Ten bombs? *Messina* was in the middle of nowhere."

"They were concerned about the fallout, remember?"

"That makes no sense, Erik. They had the antidote." She shook her head. "Now they've delivered an unknown bio-weapon into the heart of the Iraqi capital, a city of seven million inhabitants. Imagine if that virus jumps the embassy walls. Tens of thousands might be infected, millions forced to flee. How do you think that will play on the international stage?"

Mulholland took that one on the chin. "Not well," he admitted.

"Right. And if that happens, the UN will implement their Resolution. As Secretary of State, I'll be expected to manage the ensuing chaos."

"The *Messina* operation wasn't your call."

Coffman glared at her Chief of Staff. "You think that matters. Erik? My embassy, my problem, that's how this will go. I'll be expected to clear up the diplomatic dog shit, and any hopes we had of taking the White House will be gone. Permanently."

"You're wrong," Mulholland argued. "The administration will want to keep a lid on this, as will the Security Council. We're talking about what, a dozen victims? It can be managed."

Coffman ticked off the fingers on her hand. "One, you can't possibly make that judgement, and two, do you really think the Iraqis won't notice American bio-warfare teams landing in Baghdad? No," she snapped, "I will not go down with that ship while everybody else watches from the goddam lifeboats."

She took a deep, calming breath and folded her arms. Her mind was made up, but she couldn't do this alone. She had allies, yes, but she *needed* Erik. His loyalty had always been unswerving, the imposition of her will the primary goal of his political function, yet as she watched him stroke his unshaven jawline she could understand his reluctance. This was, without doubt, the biggest gamble either of them had ever undertaken. When she spoke again, she kept her voice calm and confident.

"Granted, people may die in the short term, but that's out of our control. What we *can* control is the narrative, which will put us back on course for the White House."

"By allowing this virus to spread? How can you control something like that, for Chrissakes? There are too many moving parts."

"Not necessarily," she said, stepping past him and taking a seat on the couch. "You need to trust me on this, Erik."

She smiled, and Coffman watched her Chief of Staff's eyes narrow as the penny dropped. He crossed the room and sat opposite her.

"Wait a minute. You've gamed this out already?"

"The moment they commandeered my embassy. And I took out a little insurance of my own."

"What are you talking about?"

Coffman drilled him with an unblinking gaze. "I need to know you're with me, Erik."

Mulholland looked crushed. "Jesus, of course I'm with you, Amy."

"Good, because I can't do this alone."

"I'll need to know the whole playbook."

"Absolutely."

"So, what's next?"

"We sit on this virus thing for as long as possible. Moody and the others will find out in due course, so we need to stack the deck before that happens."

"What are we talking about here?"

Coffman smiled. "We're talking about poor leadership, bad decisions, panic and chaos. A cocktail of political opportunity."

Mulholland gave his boss a hard stare. "Sometimes you scare the shit out of me, Amy."

She reached across the table and squeezed his hand. "I'll take that as a compliment. Now, get back to Ops and tell Karen to put a lid on everything coming out of Baghdad. And I want you to call Bill Jacobs personally. Tell him that his report has been received and impress upon him the need for absolute secrecy. No calls to anyone until he hears from my office."

"Yes, ma'am." Mulholland got to his feet.

"And put something in today's diary, something that'll buy me a few hours."

"I'm on it."

The Chief of Staff left the room. Coffman heard his car start outside, then accelerate away as it pulled out onto Woodland Drive. She grabbed a dark raincoat from the ground floor cloakroom, crossed the stillness of the main reception room and stepped out onto the patio. She skirted the manicured lawn, still cloaked by the pre-dawn gloom of the surrounding trees.

The outbuilding was close to the boundary wall, built with red brick like the main house, and partially hidden by dense shrubbery. Coffman let herself in, negotiating sheeted stacks of garden furniture until she stood in front of a rusted iron wood burner. She reached behind it, fished out a crumpled pack of Marlboro Lights and a book of matches. There was dry wood stacked inside the burner and she used a match to light it, keeping the flame alive to fire up a rare cigarette. She perched herself on the edge of an upturned tea chest and let the smoke drift lazily from her mouth.

As she watched the flames build, she reflected on the risk she was about to take. Lives would be lost, that was a certainty, but after the speeches and memorials, no one would care too much. Civilians who volunteered for hazardous overseas duties were generally well compensated, and anyone in uniform knew the risks of service. She felt no sympathy for either so, no, it wasn't the expected body count that gave her pause. It was the gamble itself.

She took a long, slow draw of her cigarette, savouring the hit of nicotine at the back of her throat. Erik was right, the sensible play would be to call General Moody immediately, drop this bombshell right in his holier-than-thou lap. Her presidential ambitions would immediately wither on the vine but her participation in the handling of the crisis might pay political dividends further down the road.

Might.

And that depended on the crisis being managed appropriately. If it wasn't then heads would roll, blame apportioned, and the stench of scandal and failure would follow her around for the rest of her professional life. The thought chilled her.

No, there was only one way to deal with the situation in Baghdad.

She'd made her first phone call the moment she'd walked out of the Pentagon, had met secretly with trusted friends and allies in the days that followed, her confidence boosted by their pledges of unswerving loyalty. She congratulated herself on her foresight, her certainty that the boys and girls in uniform would screw things up, that Moody and his people would cover their asses while fucking hers. She'd been cornered, manipulated, and now the crisis she'd foreseen would be dumped in her lap, a crisis with potentially catastrophic consequences. To handle a situation of such magnitude called for strong leadership and bold decisions, and Amy Coffman knew she had the balls to make them. Because that's what presidents did.

She took a final drag of her cigarette and tossed the butt into the grate.

Then she took the Baghdad report out of her coat pocket and watched that burn too.

CHAPTER 3
THE CHANCERY

THE MEETING WAS HELD IN THE AMBASSADOR'S PRIVATE OFFICE ON the fourth floor of the Chancery building.

There were six chairs arranged in a neat semi-circle in front of the Ambassador's empty desk and right now only five of them were occupied. Major Jon Roth, 1st Special Forces Operational Detachment (Delta), sat in one of them. On either side of him sat the other two uniforms in the room. On his left was Captain Young, a petite, thirty-something African American lady from the US Army's Chemical Corps, and to his right sat Gunnery Sergeant Lynch, Detachment Commander of the Marine Security Guard.

Also in attendance was Veronica Hays, the embassy's Chief Medical Officer, and alongside her sat Bill Jacobs, the CIA Head of Station and now one of only three CIA officers left in Baghdad. The sixth chair was Tom Bosco's, the embassy's Regional Security Officer. He'd just walked in, slamming the door behind him. Roth watched him ignore the empty chair and stand in front of Hays.

"Meningitis, Veronica? Is that what this is?"

Hays glanced up from the report balanced on her knee. "We've not announced that officially."

"You should. People are getting nervous. And where are the casualties from this morning's incident?"

"Take a seat," Jacobs said.

Bosco ignored him. "Who authorised the screening team outside? Had to get my blood and temperature taken before I could get into my own damn building." He held up his finger, showed Hays the bloody pin-prick on his digit.

"Consider yourself lucky," Hays told him. "We've refused entry to over a dozen personnel in the last hour. This building is now a designated safe zone."

Roth watched Bosco fume. He understood that the guy's authority had been undermined a little but this was serious, more than anyone outside this room could imagine. The RSO would have to adjust his attitude real fast.

Hays was ruffled too. She looked tired, her grey trouser suit creased, her crinkly grey hair scraped back into a bun, her lined face a little pale. Roth had trouble determining her age, but her experience was obvious. That's why he trusted her judgement. Bosco, meanwhile, was still bitching.

"Someone should've told me," the RSO growled.

"Veronica is the senior medical authority here," Jacobs told him. "She'll be taking the lead on this one." He slapped the chair beside him. "Sit, Tom. Please."

Ashcroft entered the room, and the uniforms snapped to their feet. Roth was a second or two behind them. He stood with his arms folded, dressed in tan cargo pants, scruffy Merrell boots and a navy-blue T-shirt with a faded Heckler Koch logo over his left breast. Roth wasn't overly impressed by rank or by the stature of Ashcroft's office. He'd broken bread with generals, diplomats and high-ranking politicians on many occasions. Some of them even called him Jon, but this was Ashcroft's territory and Roth was a professional. He'd give the guy the respect his office deserved.

Acting Chief of Mission David Ashcroft pulled his black

leather chair into the desk and cleared his throat. The bureaucrat's Oxford blue shirt was crisp, his red and gold striped tie knotted perfectly. The bright overheads reflected off his smooth, tanned dome, off his silver-rimmed designer spectacles and the fat silver fountain pen he placed at a neat right-angle to the legal pad on his desk. Roth thought it was a nervous gesture. Right now, Ashcroft was an unknown quantity. How he handled the next few minutes would fill in a few blanks.

Roth knew that Ashcroft was a diplomatic place-holder for Ambassador Mitchell who'd been evacuated three weeks ago. Ashcroft had spent most of his career pushing a pencil around Europe, his only significant role as Counsellor for Economic Affairs at the US Mission to the European Union. The decision surprised Roth; Ashcroft was relatively inexperienced, and possibly a little too cultured to get his hands dirty in the blood and sand of Iraq. Then again, maybe he wasn't. He shook off the thought as Ashcroft addressed the shaven-headed Marine next to him.

"Okay Gunny Lynch, let's see what all the fuss is about."

Lynch thumbed a remote control and the sideboard TV blinked into life. For the next three minutes the room sat in silence, watching CCTV footage of a naked Vann Jackson entering the commissary and attacking communications specialist Walsh.

Then the picture changed. Another room, cinderblock walls, two beds, both of them occupied. Walsh and Jackson again, side by side, bucking and screaming as they thrashed against their restraints, their medical gowns and perspex face masks covered in blood and vomit. Bio-suited figures lined the walls. Roth found it hard to watch, and not just because Jackson was one of his own. Truth was he'd never seen anything like it, except in the movies. And the noises they made —

The TV blinked off.

"Meningitis, my ass," Bosco muttered, trying to appear unruffled.

Behind his desk, Ashcroft was visibly shaken. "Who are they?"

"The assailant and his victim from this morning's incident in the commissary," Jacobs told him.

"My god," the diplomat whispered. He turned to Hays. "What the hell's wrong with them?"

"An undetermined viral brain infection."

"Meningitis?"

"That's just a cover story. I have no idea what this is."

Ashcroft waved a hand at the TV. "Can't you tranquillise them for God's sake?"

"They've both received maximum dosages of Midazolam. So far it's had no effect."

Jacobs spoke next. "Veronica is recommending an immediate lockdown. Essential movement only. I'm seconding that recommendation, sir."

"A lockdown?" Ashcroft repeated.

"It's a non-essential movement order," Hays explained. "It means shutting down all public spaces; PX, gymnasium, swimming pool, washrooms, drinking fountains, the American Club - anywhere people congregate. We close everything until we find out how far this thing has spread."

Behind his desk, Ashcroft blinked several times. "That seems a little extreme, no?"

"Veronica has been briefed on the recent *Messina* operation," Jacobs told him. "She's up to speed."

"*Messina*," Bosco snorted. "Finally, a name. That's something I guess."

"You're getting more than that," Jacobs told him. "And it stays here, in this room, understood?"

Bosco glared at the CIA man. "You've been holding out on us, Bill?"

Ashcroft cut in before Jacobs could reply. "What are we talking about here?"

"Full disclosure," Jacobs told him, "the reason why Delta and Captain Young's chemical troops are here in Baghdad."

Ashcroft sat back in his chair and folded his arms. "Well, let's hear it then."

The man was rattled, Roth could hear it in his voice. The footage, the mysterious mission, the weight of office - Ashcroft was struggling. This wasn't an alfresco lunch in a cobbled Brussels square. He refocused as Jacobs addressed him.

"You're up, Jon."

Roth stood and approached the large regional map on one of Ashcroft's walls. He tapped at a featureless point to the south of Baghdad.

"Six days ago, we assaulted a target in this area. The site was being used to manufacture a bio-weapon, one intended for global dispersal. Casualty estimates were in the billions."

It took a moment for Ashcroft to process the information. "Did you say billions?"

Roth nodded. "Fortunately, the plot was discovered before the dispersal phase could begin. The site was successfully neutralised."

"Where did you stage from?" asked Lynch.

Roth tapped a southerly point on the map. "Two C-One-Thirties out of Al-Salem in Kuwait, then a HAHO drop to target."

"Who were they?" Bosco asked. "Islamic State?"

Roth shook his head. "No, something else."

"That's why the embassy was evacuated," Bosco realised. "In case something went wrong, right? Jackson's infected with something from that site."

Roth bobbed his head. "Almost certainly." He pointed to the map again. "The weapon being manufactured at *Messina* was—"

"You keep saying that name," Bosco interrupted. "What's the significance?"

"It's a code name the terrorists used for the place. Messina is a port in Sicily. It's where the Black Death entered Europe in the fourteenth century. The plague that killed twenty million people."

No one said anything as the information sunk in. Ashcroft was the first to break the silence.

"What exactly was this bio-weapon?"

"The Angola virus," Roth told him.

Ashcroft's eyes widened behind his lenses. "The African prison bug?"

"Yes, sir."

Bosco pointed at the lifeless TV screen. "But that isn't Angola, right?"

"Affirmative. Besides, we were all immunised before the mission. This is something else. Something unexpected."

"So how did Jackson get infected?"

Roth tapped his right butt cheek. "He was wounded here, during the assault, dressed it himself, kept it quiet. Doctor Hays believes the infection spread from there."

"Why keep his mouth shut?"

Roth shrugged. "My guess is he strayed off-mission and tried to cover his ass. Literally, as it turns out. The wound passed unnoticed during decontamination."

"Asshole," Bosco growled.

Roth was torn between agreeing with the RSO or kicking him off his chair. He decided to do neither. Ashcroft asked another question.

"Why come to Baghdad at all? Why not head straight back to Kuwait?"

"That decision was made at the Pentagon. They wanted JSOC assets in the field."

"When did Jackson get sick?" the Marine commander asked.

"A couple of days after we landed here. He became withdrawn, complained of fatigue and headaches. Our medics diagnosed dehydration. A couple of days later Jackson was reported missing. At that point, I thought we might be dealing with a mental health issue, so I ordered a discreet area search." He directed his next comment at Bosco. "You checked out one of the empty State Department accommodation blocks this morning, is that right?"

The RSO nodded. "One of my guys reported a broken window in Block Two. That building was sealed after the evacuation."

"You probably just missed him."

"Who?"

"Jackson. He'd broken in, found a storeroom, burrowed his way into a pile of laundry."

"A defensive reaction to the virus that was attacking his brain," Hays explained. "Like a wounded animal seeking shelter."

"He must've been there a while because everything was soiled with blood, vomit and faeces." Roth recognised the look on Bosco's face. "Don't worry, Gunny Lynch had it sealed off," he told the suddenly pale RSO.

"I appreciate that," Bosco mumbled.

Roth got little satisfaction reigning Bosco in, but the point had to be made. They were all in this together, which meant they had to operate as a team. He retook his seat, watching Bosco wipe sweaty palms on his trousers.

"For the record, Major Roth's people have since been screened and cleared," Hays announced, "which means Jackson is patient zero. The incubator of this unknown virus."

"But he's not in the Med Centre," Bosco countered, "so where is he?"

"Warehouse Seven," Hays told him.

Behind his desk, Ashcroft raised an eyebrow. "He's where?"

"Warehouse Seven, along with Walsh, my gurney drivers and eighteen others who came into direct contact with either Walsh or Jackson, all of whom have presented with symptoms, primarily elevated body temperature and mutated blood cells. They're being monitored as we speak."

"Eleven of them are my people," Lynch added.

"If we include the additional fourteen people refused entry into this building, that's a total of thirty-six embassy personnel who are now infected with this virus," Hays concluded.

"Thirty-six," Ashcroft echoed. He shook his head. "Frankly I have no idea what Washington was thinking, cutting us out of the loop like this."

"*Messina* goes all the way to the top of the pyramid," Jacobs told him, "and that includes the UN Security Council. It's highly classified and strictly compartmentalised."

"Not for much longer it would seem." Ashcroft turned to the tired-looking CMO. "Veronica, how are we processing these patients?"

"Captain Young has established a decontamination zone inside the entrance to Warehouse Four. Patients will pass through a series of tented showers in the loading bay then change into scrubs. After that, they'll be given a dose of Xanax or Ativan and assigned a bunk in the main storage area. We will then observe the patients from an adjacent observation room."

"That's it? A shower and a tablet? How effective will that be?" Ashcroft asked. It was a few seconds before Hays answered.

"Not at all."

"Excuse me?"

"The decontamination process is nothing more than window dressing, to provide reassurance and to encourage compliance. The tranquillisers might stall the mutation in the short term but it doesn't look hopeful."

Behind his desk, Ashcroft swallowed hard. "What exactly are you saying?"

"The infected will end up like Jackson," Hays told the Acting Chief of Mission. "Whatever this thing is, it appears to be mutating exponentially, and this embassy does not have the facilities or the infrastructure to deal with such an outbreak."

Ashcroft pointed to the windows across the room. "So, we transfer the victims to Ibn Sina. That's a real hospital, and it's in the Zone."

Jacobs shook his head. "This stays in-house until we know what we're dealing with. Right now, a lockdown is our best option."

Ashcroft's face reddened. "That's not your call, Bill. I'll decide what's best for this facility."

"DC will back me on this, sir."

Ashcroft glared across his desk, and Roth felt a flutter of sympathy for the man. Brussels to Baghdad had to be a culture shock, and now he was getting publicly overruled. That had to hurt, but Jacobs was right.

"Let me understand this," Ashcroft fumed. "The only alternative to getting these people the care they need is to lie to them, then lock them inside a warehouse? That's simply unacceptable."

"We don't have a choice," Jacobs told him. "It took ten of the Gunny's Marines to restrain Jackson. Imagine another ten like him on the loose. Or a hundred. Can we take that risk?"

"How secure is that warehouse?" Ashcroft asked.

It was Bosco who answered him. "It's a Level Three facility, hardened roof, no windows, steel access doors and an administration wing. The storage area is a caged environment. Access is electronically controlled."

"Wait a minute," Ashcroft said, "those people are being kept in cages?"

"Actually, it's one big cage," Hays corrected him. "Look,

this is not an easy decision for any of us, but as Bill said, we don't have a choice. I've seen this thing up close, Mister Ashcroft. I saw a wounded and frightened young girl turn into a wild animal in less than an hour. The patients in that warehouse are already showing signs of elevated aggression though surprisingly not towards each other."

That piqued Roth's interest. "What do you mean?"

Hays turned to him and shrugged. "I can't explain it, but the infected patients appear able to differentiate between themselves and the uninfected."

Ashcroft jabbed a finger at Young. "You're being awfully quiet over there, Captain. Can you shed any light on this thing?"

Young shook her braided head. "I'm a decontamination specialist, sir, not a medical professional."

"Then why the hell are you here?" Ashcroft snapped. "Seems to me that you didn't do your job properly in the first place." He snatched at the phone on his desk. "Brenda, get me the Ops Centre in DC, would you? And schedule a call with Secretary Coffman as soon as—"

"She knows," Jacobs told him. "I emailed her office this morning."

Ashcroft glared at the CIA chief. "Cancel that," he told Brenda. He dropped the phone back into its cradle. "You emailed the Secretary?"

"Yes, sir. We've requested a full USAMRIID and CDC response." Jacobs looked at his watch. "My guess is your phone will be ringing very soon. And when it does, the folks in Washington will want as much intel as possible."

"Wait a goddam minute," Bosco blurted. "This is all connected, isn't it? The White House empty, the President in leg irons, the same in France, the UK, China; that's the fallout, right? *Messina* is Ground Zero for all of it." He eyeballed Jacobs. "Tell me I'm wrong."

Jacobs shrugged. "I can't comment on that."

"Sure you can, Bill."

"We're wasting time," Ashcroft snapped. "I'm authorising the lockdown. I take it there's an EAP for this?"

"There's an Emergency Action Plan for everything, including a WMD incident," Bosco said.

Jacobs shook his head. "That calls for the wearing of MOPP gear. That cannot be authorised."

"Why not?" Ashcroft asked.

"We can't have people wandering around in masks and protective suits," the CIA chief explained. "If word leaks outside this embassy, questions will be asked."

"We tell them it's a drill," Bosco growled.

"No. Paper masks, gloves, they're fine. And distance."

"What about meals?" Lynch asked. "People gotta eat."

"MRE's," Jacobs told him. "We've got another warehouse full of them, plus bottled water. We'll assign collection points, group them by department, issue two or three days' worth of supplies. Should be enough until the response teams get a handle on this thing."

"Collection points," Ashcroft echoed quietly, scratching a fat silver pen across a notepad.

Covering your ass, Roth assumed, but he couldn't blame him. The poor guy had been shafted on this one.

Ashcroft put down his pen and looked at each of them in turn. "Does anyone have anything else? No? Good. We'll reconvene in—"

"What happens if we're attacked?"

It was Lynch who asked the question. Ashcroft blinked behind his designer frames. "I don't understand."

"What are the Rules of Engagement, sir? If any of my people are attacked by an infected person."

"You're asking me what exactly?"

"We've all seen the footage," Jacobs added. "There's a threat-to-life issue here. We need a decision."

Ashcroft's nostrils flared, and his eyes flicked between the faces around the room. "Decision?"

"Yes. How much force the security teams can use?"

"Proportionate," Ashcroft snapped back at the CIA chief.

"That might result in fatalities," Bosco told Ashcroft.

The diplomat took off his glasses and zeroed in on Jacobs. "Let me get this straight. You keep Tom and I in the dark about this *Messina* thing and now you expect me to authorise some kind of shoot-to-kill policy? You're out of your mind, Bill."

"Sir, with all due—"

"Enough. I'll ask Washington for guidance on the matter." Ashcroft stood and everyone followed suit. "Gunny Lynch, you and Captain Young will be responsible for the security of that warehouse. No one gets out, understood?"

"Aye, aye, sir."

"And Veronica, if there's anything we can do to ease the distress of those poor people, I want it done."

"Of course."

"Okay then. Let's try to get our arms around this thing before it does any more damage."

"There's something else," Bosco told the room. "A report came in about an hour ago. There's a weather event headed our way, a *shamal*. That's a dust storm. North-westerlies have been picking up all morning and the storm will hit Baghdad by early evening."

"What does that mean?" Ashcroft asked.

"Reduced visibility, potential damage to equipment. They're pretty common out here. The good news is, it'll keep folks from wandering around the compound."

"Something else to factor into our plans," Ashcroft noted. "Keep me posted, please."

He marched out of the room and the meeting broke up. Out in the hallway Roth talked radio channels with Lynch and Young for a few moments, then headed off. There wasn't much for his guys to do, but that suited Roth. After seeing Walsh and Jackson tied to those beds, he didn't need any incentive to play it safe.

"Major Roth."

He turned around. Bosco was marching towards him. Roth waited until the shorter man stopped in front of him. His face was flushed, and his eyes radiated hostility.

"For the record, I'm holding you personally responsible for this situation." He held up his fingers. "Three days you've known about Jackson, three days in which you should've joined the dots and sounded the alarm. Instead you sat on it while your boy went nuts. This shit-storm is on you. All of it."

Roth folded his big arms. "You think I wanted this? Hey, I get it, you're pissed that you weren't cleared for the *Messina* intel. That was a bad call, but the decision to keep you guys out of the loop was made in DC."

Bosco glared at Roth. "Bullshit. You should've dialled me in the day Jackson went missing."

Roth took a deep breath and exhaled slowly. "Look, mistakes have been made, I'll grant you that. Nobody wanted this, but here we are, so I suggest we work together to—"

"*Now* you want to cooperate?" Bosco snorted. "Nice try. Best thing you people can do now is stay out of the way. You've done enough damage already. Is that clear?"

Bosco turned and marched away. Roth fumed as he headed for the stairs. The atrium was pretty empty, and as he headed towards the security lobby a scruffy Italian-American fell in beside him. He wore loose combat pants, a Raiders T-shirt and a Glock strapped to his right thigh. His hair was long like Roth's, and a thick moustache drooped over his top lip. Roth often joked that Nick Costello resembled a porn star from the seventies. Costello took that as a compliment. He was a native of Newark, New Jersey, and spoke with a heavy accent.

"What gives?" the Sergeant-Major asked.

"Not here. Where is everyone?"

"In the block, mostly. Some are out running the perimeter."

"Get 'em back. We need to talk."

"You got it."

They passed through the security lobby and out into the hot afternoon sun. Directly outside, Pope's people had erected a white tent served by a taped queue path. Several people were standing in that queue, waiting to be screened before entering the building. Parked in the shade of the tent was a sand-coloured pickup truck. Behind the wheel, the masked driver was flipping through a magazine. Three people sat in the rear, talking to another masked medic. Roth could hear her reassuring them, telling them that everything was going to be okay. He gave all of it a wide berth.

The Delta commander's eyes wandered around the embassy grounds as Costello climbed behind the wheel of a Humvee. The freshening wind was driving small snakes of sand across Main Street, and above Roth's head, the Stars and Stripes fluttered in the breeze, its snap hooks tapping against the pole. He saw one or two people in the distance, their silhouettes shimmering in the heat, but that was the only life he could see right now. There was a serenity about the compound, an oasis of calm surrounded by the chaotic crescendo of the Iraqi capital.

Yet the Delta commander wasn't fooled. His antenna was up and quivering, and the feeling in his gut persisted. Something was heading their way, something bad.

And it had nothing to do with the weather.

CHAPTER 4
HOLLY

Doug kept to the shade of the perimeter wall as he pounded the well-worn path that served as an unofficial running track around the embassy compound.

His hair was damp with sweat and he cuffed his forehead with a wristband. The sun was high and it beat down on the city like a hammer, but the wind was picking up. It gusted in short, sharp bursts, the dust stinging his eyes and skin, but Doug didn't care. The discomfort was penance, and salvation lay in keeping himself fit. He was ten months shy of his forty-fifth birthday, and he was fitter now than at any time in the last ten years. Even when he'd worn the uniform.

Ahead of him, half a dozen Delta guys in shorts and t-shirts pulled further away. Doug slowed, watching them go. For a while he'd tried to close the gap on them, match their pace, but it was a pointless exercise. Doug believed he was pretty fit, had even completed three half-marathons back home, but the Delta guys were something else. He recalled his own time in service, a three-year stint in the Army Reserve as a military intelligence systems specialist. He'd considered trying out for Ranger school, had watched the cool videos, and Doug thought that might be something he could handle. He was wrong. Truth was, he'd washed out during the intensive training phase, an embarrassing failure. He smiled at the memory as he watched the Delta guys disappear around a line of distant shipping containers. They were a different breed for sure, but US military operations were a team effort and required the many and varied skills of other uniformed personnel. It wasn't just about the door kickers.

Yeah, whatever, his inner voice mocked. Still, that Ranger scroll would've been *so* cool.

He slowed to a walk, then stopped, planting his hands against the blast wall to stretch his calves and catch his breath. He glanced up at a nearby watchtower. Twenty-five feet above him a Filipino security contractor watched the world outside the compound from behind dark glasses, a scoped weapon cradled in his arms. Doug acknowledged him with a wave but the contractor ignored him, resuming his watch across the still waters of the security lagoon and the Tigris River beyond.

A bird screeched overhead, and the sudden, grating call reminded Doug of the earlier attack. He replayed the scene in his head, the girl on the floor, the drumbeat of fists that pounded her face. It made him feel sick.

Doug squatted against the wall as his heart rate slowed. He sucked a mouthful of water from his camel pack as his eyes wandered across the compound. He felt like the only person left inside the embassy. Every road, every sidewalk, was deserted. Empty buildings shimmered in the heat. Where the hell was everybody?

The cell phone inside his pack warbled, startling him. He scrambled to his feet. Only two people had the number; the first was his line manager at the DOD, who'd hadn't called him once since he'd been in Iraq. He prayed it would be the second.

"Doug Walker."

A faint hiss, a series of clicks, then, "Doug, it's Rick Gould."

Doug took a deep breath, held it to stop his heart from racing. His daughter had been gone for two years, and a call from Gould could go either way. He closed his eyes, steeled himself. "I'm listening."

There was another delay on the line as the signal bounced around the earth.

"We have a lead on Holly—"

He exhaled, the words tumbling from his lips. "Where is she? She's not hurt, not—"

"She's okay, Doug. Take a breath, buddy."

He did, a deep one. His heart pounded. "Talk to me, Rick."

"NYPD raided an illegal squat in Brooklyn two days ago. Holly was arrested at the scene, along with a dozen others."

"She's in jail?"

"Was," Gould told him. "She was processed at the Sixty-Third Precinct then transported to Central Booking overnight. The charge was a misdemeanour - criminal trespass. She was arraigned and bailed. Ultimately the building's owners decided to drop the charges; the place is just an empty shell, so no harm done I guess. In any case, I got a copy of her sheet. The good news is, this is her first run-in with the cops."

"How was she?"

There was a few seconds of low hiss on the line.

"Holly was examined by a paramedic at the Sixty-Third. I spoke to the guy personally. He didn't do a full work-up, but she was pretty wasted. He suspected dependencies, drugs, alcohol. No needles though."

The news wasn't a complete surprise. The phone calls were often late, erratic and painfully empty. Sometimes he could hear the wail of a police siren in the background, imagined the wind whipping around her as she stood silent at a graffiti-scarred phone booth somewhere. Her breathing was always quick, angry, and Doug had to steel himself each time, for the tears, the denunciations, but they never came. Instead his daughter remained silent, refusing to answer his pleas to come home. Then the inevitable disconnect.

So, for the last two years, Doug had spent every spare dime trying to locate his daughter. He'd sold the house and everything in it. He'd moved into a trailer park in Gainesville, Virginia, and started spending the proceeds of the house sale on the first of several private investigators.

The first three took advantage of his desperation and racked up the manpower and billable hours until Doug was light by over forty thousand dollars. He took stock, then spent another month making calls and seeking recommendations. Rick Gould appeared to be the real deal, a former FBI agent with a small, dedicated team of legal and law-enforcement professionals based up in Philly. The retainer was modest, and the bills still mounted up, but Zoe's file put on some weight; a bus ticket purchase from Baltimore to Pittsburgh, a cash withdrawal in Scranton, a CCTV grab from a drug store in Harrisburg. Doug made sure her Chase card was paid up, her checking account always in credit. Holly rarely used them, but when she did, it gave them something.

Rick's voice cut through his thoughts.

"As I said, despite her obvious intoxication she checked out okay. It means she's not sleeping in tunnels or dumpsters."

"Thank God."

"There's more, Doug."

The way Rick said it spelled trouble. "Go on."

"One of the guys arrested with her was Eduardo Flores, twenty-nine-years-old, originally from Arizona and now living in Queens. Flores is a college dropout, a smart kid, handsome, charming, but he's got a record; possession, assault and battery…"

There was a pause on the line, then Gould continued.

"Last year he was arrested on suspicion of kidnapping. The girl was a runaway - sixteen-year-old Jodi Cousins from Tennessee. She was last seen with Flores, but he was never charged due to lack of evidence. I spoke to the detective on the case; Flores has links to trafficking gangs, running drugs and illegals up from Honduras and Nicaragua. The detective believes that Flores targets vulnerable young women and hands them off to gang members who put them to work. We're talking drug mules, couriers, prostitution—"

"I get it," Doug snapped. He started pacing the dirt beneath the watchtower. "Where's Holly now?"

"Still in Brooklyn. We got a hit on her Freedom card a few hours ago. She withdrew five hundred dollars from an ATM in Brownsville. It was after midnight so my guys canvassed the local hotels. The night manager at the Quality Inn on Chester ID'd her picture. It's Holly. And Flores is with her."

Doug's blood ran cold. "We have to get her out of there."

"I've got two guys out front and back, but we have to move fast. Flores asked the night manager where the Greyhound station was. He heard them talking about El Paso. Looks like they're on the move."

Doug's heart beat a little faster. "I need to come home."

"As soon as possible," Gould agreed. "We'll need you here for the intervention, Doug. That's the only way this will work. And I'll need your authorisation for round-the-clock surveillance. It's not going to be cheap, I'm afraid."

"Do what you have to."

"You're based in Kuwait, right?"

"Yes," Doug lied.

"How quickly can you get to New York?"

"I'm not sure. I'll need to talk to my boss."

"Well, I suggest you do that. We have to move fast."

"I'll get the ball rolling and get back to you."

Doug ended the call. Two years of pain, worry and sleepless nights might be at an end. He tried to imagine Holly's reaction, the moment she laid eyes on him. She'd be confused, angry and probably a little scared. He'd be hurting too, but it was a chance to reconnect with his daughter, the only one he'd had in two years. He had to take it.

Emergency leave meant paperwork and phone calls. He had to get back to the apartment, fire up the laptop—

"Hey!"

Doug saw a buggy whirring towards him. Behind the wheel was Freddie. The buggy crunched to a stop, throwing up a cloud of dust. Doug coughed as it caught in the back of his throat.

"You hear the news?" Freddie said.

"What news?"

"They just declared a medical emergency. They think it's some kinda meningitis outbreak. All public spaces have been closed, restricted movement, plus a bunch of other stuff. You need to get in front of your email."

"Meningitis? Jesus," Doug muttered. "Wait, is this related to the commissary thing?"

Freddie shrugged. "You want a lift?"

"Yeah. Run me back to my block, would you?"

Doug's accommodation was all the way over at the eastern end of the compound. He climbed into the buggy and they set off towards Main Street. As Freddie steered, Doug noticed the ill-fitting bandage on his hand.

"They didn't do much of a job on that," Doug observed.

Freddie held up his hand and laughed. The buggy veered across the road.

"Watch out!" Doug warned. Freddie yanked the wheel as the buggy missed a heavy concrete bollard by inches. "Jesus Christ, Freddie."

Freddie laughed again, then his smile faded. "Did you hear the news? A medical emergency. Everything is closed."

"You just told me that."

"I did?"

Freddie's bandage was dangling off his wrist.

"You need to get that dressing fixed."

"Did it myself," Freddie chuckled. "Fucking thing keeps coming loose."

Doug watched his friend. For a Hispanic guy from Nevada, he was sweating heavily. "I thought you were going to get that bite looked at."

"What bite?"

"The one on your hand. The guy, this morning, remember?"

Freddie said nothing. The buggy whizzed past the commissary, now cordoned off with yellow security tape.

"Did you hear the news?"

"The medical emergency?"

"They told you?"

Doug leaned away from Freddie. He had this virus thing, no doubt. Ahead, the contractor blocks were grouped in several sand-coloured ranks near the eastern security wall. As a vehicle passed them, Freddie shouted, "This is you, right?"

It wasn't, but Doug said yes. Freddie slammed on the brakes and Doug almost cracked his skull off the Perspex. He climbed out, took a few paces back.

"Hey Freddie, I really think you should go and get that hand checked properly. After all, that guy—"

"Go fuck yourself," Freddie snapped, and he swung the buggy around and drove off.

Doug watched him go. Freddie was sick. And if Freddie wouldn't help himself, Doug would make the call. This thing might be highly contagious. He had to take care of business first.

He kept moving, keen to be out of the heat and grateful for the sudden breeze that gusted between the buildings. There wasn't a soul around as he swiped in and took the stairs to the fourth floor. His apartment was at the end of the hallway and he could just about see the Tigris River if he stood on a chair and craned his neck to the top of the narrow window that was his only source of natural light.

He cracked open his laptop on the kitchen counter and logged in to the Department of Defence employee portal. He spent the next twenty-five minutes filling in forms and then he took a shower. By the time he'd dried off and got dressed, the confirmation email was sitting in his Inbox. It was only an acknowledgement, but at least the wheels were in motion. Later he would visit the Transportation Office and chase up the paperwork. He had no idea how fast the system operated but he knew he'd have to be cleared through the Zone to Baghdad International, transit to Kuwait and then transfer onto an international carrier. That took time. Wouldn't hurt to apply a little pressure. His was an emergency after all.

Then he read the email, the one from the Security Office. He read it twice, then one more time because he couldn't quite believe his bad luck. Phrases like *restricted movement* and *temporary travel ban* leapt off the screen at him. Taunted him. Doug had to restrain himself from hurling his laptop against the wall.

Bad fucking luck. It was no more than he deserved. Doug's world rolled from one crisis to another. First Karen, then Holly, then the government meltdown in the wake of the Wall Street crisis. He thought he'd found a little stability out here in Iraq, a chance to make a chunk of dough, and when Rick Gould called, he thought his luck had changed. His daughter's life had been torn apart. She'd finally been found, and Doug was in a position to get her the help she needed. And now this.

Doug swore. What was the saying? *You want to make God laugh, tell him you've got plans.* He thought about the Flores kid and his knuckles turned white. He wondered if Rick would hospitalise the guy for a few extra bucks. After Holly was safe of course.

He'd worked for Uncle Sam long enough to know that in

times of crisis his personal emergency wouldn't count for shit. So, he had to wait, pray this virus thing would blow over quickly, try to persuade Rick Gould to make the intervention without him. Failing that, to watch over her, until he could get home. Then he would connect with his little girl once again, provide the safe environment and the round-the-clock care needed to coax her out of the shadows and back into the world. Back into Doug's life.

All he needed to do was stay safe and get home.

Because nothing else mattered.

CHAPTER 5
DEEP STATE

THE CONVOY OF BLACK SUVS MADE SHORT WORK OF THE morning traffic.

It headed north on Connecticut Avenue and around Dupont Circle before cutting across the street and stopping outside a tastefully renovated period building. Blue and red grill-strobes lit up the facade as Coffman's Secret Service detail climbed out and fanned out, coats open, hands poised, heads turning in all directions. They were edgy, and Coffman didn't really blame them. They were all living through uncertain times. Coffman was going to change all that.

The reception area had been cleared in advance, and Coffman made herself comfortable on a chair. A few minutes later a pretty young thing in a grey clinical trouser suit escorted her to a bank of elevators. Coffman waved off the agents who tried to accompany her and warned them that the emergency appointment might take some time. A very personal medical matter, she explained. No one argued.

Her private physician, Doctor Kumra, was waiting for her on the third floor. He guided her into an examination room. Once inside she snapped open her small overnight case and changed into a navy Helly Hansen trench coat, pulled a black beanie over her hair and slipped on a pair of oversized sunglasses.

"How do I look?"

"Like a regular person," Kumra told her.

"What a depressing thought. How long do I have?"

"Four hours, give or take."

Coffman left by the opposite door, and she exited the building unmolested through the loading bay on Eighteenth Street. Mulholland was waiting in a nondescript brown Chevy Malibu, a baseball cap pulled low over his brow. She climbed in beside him.

"I barely recognised you."

"Let's go," ordered Coffman. "We don't have much time."

Mulholland dropped the car into gear and headed north on Columbia. He reached into his pocket and handed her a folded sheet of paper.

"What's this?"

"A weather alert," he told her, "for the Baghdad area."

Coffman speed-read it. "A dust storm?"

"Came into ops a short while ago, from the weather station in Kuwait. They're predicting a major dust event in the next six hours. The embassy has been notified."

Coffman re-read the alert message. It spoke of wind speeds and atmospheric pressures and visibility estimates. The words sang to her like a chorus of angels.

"This is a sign, Erik. You see that, right?"

"I see unpredictable weather."

"Oh, ye of little faith. Now be quiet. I need to think."

Coffman stared out the window. She was committed now, in every way possible, but the prize was like no other. The thought of occupying the seat inside the Oval Office made her stomach flutter with excitement, and the man they were going to meet could make it happen. It had been a while since they'd met, but Coffman's gut feeling was a positive one.

The Chevy continued north on Sixteenth. At Rock Creek,

it turned into a construction site. The partly finished building was an unremarkable two storey concrete shell that looked like any other commercial project. A couple of construction workers wearing orange vests and hardhats swung open the chain-link gates and waved them through.

"What is this place?" Mulholland asked.

"A DOD network hub."

"Here?"

"*Hidden in plain sight.* That's the phrase Bob used. Drive down the ramp."

Mulholland obeyed, steering the Chevy beneath the structure. There were other vehicles parked in the gloom, a couple of mud-splattered SUVs and several pickups. Mulholland found a spot and killed the engine.

Coffman swiped off her sunglasses and climbed out of the Chevy. Footsteps echoed off the walls, off the low concrete ceiling. Two men emerged out of the gloom. Hands were extended, shaken.

"Did you make the call?" Coffman asked.

Robert Blake, wearing a button-down shirt, jeans and a black puffer coat, handed her a small card. "His name is Gatekeeper. It's a code name. Matt thought that one up."

Matt Sorenson, the thin, bald fifty-something standing next to Blake, smiled. "Gatekeeper developed the routing software that controls all DISA traffic coming out of Baghdad. He can turn the tap on or off."

"Good." Coffman handed the card to Mulholland. "Is our friend here?"

"Right this way." Sorenson led them across the parking lot as he talked. "Perimeter security is in place, the room has been swept and there's a signal blocker operating. You can talk freely."

They headed up a short flight of stairs. The makeshift canteen was populated with several rows of wooden picnic tables and the air stank of fried food. Coffman saw him at the end of the furthest row, toying with a cell phone. She reached into her pocket, checked her own device: *No Signal*.

The man saw Coffman approaching and got to his feet. Hamid Aswad was fifty-four-years old, his dark hair and beard neatly styled, his jeans pressed, his shirt and sweater of obvious quality. A dark raincoat was draped across the back of the chair next to him.

Still handsome, Coffman noted. Aswad was an MIT alumnus, with degrees in engineering and business administration. He owned a successful biomass factory in Texas and a variety of agricultural and engineering businesses across Europe. He'd won the Goldman Environmental Prize for his part in the post-war clean-up of Iraq's southern marshes and continued to serve as an advisor to the Middle East Research Institute. He was a proud Iraqi, Coffman knew. He was also a politician, albeit a silent player, with a reputation for discretion. If that was no longer the case, well, there was a plan for that too.

Coffman found herself returning his wide smile. They shook hands and Aswad leaned in, pecking her cheeks. She caught the scent of his cologne and was reassured by the physical contact. Aswad was a Shia Muslim by birth, but one whose extended family included a varied mix of Assyrian Christians, Kurds and Turks. She watched his dark brown eyes travel from her face to her body and back again. They might have been lovers once, but the timing was wrong and the potential liaison held no political cache for her. *How the tides can change,* Coffman reminded herself.

She'd met Hamid on many occasions, both formal and otherwise. She'd always been impressed by his ambition, his vision of a transformed Iraq. He believed Iraq had the potential to become a beacon of secularism and modernity that would be the envy of the region. His brother, Ahmad Aswad, the current President of Iraq, shared that vision, and Hamid had his brother's ear. A meeting with the younger Aswad was like meeting the president himself. "It's good to see you again, Hamid."

"Likewise, Madam Secretary. Or should I say, *President-elect*?"

"Amy, please. We're all friends here. You remember Erik?"

Aswad gripped her Chief of Staff's hand. "Yes, of course."

Coffman invited Blake and Sorenson to join her around the beat-up table. She pulled off her beanie and smoothed down her hair, careful to avoid the dark patches of grease and ketchup stains dotted across the table. She gestured to the men alongside her.

"This is Bob Blake and Matt Sorensen, founding partners of Kroll Industries. This building is one of their many projects."

Aswad nodded and asked, "I'm curious, what is this place?"

"Bob and Matt are also very good friends," Coffman continued as if she hadn't heard. "We've known each other for a long time, supported each other over the years. We're all friends here."

Aswad smiled. "Let's dispense with the mystery, shall we, Amy? Why are we meeting?"

Coffman tapped a finger on the table. "Let me start by saying that our only priority is to ensure the security and prosperity of your country. First and foremost, we are allies, Hamid."

"I'm not sure many Iraqis would agree with that statement."

"Things are about to change. A new era dawns in US-Iraqi relations, a dawn that will see the forging of a genuine and lasting friendship. It's important both you and your brother remember that."

Aswad's eyes narrowed. "Perhaps this is something he should hear for himself."

"No," Coffman said, shaking her head. "The only way this

will work is through back-channels. Thousands of lives depend on it. Iraqi lives."

"Get to the point," Aswad said, his face darkening.

He was worried, and Coffman knew why. Iraq had twice borne the brunt of American foreign policy decisions based on fabricated evidence, and right now that same superpower was a rudderless behemoth. She needed to stoke that fear.

"It concerns the United States embassy, in Baghdad. We have a problem there, a medical emergency to be exact. An unknown virus has broken out within its grounds. It's highly contagious and almost certainly life-threatening. Erik?"

Mulholland pushed an iPad across the table. "Tap *play*."

Aswad did as he was told. Coffman studied his face as the Iraqi played the video of Jackson convulsing in his sick bed, the tinny shouts and screams echoing off the concrete walls. She watched Hamid's eyes narrow, then widen, his Adam's apple bob as he swallowed involuntarily. Mulholland took the iPad back.

"Tell me you have this contained."

The pitch of his voice had dialled up a notch, Coffman noticed. Like everyone who'd seen the video, their first reaction was fear. Time to stoke that a little.

"I'm afraid not. At eight am local time there was one confirmed case. Now over thirty people have presented with symptoms. What little control we thought we had, we're losing fast."

"What is it?"

"We don't know."

"You don't know?" Aswad stroked his beard as he processed Coffman's response. "But you must have plans in place for this type of scenario, right? Protocols, that sort of thing?"

"Of course. There's a team on the ground, but controlling the virus is beyond their scope."

"You have bio-warfare experts in Baghdad? Why?"

"It's complicated."

She paused for effect as if struggling with some internal conflict. "As you know, Hamid, western governments have been in turmoil for several weeks. Our former president is in prison, along with many others, the reasons for which are varied and complex. The truth is, the world has come dangerously close to catastrophe, a terrorist attack on a scale unseen in human history. Its base of operations was located in the desert south of Baghdad. It is from there that the weapon was to be deployed."

"What weapon?"

"The Angola virus."

"Angola?"

"Correct. A man-made pathogen as it turns out, and one intended for global dispersal. The plot was foiled by US Special Forces—"

"Thank God," Aswad breathed. "For a moment I thought—"

Coffman silenced him with a raised hand. "I'm not finished. The Pentagon drew up a contingency plan to ensure that, should something go wrong, any potential contamination would be contained within Iraq's borders. Specifically, Baghdad. It's why my embassy was evacuated."

"I didn't know that."

"How could you? This is all highly classified. In any case, something *was* brought back to the embassy. Something unknown, and far more terrifying."

Aswad didn't answer immediately. Coffman knew he was smart, a pragmatist who would eventually see the opportunities ahead, but time was one luxury neither of them had.

"So, you see the problem, Hamid."

"You mean Iraq's problem?"

"This is *our* problem. Even as we speak, others are succumbing to this ghastly infection. Panic will set in. People will become desperate, attempt to reach safety at the consulates in Erbil and Basrah. If that happens there is a very real possibility that this contagion will find its way into the International Zone, then Baghdad itself."

She saw the look in his eyes, the scenario taking shape in his mind. She pushed on.

"If it does, the city will quickly fall into chaos. At that point, they will initiate *Operation Lightning Strike.*"

"Who are *they*?" Aswad snapped, "and what is *Lightning Strike*?"

Coffman held the Iraqi's gaze. "*They* are an international coalition of G7 countries. *Lightning Strike* is the total destruction of Baghdad by nuclear weapons."

Across the table, Aswad's olive skin paled significantly. He shook his head slowly. "I don't believe you."

"The UN Security Council has already approved the Resolution," Coffman told him. "US Navy nuclear assets have been deployed to the region for that very purpose. Once your capital city has been erased from the map, the same coalition will assume control of the country. Naturally, the oil must continue to flow."

She inched her chair a little closer, dialled her tone down. She needed the Iraqi onside, and quickly.

"You feel betrayed and angry, Hamid. Iraq has been used as a chessboard for the political and economic gain of others for decades, and the only losers have been the Iraqi people. We've spoken about this before, you and I, on many occasions."

Coffman was surprised to discover a degree of emotion had leaked into her voice. That sometimes happened when she truly believed in a cause, and female emotion often proved to be a powerful advocate. She had Aswad's full attention now.

"I share that anger, that betrayal. I too have been manipulated, my office disabused, my people placed in harm's way without their knowledge or consent. But what I'm about to propose will save Baghdad. More than that, it will cement your brother's power base for years to come, time that can be used to invoke the transformation that you've so often spoken of. A future where Iraq is a peaceful, prosperous nation, with the United States as a strong ally and economic partner. Everything you and your brother have always dreamed of is now within your grasp, Hamid. The alternative is unthinkable."

She watched the Iraqi's shoulders sag as he absorbed her words, the imagined death of his country a physical burden.

"What can we do?" he asked, a tremor in his voice.

Coffman spread her hands on the table, no longer concerned by the stains.

"An evacuation of US personnel cannot be allowed to take place. Our only hope—Iraq's only hope—is to eradicate the problem before the world learns of the danger. And when it does, we will control the message. To do that, we'll need your help. Your brother's, to be accurate."

"How?"

"As I mentioned, Bob and Matt handle many of this country's defence contracts," Coffman reminded him, waving a hand at the Kroll executives. "One of their responsibilities is external security for the Baghdad embassy."

"Run by a subsidiary of ours, Northridge International," Sorenson explained. "The security force over there is made up of Third Country Nationals, private contractors whose allegiance is to Northridge."

Aswad shrugged. "What's your point?"

"When the time comes, they'll withdraw that security. They'll also stop anyone from leaving," Coffman added.

"Okay, but what do you want from us?" Hamid asked.

"A covert withdrawal of all Iraqi forces from the streets surrounding the embassy. We'll also need a disruption of the power network and the suspension of all communication services to the International Zone, including cell coverage."

"But the Prime Minister's office, Parliament—?"

"The work day is winding down," Coffman said, tapping her watch. "It's the next twelve hours that are crucial."

"Why? What are you planning to do, Amy?"

"Save seven million Iraqi lives." She reached into her pocket, pushed a USB thumb drive across the table. "The document on there outlines the steps that need to be taken."

"It's pretty straightforward," Blake smiled. "Basically, you leave the room and turn the lights off on your way out."

"There's something else," Coffman said, passing the folded weather alert across the table. "A dust storm is due to hit Baghdad this evening. The timing couldn't be more perfect."

Aswad took the report and read it. Then he stared at Coffman. "You could go to prison for this, Amy. Conspiring with a foreign national—"

"A friend," she corrected him, offering a smile. She tapped the USB drive between them.

"This represents hope, Hamid. Hope for Iraq's future, the one you and your brother have always dreamed of. If the virus gets out, that hope—all hope—will evaporate."

Aswad pocketed the drive. "I'm going to have to talk to my brother—"

"—Who is currently at the United Nations in New York for an Economic and Sustainability Council meeting. I have a jet waiting at Dulles."

"He'll need assurances."

"Which we'll discuss at a later date."

She understood Hamid's plight of course, but their friendship had been forged on the back of a quiet disgust for her country's record of military interventions. A thought occurred to her; *maybe that was the reason she was never invited to join The Committee.* Maybe they'd felt that she didn't have the stomach for spilling blood. Well, she did. And the next few days would prove that.

"You should leave," she urged the Iraqi.

"If Ahmed agrees—"

"He must."

"And what about your end, Amy? My brother and I were hoping to have a friend in the White House. If Americans die, there'll be outrage, an investigation. If you're implicated, you're finished."

Coffman silenced him with a raised hand. "Not if we control the narrative. This will be a story of heroism, of American sacrifice and Iraqi fortitude. And when it's all over, US imperialism will have died too. Our countries will be reborn, Hamid. *That* is the future, and the message you must convey to your brother." She got to her feet and walked around the table. Aswad grasped the offered hand. "Matt will accompany you to New York. Godspeed, Hamid."

Sorenson escorted Aswad from the room. Coffman sat in the Iraqi's recently vacated chair. It was still warm.

"You think he bought it?" Mulholland asked.

"You saw his face. The Iraqis are no strangers to the prospect of nuclear war, and they have good cause to mistrust both us and the UN. President Aswad will believe the threat is real. He'll also see this for what it really is—a chance to lead his nation out of the dark ages." She turned to Blake. "Are you ready, Bob?"

"We've got a temporary control suite on one of the lower levels. Gatekeeper will plug us into Baghdad once you give the word."

"We'll need footage, Bob. The world will need to see the horror, the sacrifice."

"Leave it to me," Blake smiled. "Will you be coming back?"

Coffman shook her head. "Only to cut the tape during the opening ceremony. As President."

Blake's smile widened. A President Coffman in the White

House would benefit them all. "Stay in touch, Bob. I want regular updates."

"Yes, ma'am."

Mulholland had said nothing, not until they'd driven through the security gates and were heading south on Sixteenth.

"So, who's this Gatekeeper guy?"

"That's the insurance policy I mentioned."

Mulholland checked his mirror and accelerated past a slow-moving truck. "Can we trust Bob and Matt? And the Aswads? This thing has got a lot of moving parts, Amy. If things start to—"

"What's wrong with you, Erik? You never used to be this much of a pussy."

Mulholland snatched a quick look at her. "We've just gone all in. Biggest goddam hand we've ever played, and there are things I still don't know. You promised me full disclosure."

Coffman smiled and patted him on the thigh. "Relax, Erik. We keep a lid on things until it's too late and then we press our advantage. Gatekeeper will ensure that things go from bad to worse over there."

"And how will he do that, exactly?"

A suburban passed them in the next lane, a couple of snot-nosed kids pressed against the glass, pulling faces at Coffman. She pulled her beanie down a little further and adjusted her sunglasses.

"Patience, Erik. You'll see."

CHAPTER 6
READY, FREDDIE?

Roth stood on the roof of the Military Liaison Building, a pair of rangefinder binoculars pressed to his eyes.

He did a slow sweep of the whole compound, paying particular attention to the watchtowers along the walls. Inside each one was a foreign national, contracted through the US government to provide perimeter security for the embassy. They could never be trusted to set foot on US soil of course, and Roth knew that whatever was happening inside the embassy, those guys would have the best seats in the house. As far as the Delta commander was concerned, that was a problem, and something else to add to his report.

He continued his sweep. Due west, just three open-air basketball courts away, was the commissary, now shut down and taped off. Two hundred metres to the south-west, also ringed with security tape, stood the apartment block where Jackson had holed up before launching his attack. Roth kept rotating, his high-powered optics sweeping across buildings and roads, security gates and walkways. He saw very few people.

Due south, across Main Street, he could just about see the entrance to Warehouse Seven, and every time Roth looked, someone was disappearing inside. Someone with a headache, or aching limbs, or mild disorientation. Someone who wasn't getting out.

Behind him, Costello climbed up through the hatch and onto the roof. He stood next to Roth who continued his surveillance of the warehouse.

"Poor bastards," Costello muttered, following Roth's line of sight.

"I've counted fifteen new admissions in the last thirty minutes."

"The EAP was pretty explicit," Costello said. "You feel sick, you head to Warehouse Seven."

Roth lowered the binoculars. "How are the guys?

"Spitballing tactics and gear," Costello told him.

Roth's briefing and subsequent Q & A had lasted for just under two hours. His men already knew that the meningitis cover story was exactly that. They knew that Jackson was infected with something unexpected, that it was mutating and spreading, that a lockdown was in place and help was on its way. Afterwards, they'd gamed out the scenarios; what happened if the lockdown lasted weeks? If a full evacuation was ordered? If this thing got seriously out of control? And the question they'd debated for some time, the question that Ashcroft had failed to answer during the meeting—what are the Rules of Engagement in such a scenario?

"The guys all have their suppressors fitted?"

Costello nodded. "Affirmative."

"Perimeter security?"

"We've got steel drop-shutters protecting every door and window on the ground floor. They're testing them as we speak."

Costello took the binoculars from Roth and scanned the area to the north of their building. A couple of hundred metres away the embassy's main gates were closed. Out on Kindi Street, the Northridge contractors manning the vehicle checkpoint had nothing to do. Beyond that, the Green Zone was still.

"It's quiet out there," Costello noted.

"Quietest I've ever seen this place," Roth agreed.

Costello lowered the binoculars. "Doesn't seem right."

Roth rolled his eyes. "This again?"

"C'mon, Jon. This ain't how we operate. Delta don't sit on their asses."

"Things are fluid in DC right now. They say we need to be here, they must have a good reason."

"This is bullshit," Costello said. "Even the guys think so. And this Jackson thing has got them pretty spooked."

"Then it's our job to keep them focused. You and I are going to organise a training rota. There's forty of us in a building designed for five hundred, so we're going to clear out a couple of offices and put them to work. Weapons, combat medicine, PT, as if we were cycling through Bragg on a refresher. We stay sharp, busy, we get through this in no time. And when JSOC decides to sic us on the bad guys, we'll be ready."

"Sounds like a plan," Costello conceded.

"And I want a perimeter established. Nothing complicated, just a line of security tape around the building. That'll keep folks away. And we use one door for entry and exit, and I want it manned twenty-four-seven. No one in or out without us knowing why."

"Got it."

"From here on in we stay behind our perimeter. How's our ammunition count?"

"We're maxed out. They got enough munitions stored in this facility to take on the whole Iraqi army." He looked at Roth and said, "Think we'll need it?"

Roth closed his eyes and raised his chin to the sky. He felt the heat on his face, tempered by a stiffening breeze, and he wondered if he'd ever feel that heat again, as a Delta Force commander. *Doubtful.*

"I'm sorry I snapped," he told Costello.

The Sergeant-Major shrugged. "Forget about it."

"When this is over, they'll want a scalp."

"Wait, they can't pin this thing on you, Jon. The intelligence was solid, remember? There was absolutely no mention of any other bio-threat, none. Whatever Jackson's got—"

"It doesn't matter. I wasn't paying attention."

Costello's face darkened. "The kid kept his mouth shut, hid the wound. No one noticed."

"That's not the point. You saw what he did to his mattress, his kid's pictures. PTSD my ass. I should've called it right there and then. The RSO's right, this is my fault."

Costello took a step closer. "Fuck that guy. Say the word and we'll close ranks, spin our way out of this."

Roth shook his head. "Appreciate the support, but lying don't sit right with me." He pointed at the distant warehouse. "Right now, that virus is eating away at the brains of those people in there. Soon enough they'll end up like Jackson and that poor kid Walsh. They'll probably die too. All that is on me."

The enormity of his mistake hit him then, and Roth's stomach churned with acid. He leaned against an air-con unit and hung his head. "Jesus Christ," he muttered. He felt Costello's hand on his shoulder.

"Don't beat yourself up, Jon. I missed it too. We all missed it. You can't claim sole responsibility on this one."

"Fuck!" Roth cursed. He straightened up, eyes glued to the distant warehouse. "Worse thing is, we'll never know what happened to Jackson."

"Unless they find a cure. How long 'til those outbreak teams get here?"

"A day, maybe."

"So those people down there have a shot, right?"

"Hays said the virus is mutating too fast."

"She's not an expert. Maybe she—"

"Enough, Nick." Roth turned to face his Sergeant-Major and friend of eleven years. "What's done is done. All we can do now is pray this thing doesn't spread. Which brings us back to the problem at hand. ROE."

Costello shrugged. "That's gotta be your call, Jon."

"Plan A, we avoid all contact, wait for the response teams. With any luck, they'll squash this thing fast."

"And if they can't? If it gets out of control and we're backed into a corner, what then?"

Roth had been pondering the question since the meeting in Ashcroft's office, had debated it with the guys downstairs. And here, on this baking rooftop, he'd turned the problem over again and again—faced with a direct threat, what were the Rules of Engagement?

"I'm not going to risk any more lives," he told Costello. "If it comes down to it, if any of us are threatened, we shoot."

"It's the right call," Costello said.

"Let's hope it doesn't come to that. Now, let's see about that training rota."

Costello climbed down the ladder first. Roth followed, slamming the hatch behind him.

TWO HUNDRED AND TWENTY METRES AWAY, FREDDIE CRUZ swung the wheel of the buggy and drove it into the wall of his accommodation block. The plastic hood shattered with a loud *crack* and Freddie was catapulted out of his seat, smacking his head against the canopy. A cloud of dust wrapped itself around the vehicle, and Freddie dragged himself out, heading towards the block's main entrance. He pushed the door but it didn't budge. Freddie was confused. He'd been inside before, he was sure of it. This is where he lived. Or was it? He turned around. The building opposite looked the same. Maybe it was—

The door buzzed and swung outward. Freddie caught it as another man left the building. He was smaller than Freddie, with a pot belly that hung over his shorts. The man glanced at him, then stopped.

"Hey man, d'you know you're bleeding?" The paper mask that covered his mouth smothered his words.

Freddie touched the side of his head. His fingers came away sticky with blood.

"You should get that looked at."

"Mind your fucking business," Freddie snarled and slammed the door behind him.

"Where's your mask?" He heard the man shout after him. "*Asshole.*"

Freddie felt a sudden rush of adrenaline and he bolted up the stairs to the third floor. He stopped on the landing, chest heaving. Apartment doors stretched away in each direction. Freddie frowned, uncertainty nagging at him. He sniffed the air and thought he caught a scent of something familiar, something comforting. He followed the scent along the hallway until it filled his nostrils. He stopped outside a door, twisted the handle and stepped inside.

His place, he realised, and he slammed the door behind him. The room felt cramped, just a bed, a side locker, chairs and a small dining table. There were photographs in frames on the window ledge. Freddie looked at them, failing to recognise the fat, ugly faces that gawped at him. He threw them onto the floor and sat on the bed. The heat was unbearable and sweat ran down his face, soaking his underclothes.

He ripped off the bandages and inspected the wound on his hand. He rolled up the sleeve of his coveralls. The teeth marks were still there, only now a pattern of tiny blue veins had spread past the elbow of his left arm. He got to his feet and pulled off his T-shirt. The strange pattern had spread all the way to his shoulder and across his chest. He traced the small blue lines with his finger and strange, disjointed images filled his mind. The man who'd bitten him, Freddie no longer feared him, what he had inflicted. They were the same now. There were others too. He'd seen them all day, wandering around the compound. He was not alone.

He pulled off the rest of his clothes. He felt something uncoil inside him, a black, glistening thing that dwelt in a dark corner of his mind. He felt a rush of anger and hurled a chair across the room. He set about the rest of his furniture until it was all shattered. He stood in the middle of the room, his chest heaving, sweat running down his naked body, his hands lacerated and bleeding.

You're sick, a voice inside him said, but it was a timid, pussy-assed voice. The serpent hissed and the pussy-voice stopped talking.

Freddie vomited, the yellow fluid hosing the wreckage of his room. He staggered into the compact bathroom and gripped the sink. The reflection in the mirror angered him. It was the teeth, he decided. There was a purity about them, a whiteness that pained him, that triggered a dark, black rage. He tilted his head back and brought his mouth down onto the edge of the sink. The first blow cracked his front teeth. The second and third blows destroyed what was left. He spat blood and splinters into the sink, plucked root threads from his gums. He looked at his reflection again.

Better.

"Are you okay in there?"

Freddie frowned. Someone was outside, tapping, whining, like the pussy-ass voice he'd heard earlier. He yanked it open.

The woman on the other side stared wide-eyed at him. Freddie thought he recognised her but couldn't be sure about anything anymore. He grabbed a handful of hair and dragged her into his room. She screamed, so Freddie swung her around as hard as he could. The woman careered across the room and crashed into the mess of broken furniture. He slapped the uprooted hair from his hands and leapt on top of her. She slapped at him, her voice still whining, and it fuelled his rage. He sunk his thumbs deep into her eye sockets until the blood pooled over his knuckles.

Freddie staggered to his feet, panting. He watched her as she whimpered, her fingers exploring the useless mush of her eye sockets. Then she rolled over and began to crawl through the debris, one hand in front of the other. She crossed the room and found the door, ran her hands over it, used the handle to pull herself up. Then she turned towards him.

Freddie cocked his head. Even though she had no eyes, he understood that she was like him now. Her shallow breaths sucked the paper mask in and out, but soon her strength would come. Then she would test it, just like Freddie had. She was already moving out into the corridor. Freddie heard her feet scraping along the floor, the brush of her hands against the wall, the muffled rattle of her breathing. He followed her outside.

Freddie heard music and voices, and he saw the woman heading towards an open door. Then he heard more sounds, more voices above him. Freddie crept towards the stairs, his body feeling another surge of strength. He scampered up the stairs and paused on the landing. He swayed on his feet as he urinated, the liquid splashing over his legs and feet, pooling across the floor. He crept forward, his bloodied hands outstretched like claws, his fingers flexing. There were others at the end of the hallway, distant shadows, their urgent voices travelling down the hall. Freddie neither understood the words nor cared what they meant. His only urge now was to tear into them.

He broke into a run, his feet slapping against the floor, the scream of rage building in his chest and exploding from his toothless mouth. He saw their faces turn towards him, heard their yelps of fear. Rage gave him speed and power. He raised his hands, ready to rip and tear. They scattered like cock-roaches. Doors slammed along the hall. Some panicked and froze. Others were simply not quick enough.

Freddie charged into them.

Their screams filled the building.

BOSCO HEADED BACK TO HIS OFFICE ON THE FOURTH FLOOR OF the Chancery. The outer office was staffed with a handful of administrators and agents, all tapping away at their comput-ers. Bosco strode past them without a word and slammed the door behind him. He flopped into his chair, kicking his shoes up onto an open drawer.

The virus thing had him spooked, and the screening team in the lobby didn't reassure him. Hays said the virus was mutating. Did that mean that someone might pass the screening downstairs and *still* be carrying the virus? He'd meant to ask her, but he'd been spooked by the video of Jackson and Walsh. Now things had changed. They no longer thrashed against their restraints, Hays had told him. Instead, they sprayed vomit on anyone who entered the room they were being held in. Hays had shown him the video file.

He saw one of Captain Young's bio-suited soldiers enter the room. Jackson and Walsh's heads had turned in unison, tracking the soldier as he moved around the walls. And when he'd got close, they'd barfed at him, like cobras spitting venom. Hays believed that they were trying to recruit the soldier by infecting him. *Recruit?* Bosco had made his excuses and left the warehouse. He was feeling increasingly unnerved by the whole crisis. He hoped those specialist teams would arrive sooner rather than later.

He got to his feet. He had a corner office and he went to the window that overlooked Kindi Street and the Green Zone beyond. The sun was dipping towards the horizon and the sky to the east had taken on a yellowish tinge. Across the

Zone, the taller palms were getting teased by the strengthening breeze and dirt was being whipped off the rooftops. Bosco thought that the coming storm might be a bad one. He'd seen enough of them in his time.

He swore under his breath. First the bump to RSO, then they handed him Baghdad. That was more than a career booster. Granted, the facility had been undergoing a continuous drawdown for some years now, and since the crisis in DC the headcount was even lower, but it was still an honour to be handed such a responsibility. It was the biggest of Bosco's career, but now, thanks to Roth, it could prove to be his last. Everything he did now, every action and decision, had to be carefully considered. This would probably end in a Senate hearing, and Bosco had to make sure he was prepared for—

The phone on his desk rang. He snatched it up.

"Bosco."

"This is DC Ops Centre. Confirm ID please."

Bosco reeled off his personal confirmation code.

"Acknowledged. Are you in a secure location?"

"Affirmative."

"Hold, please."

Bosco waited for less than three seconds. The voice that spoke to him next was unmistakable, the urgency, evident.

"Mister Bosco, do you know who this is?"

Holy shit…

"Yes, of course, Madame Secretary." He'd never met Coffman but he knew that right now she was the most powerful woman in Washington. And pretty soon, if the media had their polling right, the world. Bosco felt a rush of excitement. Whatever she needed, Bosco would make it happen.

"I appreciate you taking care of my embassy over there, Mister Bosco."

"The honour is mine, Madame—"

"Time is short, so I'm going to hand you off to someone else. Listen very carefully to what they have to tell you. And Mister Bosco?"

"Yes, ma'am?"

"When this is over, I expect to see you in DC. To thank you personally."

And then she was gone. Bosco heard another click on the line, and then a voice he didn't recognise spoke to him.

"Mister Bosco, my name is Mulholland, Secretary Coffman's Chief of Staff. You have a situation there, correct?"

"Yes sir, a serious public health issue. I believe Bill Jacobs sent a report to DC earlier this morning."

"And you've been briefed? About *Messina*?"

"By Jacobs himself," Bosco confirmed. "And my belief is that this situation could've been contained much sooner if the Delta commander had—"

"We'll get to all that later," Mulholland interrupted. "How many people are sick?"

He recalled the warehouse, the people wandering around inside the cage, frightened, angry. *Infected.* "Seventy-eight," he told Mulholland. "Doctor Hays expects that number to rise."

There was a crunch of static over the line. "Are you there, Tom?"

First names, now? Things must be serious. "Go ahead."

"Tom, you need to listen very carefully to what I'm about to tell you."

"Yes, sir."

"The political situation in Washington is deteriorating. Trust between the Pentagon and the temporary administration is at breaking point. Powerful interests in the military see an empty White House and they smell opportunity."

Bosco pressed the phone a little tighter against his ear. "Excuse me?"

"There are forces at work, right here in DC. They're trying

to undermine the political process, derail the presidential election."

Bosco picked up a pen and wrote *election* on a notepad. He put a question mark after it and circled it several times as his thought processes played catchup. "That's illegal," he told Mulholland. "And who's *they*?"

"Look, we don't have much time. The interests I speak of, they have friends in the Pentagon, the Crisis Committee, in Homeland Security and the House. There's talk of waiving the Posse Comitatus Act—"

Bosco felt the blood drain from his face. "They can't do that."

"Let me tell you what they *did* do. When Jacobs' report landed on Secretary Coffman's desk, her first reaction was to mobilise the USAMRIID and CDC teams, get them to you ASAP. That order was countermanded." There was another crackle of static on the line, then Mulholland said, "No one is coming to the rescue, Tom."

Bosco felt a chill deep inside his stomach. Without that help, they were going to be in serious trouble. He had a sudden vision of himself, strapped to a hospital bed, spitting blood and screaming. He heard Mulholland talking and refocussed.

"—Coffman told the Pentagon that those responsible for transporting that virus into your embassy will be held accountable for their actions. They're not going to allow that to happen."

"What do you mean?" Bosco asked him.

"A Pentagon whistleblower has spoken to Secretary Coffman. They want the virus to run out of control and spread into Baghdad—"

Bosco thought he'd misheard. "What? Who does?"

"Listen to me, Tom. If the city falls, it'll destabilise the country, maybe the region. If that happens, the world will demand swift action. The State Department will be blamed and the military will assume authority here in Washington to —quote—*deal with the crisis*. The elections will be postponed, maybe indefinitely. Democracy will be finished, Tom. We can't let that happen."

"Jesus Christ," Bosco whispered. He switched the phone to his other hand, wiped his sweaty palm on a trouser leg. "What is it you need me to do?"

Mulholland's voice crackled with static. "Keep that virus contained, any way you can. Use any means necessary. We'll try to get those response teams mobilised but we've got a fight on our hands here. It may take some time."

"I understand."

"And be advised, they may have assets in the compound there, allies, saboteurs perhaps. Stay alert. Watch for red flags."

"Stand by." Bosco lowered the phone. Like almost everybody else at the embassy he'd been cut out of the loop, and now Delta had put all their lives in danger. The military posed a threat, Mulholland said. That was a tough pill to swallow, but governments had fallen across the world, including his own. Power vacuums had been created. Anything was possible right now. Yet his loyalties—no, *his future*—lay with Secretary Coffman. Whatever she needed, Tom Bosco would get it done.

"The legal ramifications of all this, I—"

"You'll be protected, Tom. You have Secretary Coffman's word on that."

Bosco took a deep breath. "That's good to know."

"There's something else. You need to get everyone inside the Chancery, in preparation for an emergency evacuation. We don't have much time. Are you listening, Tom?"

Bosco sat a little straighter in his chair, pen hovering over his notepad.

"Go ahead."

CHAPTER 7
BAGHDAD UNPLUGGED

IN THE PRIVACY OF HER OFFICE, COFFMAN LEANED BACK IN HER chair and studied the high-definition toad on her computer screen. David Ashcroft was a decidedly unattractive man, but he hadn't been chosen for his looks. Or his political smarts.

The feed from Ashcroft's built-in computer camera gave Coffman an up close and personal view of the diplomat's fat head. He was polishing his glasses, his bulbous eyes flicking to the screen every couple of seconds. He had no idea Coffman was watching him from over six thousand miles away.

She peered over the top of her computer as Mulholland strode into the room. He dropped into the chair in front of her desk as the door swung shut behind him with a sound-proofed thud. The casual clothes were gone now, replaced by a smart grey designer suit and red tie, his thick grey hair neatly groomed.

"Well?"

"Bosco's onboard."

"And the Aswads?"

"The President came through. With conditions."

"We don't have time to negotiate."

"He's prepared to wait. He spoke about reparations."

"Naturally," Coffman said, her eyes flicking to the toad. "Is everything ready?"

Mulholland held up a compact cell phone. "Gatekeeper's waiting for the word."

"Then let's get on with it."

Coffman sat a little straighter in her chair and smoothed the arms of the smart navy business suit she was now wearing. She leaned forward and clicked the *privacy* icon on her screen.

"Good morning, David," she began.

Six thousand miles away, Ashcroft's fat head snapped up. He fumbled his glasses on and cleared his throat. "Madame Secretary," he stuttered. "It's an honour to speak to you."

Coffman glanced at the row of clocks on the wall. It was early evening in Baghdad.

"We're short on time, David, so brevity is vital."

On her computer screen, Ashcroft nodded. "I understand, in which case I think we should discuss medical priorities—"

"There's no time," Coffman told him. "The political situation here in Washington has taken a disturbing turn. There are forces at work, rebellious elements in our military."

The toad leaned into the camera. "Excuse me?"

"The RSO has been briefed. And whatever he tells you, it stays between you both, do you understand, David?"

The high definition camera picked out the sheen of sweat on Ashcroft's top lip, the confusion in his eyes. She heard the tremor in his voice. "Madame Secretary, I don't—"

"Listen to me, David." She leaned closer to the screen. "Are you listening?" Ashcroft nodded several times. Coffman furrowed her brow, delivering a well-practiced expression of deep concern. "You and Mister Bosco are the only two people I can trust right now. Not the military, nor the CIA. Talk to each other, work together. You need to make sure that the virus does not escape from that embassy, do you hear me?"

"Yes, Madame Secretary. Can I ask—"

"Thank you, David. I'll get back to you shortly." She terminated the feed with a click of her mouse. "Make the call, Erik. Cut them off."

She watched Erik send the message, heard his phone beep with a reply. "It's done," he said. He punched another number. "Karen, let's get the Secretary's computer wiped, please. Make sure you delete all the backups too." He slipped the phone into his jacket pocket. "I hope you know what you're doing, Amy. I don't want to be wearing an orange jump suit for the next thirty years."

"It won't come to that. They'll give us the needle."

Mulholland paled. "This isn't a joke."

"I'm serious." She was too. The country would demand it. "Stop worrying, Erik. We have a plan."

Mulholland wasn't convinced. "You know what they say about the best-laid plans."

Coffman said nothing because she knew Erik was right. Empires had unravelled as a result of seemingly unrelated and innocuous incidents, but her Chief of Staff had misread her. She wasn't complacent at all. It was fear that caused the sudden shaking of her hands, the acidic knot in her stomach. Baghdad might be cut off, but what happened behind its walls in the next twelve hours would make or break her presidential ambitions. She was at a fork in the road; one branch led to the Oval Office, the other to Erik's orange-clad perp walk. The thought of the latter made her nauseous.

"It's time to double down, Erik. Now that we've lit the fuse in Baghdad, we're going to spin our narrative and get the administration onside. I'll deal with Moody and his little Band of Brothers at the Pentagon, but you're going to have to reach out to our friends in the Crisis Committee, Homeland Security and the Supreme Court. And you'll have to spin them hard, Erik, because painting Moody as a bad guy is going to be a tough sell."

"So, how long before we break this?"

Coffman took another sip of water and settled back into her chair. The fear left her then, like a silk scarf slipping from her shoulders. What she felt now was excitement. Yes, there were many unknowns, but Coffman trusted her instincts. She trusted the outcome would be favourable, and that the next seat she occupied would be in the Oval Office.

"Another hour," she told Mulholland. "Long enough for the seeds of chaos to take root."

Bosco marched through the executive suite and into Ashcroft's outer office.

"Is he in?" he barked at Ashcroft's PA. She nodded, but before she could announce him, Bosco was already inside the inner sanctum, slamming the door behind him. Ashcroft scrambled out from behind his desk and met Bosco halfway across the room.

"I've just spoken to Secretary Coffman," Ashcroft whispered.

"Likewise," Bosco told him. He relayed his conversation with Mulholland. Ashcroft's face turned white.

"A traitorous military? I don't believe it."

"We can't trust anyone, David, especially them. It's just you and me."

"But why would they want this virus thing to spread? What good will that do?"

"Imagine if the virus gets out, David. In a city like Baghdad, it'll spread like a medieval plague. People would flee, seek safety in neighbouring countries. Iran, Saudi, Jordan, Syria, they'd all be in the firing line. Tens of millions will die and the whole region will be quarantined. They'll beg for help, and we could dictate terms—"

"C'mon, Tom, you can't be serious," Ashcroft blurted.

"*Rogue elements in the military*, that's what Mulholland

said. Think about it, David. The only reason you and I are standing here now, in this billion-dollar embassy, is because of falsified evidence." He saw the vacant look on Ashcroft's face and said, "Saddam Hussein? WMDs? The whole world now knows it's bullshit, yet here we are."

"You're right," Ashcroft whispered.

The man was frightened, Bosco could see that. He was too, and given the circumstances it was understandable. American lives have been sacrificed on the altar of political expediency many times in the past. He didn't want *his* name carved into the Memorial Wall.

"But it doesn't make any sense," Ashcroft persisted. "If they want the virus to spread, why the lockdown, why quarantine the sick?"

Bosco shrugged. "I don't know. Political cover, reassurance, maybe—" He frowned. "Wait a minute, the attack in the commissary, maybe that was some kind of test. Maybe they *wanted* that to happen. It would explain why Roth kept his mouth shut about Jackson going missing."

Ashcroft's face darkened. "That sounds plausible. And if Delta pose a threat, we probably shouldn't trust Lynch or his Marines."

"Agreed."

"So, what happens now?"

"We start moving everyone into the Chancery. I'm implementing EAP Annexe D. All personnel to fall back to this building."

"Everyone?"

"Anyone who's not sick. Mulholland's idea."

"Why?"

"All the good guys in one location, plus it'll make any evacuation easier to manage. We've got a kitchen, lots of empty floor space and plenty of supplies. Mulholland believes that common sense will prevail in DC, but, in any case, we need to be ready."

"Should we start burn procedures?"

Bosco shook his head. "Not yet. State will advise on that. In the meantime, I'll send you a couple of my guys to beef up security."

Ashcroft offered a grateful nod. "Thank you, Tom." He walked around his desk and sat back down. "I'll leave you to it then. Keep me updated, would you?"

Bosco watched him spin in his chair and start typing on his keyboard. Making a record, no doubt. Bosco knew he'd have to do the same at some stage.

Despite Mulholland's assurances, his ass still needed to be covered.

"STATE YOUR BUSINESS," BARKED THE MARINE AS DOUG STEPPED into the tent erected outside the Chancery.

A bunch of uniforms in desert pattern LIST smocks stared at him as the wind rattled through the temporary structure. All of them wore Perspex face masks and latex gloves. They stood behind a table filled with neat rows of swabs, wipes, vials and a row of laptops.

A bio-warfare team, Doug realised.

The Marine had a paper mask over his mouth and a rifle slung across his chest. He seemed edgy. Doug tapped the laptop case slung over his shoulder.

"There's a hardware fault down in The Hub. Got a Severity One message from the monitoring software if you'd like to see it?"

He didn't. "Drop the bag and step forward," the Marine ordered.

Doug obeyed. A black female fired questions at him from behind the table as she scanned his SAP card.

"Are you running a temperature? Do you have a headache? Are you feeling disorientated, confused?"

Doug answered in the negative. He winced as one of the

bio team pierced his thumb with a lancet and took a blood sample. Next to her, a colleague was cleaning the surface of his bag with a disinfectant wipe.

"Step back," the Marine ordered. Doug did so, feeling his heart rate rise a little. The man was geared up, tactical vest, gloves, eye protection. Two bio-suits were pointing at the computer screen.

"He's clear," the black lady announced.

Doug swallowed. "You had me worried," he joked, but his voice sounded a little reedy.

He took his laptop bag and walked through the tent to the Chancery doors. He continued through the security lobby and out into the atrium, which seemed busier than before. Doug didn't give it much thought. Getting home as fast as possible was his priority now. After he was done downstairs, he'd visit the Transportation Office, see what his options were.

Service Corridor A took him down to The Hub. He swiped his SAP card and shouldered the door open.

SIX THOUSAND, ONE HUNDRED AND SIXTY-EIGHT MILES AWAY, IN A similar sub-level basement located beneath the NSA's Fort Meade complex, an incoming message rumbled on Gatekeeper's burner phone. He put down his coffee mug and snuck a peek over those same monitors. Across the room his colleagues were working an ongoing DISA problem. No one was watching Gatekeeper.

He read the message. *So, it's time.* All he needed now was someone to take the heat. He tapped a few commands and brought up The Hub's door-entry log. *Great, there's someone in The Hub right now - Doug Walker, DOD Communications Specialist.* He pulled up the CCTV feed on another monitor and eyeballed Unlucky Contestant Number One. Walker was dressed in navy cargoes and a white T-shirt, and he was unpacking his laptop on a workbench. Gatekeeper felt a momentary twinge of sympathy for the man, but that's all it was.

Bad timing could make or break a person, and Mister Walker was about to find himself in a world of hurt.

Doug made his way between the server cabinets until he found the faulty system. He opened the cabinet door and took a careful look at the server rack. On the display above the faulty transceiver card, a red light winked at him. Doug was reasonably familiar with the system and knew that card replacements were dynamic - all he had to do was switch them out. Easy-peasy. He plugged in his laptop to the management port. It wouldn't hurt to run a diagnostics check afterwards.

He found a replacement card in the storage cage and went back to the cabinet. Doug slid the system out on its rails and popped the cover. Inside, complex electronics hummed quietly. Doug located the faulty card and flipped up its locking pins. He hesitated for just a moment, double-checking one more time that he was about to pull the correct module. *Measure twice, cut once*, as his grandpa used to tell everybody.

Satisfied, Doug gripped the card's edges and yanked it from its runners.

Overhead, the lights flickered and died.

Gatekeeper saw the feed from that distant room terminate.

He crabbed his chair across the floor to a bank of routing management terminals and ran the program he'd buried deep in the system code some time ago. The software suppressed all confirmation messages, and he watched the Baghdad systems acknowledge the update and begin their reboot sequences. As they did so, Gatekeeper ran his own checks, sending data packets across tens of thousands of miles of fibre optic cabling and through a myriad of secure routing networks until he was certain. Then he tested it again, and after he'd ticked off his mental checklist, he checked everything one more time. Gatekeeper liked to measure twice and cut once too.

Because Gatekeeper had to be certain. He was playing a high-stakes game and his life probably depended on it. No one had threatened him directly but the understanding was clear. If he fucked up, it would only be a matter of time before they came for him. A home invasion gone wrong, a hit and run, a heart attack; in every case, Gatekeeper would be history, so getting it right was important.

Because they knew about his messy divorce, the twins' college tuition fees, the Florida nursing home where his folks resided, all of which were slowly crushing him. They knew about his secret trips to Atlantic City too, which was *verboten* to anyone with his security clearance. They knew it all, but instead of the stick, they offered him a big, fat juicy carrot. Enough cash to pay off the bitch, to settle Dartmouth in full and get the nursing home administrator off his back. And after all that was taken care of, he'd still have enough squirrelled away to ride the tables at the Borgata long into old age.

When they'd laid *that* deal on the table, Gatekeeper had hesitated for less than three seconds.

He crabbed his chair back again, wheels rumbling across the tiled floor. He checked the visual displays this time, the big HD screens around the walls and saw the routing maps glowing green, all the way from Iraq to the continental United States. As far as the NSA or anyone else was concerned, Baghdad was live on the grid. He yanked a tissue from the box by his workstation and dabbed at the pearls of sweat that dotted his forehead.

So, now he really was the Gatekeeper.

He had full control of the Defence Information Systems

Networks, the global video systems, the messaging service and the wireless, mobile and satellite networks. That last one was crucial and Gatekeeper had taken special care to ensure that local access was disabled for the COMSATCOM, ARABSAT and INMARSAT networks. Anyone with a satellite phone in the greater Baghdad area would find their handset useless until Gatekeeper restored access. He was officially past the point of no return.

He sent an email from his personal laptop, a request for more information regarding a spa resort in Vermont, a place he'd never been to nor had any intention of ever visiting. The reply was almost instantaneous, registering his interest. *Confirmation received.* That would be Blake, sitting at his own suite of command consoles at Rock Creek. As of that moment, Blake was juiced in too.

Sit back and wait for the all-clear, that's all he had to do now. He wondered about the other guy, Walker, the patsy in Baghdad, and imagined the heat the poor schmuck was about to catch. Gatekeeper didn't envy him.

He raised his coffee mug in a silent toast.
Good luck, buddy.

THE LIGHTS STUTTERED BACK INTO LIFE.

Doug blinked several times, his hands gripping the cabinet, a cold sweat on the back of his neck. The room had been plunged into total blackness for at least a minute, and now it was filled with the beeps and clicks of rebooting systems.

Doug looked around him. Scratch that - it looked like *every* system was rebooting. Right around the room, in every hardware cage, processor lights were blinking and hard drives were grinding. Doug wondered why the battery-backups hadn't kicked in and that worried him. He thought about the potential data loss and its implications. After all, Doug was the only person in the room. Questions would be asked, answers demanded.

Fuck.

He tapped the keys of his laptop but the screen was blank. He held his finger on the power button and a BIOS message appeared, a flashing cursor, a single sentence:

No operating system found.

Doug frowned. *What the hell?*

He heard a click and a buzz as The Hub door opened. A moment later Howard Reed appeared at the end of the aisle and marched towards him. Reed was the IT manager and he looked seriously pissed. A couple of tech guys hurried after him. Reed spread his hands as he approached Doug.

"What did you do?"

"Excuse me?"

"Everything is down. Intranet, messaging, phones, cloud services, everything. We've lost the consulates at Erbil and Basrah, plus the hard lines to Kuwait. You were the only person in here so I'll ask you again, what did you do?"

He saw Doug's laptop and practically shouldered him out of the way. "What's this?"

"My DOD laptop. I was swapping out a transceiver board," he explained.

"Tell me what you did. Exactly."

Doug told him.

"Who ordered you to do that?"

"I received an automated system message."

"Show me."

Doug pointed to the laptop. "I can't. My operating system has disappeared."

Reed unplugged the laptop and handed it back to one of his techs. "Take that to my office."

"Hey, that's my property," Doug protested, but his voice lacked conviction. All around him systems were still running up to speed. The air hummed with feverish electronic activity.

Reed held out his hand. "Give me your credentials."

Doug shook his head. "You don't have the authority."

Reed dropped his hand. "We'll see about that." He turned to the remaining tech guy. "He stays here and touches nothing."

Reed marched out of the room. The other guy smiled sheepishly and shrugged. "We lost everything," he said.

Doug held up his hands. "It was hardware swap, that's it. This doesn't make sense."

His stomach churned. He'd effectively rebooted the embassy, and he prayed that everything would come back online. If it didn't, a couple of things would happen. The first would be the withdrawal of his SAP clearance. The second would be his expulsion from Iraq. That one wasn't so bad - he needed to get home - but the loss of the contract would be a major blow. His security clearance would almost certainly be downgraded. He'd lose his job at the Naval Yard, and with it the big contracting bucks. The DOD would probably cut him loose, and the private sector would avoid him like - well, like someone carrying that goddam virus.

He pushed past the tech and sat down at a workbench. *You're panicking. The systems will reboot and this will be chalked up to a hardware glitch. It'll be okay.*

Doug sat in the chair and stared at his sneakers.

Forty-three feet below Doug's Nikes, in a dark, concrete chamber buried deep below the Chancery building, another system bleeped and hummed into life.

It was roughly the size of a Chevy Spark, rectangular, with a single command terminal built into its front panel. From its sleek black sides eight thick pipes disappeared into the ground at right angles, each one containing a loom of fibre-optic cabling that connected it to its component parts located all over the embassy. The system had lain dormant for some time, but now a remote command had woken it from its electronic slumber. And it had work to do.

Its first task was a full systems check, and the subsequent acknowledgement packet travelled through the two hundred and forty-seven miles of cabling buried in a network of fortified pipes beneath the compound. All nodes registered the acknowledgment and answered the wake-up call in under nine seconds.

Now that communication had been established, the system interrogated the status of the hardware located at those nodes. It checked motion detectors and hydraulics, ammunition stores and firing computers, until it was satisfied that everything was online and functioning.

Logic dictated that the next test was a physical one, and the system checked its internal log to find out when that had last occurred. *One year, three months, two days, eleven hours and fifty-one seconds ago.* It logged a recommendation for a physical systems check.

There was one more component that required a diagnostic test. It was a system that could only be triggered manually, however a recent update to its firing software had overridden the need for physical human interaction. The system checked when that update to its operating system had been made.

Eight minutes ago.

It was now fully autonomous.

Developed by the technicians at Kroll Industries, the highly classified Grand Slam Close-In Combat Defence System waited quietly in the dark like a huge black spider, its myriad red eyes winking in the darkness.

Just under a mile away across the International Zone, a grey Nissan SUV pulled into the parking lot behind the Al-Fardan telephone exchange building.

Two men climbed out of the vehicle and approached the

building's main entrance. Both of them were dressed in dark suits and open-necked shirts, but only one of them carried an SR2 Veresk submachine gun in a special harness under his jacket. He was the older of the two, a presidential bodyguard and experienced warfighter capable of sudden and extreme violence should the circumstances arise. So far today they hadn't.

The other man was younger, bespectacled, his collar-length black hair swept back off his forehead and confident to the point of mild arrogance. He punched a four-digit code into the building's entry system and yanked the door open. The man with the gun followed him inside and scanned the lobby, his hands ready to reach beneath his open jacket and bring the weapon to bear. Neither man was expecting trouble, however. It was cooperation they sought today.

The younger man had never been inside the modern two-storey building but he knew it had been built by the Americans after the invasion of oh-three. He also knew it provided a digital switching capability that served the whole of the International Zone, including the phone networks that served all the foreign embassies and consulates. He himself was an electronics engineer and today he'd been busy.

His first stop had been the electricity sub-station at Karkh, where he'd ordered the management to carry out a limited shutdown of their network. He repeated that order at the offices of Asiacell, Korek and Zain Iraq, with a special emphasis on the cellular towers that served the International Zone and surrounding districts. His orders were not questioned - the bespectacled man's reputation and impeccable political connections spoke for themselves. The hard-faced man with the black gun reinforced that spirit of cooperation. The Al-Fardan telephone exchange was their last stop.

The first person to encounter them was a hijab'd woman who crossed the lobby in front of them. The younger man demanded to see the duty manager. The older man stood behind him stony-faced, the black metal of his submachine gun clearly visible. The woman scurried away. The duty manager appeared soon after.

Their conversation was short, the younger man's authority quickly established, the order implicit - an immediate shutdown of all local and international circuits, except those that served the American Embassy.

The duty manager was confused. His mouth opened to say something, but then he glanced at the hard-faced man and decided against it. Instead he invited the men to join him in the control room. His staff consisted of eleven engineers, eight men and three women, all of them dedicated telecommunications professionals, the manager proudly told the interlopers. He then repeated the shutdown order. The engineers went to work immediately.

It took approximately eighteen minutes for the telephone systems to be shut down and for the cell repeaters to be disabled. It wasn't uncommon for networks to fail in Iraq but an outage of this magnitude would not go unnoticed. Neither would their cooperation, assured the bespectacled man. A nervous smile spread across the manager's sweaty face.

A *shamal* was coming, the young Iraqi informed the assembled staff, and he ordered them to take their belongings and go home until further notice. He saw another question form behind the manager's lips, and once again the man decided against opening them. Instead he nodded and tugged his jacket off the back of his chair.

Outside in the parking lot, the bespectacled man watched the manager lock the building and climb into a waiting car. When all the staff had left, he took a heavy chain and padlock from the trunk of the SUV and secured the doors. He climbed back into the SUV and they drove away.

The bespectacled man checked his phone, satisfied with the *No Service* legend on his phone's display. Now they would have to drive several miles, to the villa just outside the city where he would make the call. He had no idea why his uncle wanted the International Zone cut off from the outside world, but neither did he care. The future of his country was at stake, and the bespectacled man felt as strongly about that as his uncles did, so he didn't question it.

The Nissan headed north, leaving the dead zone far behind them.

CHAPTER 8
PRIMATE

Doug heard the drum of footsteps approaching The Hub door. He got to his feet. *Here we go.* The door buzzed and swung open.

The Regional Security Officer strode in. He saw Doug and veered towards him. He was followed by Reed and four Diplomatic Security agents. They wore tan combat pants and black shirts with the DS logo on their chests. They also carried sidearms.

Bosco stood in front of Doug and held out his hand. "Your SAP credentials, right now."

Doug lifted the lanyard over his head and dangled his ID into Bosco's waiting hand.

"Who issued your clearance?"

"DOD," Doug told him.

"Your laptop has been wiped clean."

"It was working just fine before this happened."

"Don't get smart. You've compromised the security of this embassy."

"I was just doing my job. A routine maintenance thing."

Bosco said to his agents, "Escort Mister Walker upstairs."

A few minutes later Doug was being escorted along the

carpeted corridor of the Executive Suite. He was steered into a brightly lit conference room and ordered to take a seat at the large conference table.

The twenty or so people in the room stared at him like he was on trial. Some were military personnel, others civilians. Half the room was sitting around the table while the remainder lined the walls. No one said a word. Everyone was eyeballing him, and Doug suddenly realised that this situation could result in something far worse than the termination of his contract.

Bosco marched into the room a moment later, and Doug saw him hand over his credentials to the bald man sitting at the far end. He studied them for several moments, then looked up over his spectacles at Doug.

"Doug Walker," the man said.

"Yes, sir."

"I am Acting Chief of Mission Ashcroft."

Doug nodded. "Sir, let me start by saying—"

"Quiet," Bosco growled.

Doug swallowed a flash of anger. He didn't appreciate being scolded like a fourth grader. Ashcroft continued, reading from a sheet of paper on the table in front of him.

"Your area of expertise is communications and you have DOD clearance to SAP level, is that correct, Mister Walker?"

Doug nodded. "Yes, sir."

Ashcroft dangled the sheet between his fingers. "This is the receipt you signed for your entry swipe. Right now, that's all we know about you, Mister Walker, because whatever you did, you've managed to cut this embassy off from the outside world."

"I didn't—"

"What's our status, Mister Reed?"

The IT manager hovered by the door. "No change, I'm afraid. All systems are functioning normally, but the DOD cloud is just not there. Telecoms systems are all operational but there's no routing beyond our own exchange. Dedicated links to Erbil and Basrah are down too. I've got the whole team working on it."

Ashcroft waved a hand at the wall. "What about satellite communications? We've got all kinds of dishes out there."

"We do. Our main earth station feeds satellite signals to the Air Force's WGS system which relays that traffic to—"

"Is it working or not?" Ashcroft cut in.

Reed shook his head. "No, sir."

"I've got no cell signal," said an older guy at the table, his sleeves rolled up to his elbows. He held up his Samsung. "Anyone got anything?" His question was met by a chorus of troubled murmurs.

Ashcroft pointed a finger at Doug. "You're telling me this man has cut us off from Baghdad's cell network too?"

"Is that even possible?" someone else asked.

Ashcroft looked at Reed who shook his head. "That's out of our remit. We have two cell repeater towers on site but they're nothing more than signal boosters. The International Zone is normally well-served by the local network."

"Thank you, Mister Reed. Don't let us keep you," Ashcroft said, staring over his glasses at the IT Manager. Reed took the hint and left the room, followed by his tech guys. The embassy chief shifted his gaze to Doug. He looked nervous, Doug thought.

"Well, Mister Walker, from where I'm sitting this looks like wilful sabotage."

"Sir, all I can tell you is—"

"No more hiding behind the DOD's skirts," Bosco warned, "unless you plan on spending the next twenty years in Leavenworth."

Doug knew he was in serious trouble. He was innocent, he knew that too, but how was he going to prove it? All of his communications with the DOD were conducted through the secure portal on his laptop. In fact, everything he did out here, from email to web browsing, to running his daily checks, was carried out on that laptop.

"I want to help, believe me. The truth is I have no idea what happened. I was carrying out a simple task and—"

"On whose orders?" a suit to his right asked. "Who gave you the authorisation?"

Doug shrugged. "I don't need it for a job like that. I must've carried out at least a dozen hardware faults in The Hub since I've been here. Check the logs."

He turned back to Ashcroft.

"Sir, I'm a communications specialist working under contract through the DOD's Joint Force Information Network. I'm cleared for Top Secret work. My last job was upgrading VLF boards on the USS Colorado, one of the Navy's latest attack subs. I've held a variety of high-level clearances for over eight years, and I've also served my country. I'm a patriot, sir. Harming the interests of the United States is not in my DNA."

No one said anything for several moments. Doug made eye contact with some of the faces around the room, daring them to question his loyalty. There were no takers. A DS agent entered the room and approached Bosco.

"His place is clean," Doug heard him say.

"You searched my apartment?"

"It belongs to the US government," Bosco told him, glaring down the table. He leaned into Ashcroft and said, "I suggest we detain Mister Walker until we're back online and we can verify his credentials."

Doug's eyes widened. "What?"

A DS agent grabbed Doug's arm. Doug sprang to his feet, shoved the guy away. "Take your hands off me."

The room erupted. Doug was pinned to the table by half a dozen agents and he stopped struggling. It would only make things worse.

"Clear the room," Ashcroft ordered. He jabbed a finger at Doug. "Not him."

The agents released him and dumped him back into his seat. The room cleared in less than ten seconds. Now it was just Ashcroft and Bosco.

"You can see how this looks," Ashcroft told Doug.

"All due respect, it looks even worse from where I'm sitting."

"He could be a sleeper," Bosco speculated. "He crippled The Hub, wiped his laptop. Who knows what else he's been—"

Bosco clammed up as the door opened and another man entered the room. He wore dark trousers, a white shirt and blue tie. He was middle-aged, authoritative. He glared at Doug.

"Is this the guy?"

"That's him," Bosco confirmed.

Ashcroft pointed to the new arrival. "Mister Walker, this is Bill Jacobs of the Central Intelligence Agency."

Doug nodded, swallowed hard. This was getting way out of hand.

Jacobs stood across the table from Doug, his arms folded. "What did you do, Mister Walker?"

Doug told his story again. When he finished, he said, "Whatever happened in that room could not have been triggered by a simple card swap."

"Did that wipe your laptop too?"

"I can't explain that," Doug told him. "As I've said before, I've been working DOD contracts for almost a decade. I've worked at several classified facilities in the States and overseas. I've worked on US Navy missile boats and at Air Force intelligence reconnaissance bases—"

"You mean drones," Jacobs said.

Doug nodded. "Right. Joint JSOC/CIA programs. My

bona fides are valid, Mister Jacobs. In fact, I've probably got higher clearance than most of the people in this embassy."

"So did Edward Snowden," Bosco told him.

"He was a fucking traitor," Doug snapped. "I'm no goddam traitor."

"Take it easy," Jacobs cautioned. He looked at Ashcroft. "My office has lost all comms. The Baghdad cell network is out too."

"Maybe he's working with someone," Bosco speculated. Doug saw him exchange a look with Ashcroft. The embassy chief addressed him.

"Tell me something, Mister Walker, if this wasn't deliberate, how do we fix it? You're the specialist after all."

Doug shrugged. "Well, it sounds like everything is working okay, which means it's a connectivity issue. A fault outside the facility. I'd probably send someone out into the Zone, make a call from elsewhere. Another embassy maybe?"

There was a moment of silence as everyone looked at each other. Ashcroft was the first to speak.

"The Danish Embassy is right across the street."

Jacobs shook his head. "Their government has been a little hostile towards the US since the financial scandal." He snapped his fingers. "There's an Iraqi Radio Shack-type store in the Zone. We take a vehicle and go buy some Sat phones."

"Is that secure?" Ashcroft asked.

"They're encrypted, but not to government spec. In any case, it's a short-term fix. We call State, the Pentagon, get this problem fixed."

Doug saw another exchange between Bosco and Ashcroft. It was subtle, a momentary eye contact, and Jacobs wasn't included. Bosco checked his watch.

"That store will be closed now."

Jacobs shrugged. "So, we find the owner, get him to open up."

"And let the Iraqis know our comms are down? Not a good idea."

"Those phones could be for anything," Jacobs argued. "We send one guy in, make the purchase, then we contact Erbil. They can relay messages with DC."

"Tom's right, it's a security risk." Ashcroft plucked at his lower lip. He stared at Doug again. "I prefer Walker's suggestion. We'll send a delegation to the Brits. They can be trusted, right?"

Jacobs nodded. "Absolutely."

"Good. So, we contact State from there. How's the weather looking?"

"Deteriorating," Bosco replied.

"We'd best move quickly then." Ashcroft looked at Jacobs. "Set it up please, Bill."

Jacobs looked surprised. "Don't you want Tom's office to handle it?"

"I'd rather you take care of it. National security and so forth." Ashcroft got to his feet. "Tom, we need to talk."

"What about Walker?"

The Acting Chief of Mission gave Doug a long, cold look and said, "Detain him."

Doug shot to his feet. "Wait!" The agents stepped closer, boxing him in. Doug kept his tone measured. "Sir, I have a daughter, Holly. She's been missing for some time, but now she's been found and she's in serious trouble. Health issues and suchlike. She needs me. I have to get home, sir."

No one said anything. Doug looked at the three men in turn, hoping for something positive. Anything. It was Bosco who spoke first.

"This facility is on lockdown. No one goes anywhere until that's lifted."

"Do you have kids?" Doug asked him.

"We all do." It was Ashcroft this time. "I'm afraid Mister Bosco is right. I'm sorry, but there's nothing we can do."

"Put him in one of the interview rooms," Bosco ordered the agents.

"Sir!" Doug looked straight at Jacobs. "When you get to the Brit embassy, would you make a call for me? The guy's name is Rick Gould, a former FBI agent. He's the guy who found my daughter. Would you get a message to him? Please?"

Jacobs shook his head. "Maybe later. When things have settled down."

Doug watched everyone file out of the room. He felt a hand on his shoulder.

"Let's go, buddy."

Doug's heart sank. He felt physically sick as they escorted him downstairs. The clock was ticking. If he didn't get home soon, Holly would disappear with that Flores kid. Doug might never see her again.

Down in the atrium there were a lot more people and a lot of chatter. Something was going on, and Doug had a terrible feeling that the situation was only going to get worse.

He was escorted through a few security doors and directed into a small room. A table, three chairs, sound-proofed walls - a standard interview room.

"Take a seat," the lead agent said to him. The name on his ID card read *Murphy*. "You want a coffee?"

"Sure," Doug nodded. "Thanks."

Murphy hesitated. "I got a daughter too. The minute comms are back up, I'll get you to a phone."

Doug could've hugged the guy. "Thanks, man. I appreciate that."

The door closed behind him and Doug heard the lock being thrown. He dropped into a chair and held his head in his hands.

. . .

Veronica Hays stood in the doorway of Warehouse Seven and studied the line of patients shuffling towards the loading bay. She kept to the shadows as she smoked a cigarette, ticking off the heads until she reached twenty-seven. She couldn't see the end of the line because it continued around the corner of the building across the street, but there were probably a few more waiting back there too.

They were a mixture of diplomatic staff, utility workers, facility contractors and military personnel. Their faces were obscured with paper masks and all of them wore latex gloves on their hands. There was a gap of at least six feet between each of them, strictly policed by Lynch's Marines.

Including the twenty-seven she could see, that made it over sixty victims in the last hour. The infection rate was rising fast, and again Hays considered door stepping Ashcroft and demanding an ETA on those response teams. There'd been no news all day, which was deeply troubling. This thing was way beyond her experience.

And Captain Young's too, she'd discovered. The Chemical Corps officer had confessed that she'd spent most of her career decontaminating vehicles rather than people. Her brief had been a simple one - provide post-mission facilities for the returning Delta team. Deluge showers for personnel and kit. Nothing more. And just like Hays, Young was scared too.

She took another hit on her cigarette and studied the people in the line. She was looking for signs that were now all-too-familiar; increased levels of anxiety and aggression, that translated as raised voices, hand waving, a marked lack of patience. Right now, all of them seemed pretty calm.

She saw a pale-faced young man in combat uniform near the head of the line, twisting his forage cap in nervous hands. That was anxiety, but not particularly pronounced. Hays guessed he was in his mid-twenties. Poor kid had his whole life ahead of him, a career, family, all about to be erased by a simple pinprick.

She saw him step over the Judas gate and disappear inside the warehouse loading bay. The first thing he'd encounter would be the screening team; blood sample, body temperature and a saliva swab that indicated a viral infection. Once the soldier had been screened, he'd pass through Young's three large, inflatable tents.

In the first, he'd strip and bag his clothes for disposal. In the second, he'd stand naked beneath a lukewarm antiseptic deluge shower. It was in the third that his fate would be decided.

Hays had named it *purgatory*. The tent had two inflatable exit tubes. One led to heaven. The other - well, there really was no other word for it.

The lucky ones took the tube on the left. Once in the admin wing beyond, they were issued with a green utility T-shirt and a set of camouflage trousers, stockpiled since the Iraq War. They were then ordered to leave the building via the recessed doorway. No one needed telling twice. Since that morning, only four people had tested negative and had fled the warehouse damp-haired and barefoot.

The unlucky ones were directed through the other tube, where piped music drifted from temporary speakers and all instructions were scrawled on sheets of paper taped to the inflatable walls.

Please wear the scrubs provided.

Please pass through the door ahead.

Please close the outer door before proceeding to the treatment area.

Please wait for the door to buzz before attempting to open.

Please continue into the facility.

Thank you for your cooperation—

Hays took another hit of her cigarette. The wind gusted, buffeting the line with dirt and grit. Some people turned away, shielding their eyes. Others stood immobile, and Hays knew from her limited experience that those people were at a later stage of infection.

The door buzzed and opened behind her. Hays stepped back as the young Marine exited the building, his dark hair still damp, his feet bare beneath his dated camouflaged trousers.

"You're a lucky guy," Hays told him. "Now head straight for the Chancery. Don't stop for anything."

"Yes, ma'am," the kid said without slowing down.

She watched him hurry away, relief lending speed to his retreat. That was the order, straight from Ashcroft's office. The sick were to be detained without exception, the healthy sent to the Chancery. By tomorrow morning, all twelve hundred or so personnel would've passed through screening and then they would know the numbers. She wondered on which list her own name would appear.

Just be careful, Veronica.

She stepped on her cigarette and went back inside. She walked along the hall of the admin wing and joined Captain Young in the makeshift observation room. Young was typing notes into a laptop.

"What's the tally?" Hays asked.

Young glanced at a pad on the table. "A hundred and fifty-eight, plus we've got another fourteen on their way up from the Chancery team. How many outside?"

"Thirty or so. We have to process them quicker," Hays warned. "The weather's getting worse."

Young nodded her braided head. "Roger that. We can cut the shower time down. Maybe get everyone to remove their footwear outside? That'll shave something."

"See to it, would you?"

Young stood and left the room. Hays snapped the lights off and walked towards the rectangular window that ran the length of the wall. She twisted the plastic stalk, cracking open the blind.

Beyond the glass was a steel mesh cage the size of a football field, lit from above by an array of bright fluorescents. The scene inside that cage - as far as Hays was concerned - resembled a far more terrifying vision than anything that could be conjured from Dante's dark and twisted imagination.

Almost two hundred now, some clothed, some naked, but all infected and devoid of anything resembling human behaviour.

Aggression levels were varied, Hays observed. Some barrelled around the cage with unrestrained energy, running in wide circles or climbing the walls of the cage, spitting their rage in sharp barks and anguished howls. Others stood immobile, or squatted on the ground, inspecting the blue-veined patterns that had formed across their skin. Their physical actions - and interactions with each other - reminded Hays of primates. The cage itself was certainly turning into something resembling a zoo. Clumps of faeces and pools of urine dotted the concrete floor, and the window that Hays observed them through was also spattered with excrement; the inmates directing their anger at their captors behind the glass. When the sun came up tomorrow and began cooking the roof, the smell would be unbearable.

The vomiting was also a problem, highly infectious and often projectile. What they were doing wasn't humane, but Hays knew they had no choice. When the response teams got here, they would see for themselves.

She watched another group of new arrivals enter the cage in their newly issued scrubs. Like the others before them they were terrified and cowered near the door, screaming and pleading to be let out. Hays had found that hard to bear at first, but the terror would soon turn to confusion when the new arrivals realised they were not in any danger. Then, as the infection accelerated, they would become angry, then furious, and finally insane. And then they would join the others.

She peered through a narrow gap in the blinds, saw one of the infected charge through the crowd and throw himself at the cage directly opposite the window. He was one of the original group of Marines from the commissary. He was a big guy, the muscles of his chest and arms covered in those strange blue markings. He stared at Hays from less than six feet and it unnerved her. She watched him thread his fingers through the fence and shake it, all the while fixing her with a dead, red-eyed stare that chilled her. She closed the blind and stepped away from the window.

She sat on the edge of a table and wondered how the response teams would deal with such an outbreak. There was much to be learned, and Hays hoped she would be involved in the process. If she survived. She just had to be very careful, that was all, which was why she intended to keep as far away from the infected as possible.

She was distracted by a sudden and inexplicable silence. Beyond the window, the barking and growling had died down. She crossed to the blind and slowly twisted the stalk.

The Marine had been joined by dozens of others. They crowded the fence and stared at Hays with dead eyes.

The doctor slapped the blind closed and backed away from the window.

CHAPTER 9
DARK IS THE NIGHT

"And let's get one thing clear, General Moody; whatever's happening inside that embassy, I'm holding you and anyone else involved personally responsible, is that clear?"

The conference room erupted. State Department officials jabbed accusing fingers at their Pentagon counterparts, and Crisis Committee members whispered urgently into each other's ears. In the eye of the storm, Amy Coffman sat in silence, glaring at the cluster of green, black and blue uniforms across the conference table. Most of them were middle-aged white men, and the hawks amongst them stared right back at Coffman with borderline contempt.

Oh, how she'd enjoyed the last few minutes, laying bare their incompetence, exposing their arrogance and their disdain for civilian authority. Across the no-man's-land of polished mahogany, General Moody twisted the chunky class ring on his finger and stared right back at her. She saw the frustration in his grey eyes - and more than a little resentment - but there was something else too. Regret, perhaps? Failure? Whatever it was, Coffman intended to exploit it as far as she could, because right now she had both of Moody's tits in the wringer, and she'd just cranked the handle.

She caught Erik's cologne as he leaned into her ear. "If looks could kill," he whispered behind his hand.

"You think he got the message?"

"I think the whole damn room did. Nicely done."

"Let's wrap this up, shall we?"

Mulholland brought the room to order. Coffman stared across the table at Moody, at his uniform with the black Marine Corps lapel pins, the multi-coloured board of medal ribbons above his tunic pocket. A proud man for sure, a patriot without doubt, but he was naive in the ways of DC politics.

The room settled, all eyes on Coffman.

"So, General, we've established the cause of the problem in Baghdad. Now we've lost all communications and it's clear to me that the two must be connected. That infrastructure falls under the defence establishment's purview. So, my question is, how does the Pentagon plan to deal with it?"

Moody glanced down at his notes. "I've spoken to Lieutenant General Howell at Fort Meade. They're working the communications problem as fast as they can. The outbreak response teams have also been mobilised—" He checked his wristwatch, "—and by this time tomorrow they should be on the ground in Baghdad."

"What about the Iraqis?" asked a voice from the Crisis Committee delegation. "They'll need to be informed if we're sending military assets into Baghdad."

"We'll tell them it's an exercise," barked Admiral Schultz, the white-haired Chief of Naval Operations. "They'll play ball if they know what's good for them." He glared at Coffman, his braided arms folded across the table. "Unless the Secretary has another suggestion?"

Coffman shook her head. "No one likes a bully, Admiral.

We've spent years building relationships with the Iraqi administration and I'm not going to jeopardise—"

"They can't know about *Messina,*" Moody cut in. "That's still highly classified."

"I'm well aware of that, General, but there are twelve hundred American lives at stake here and our job is to protect them as best we can. If that means bringing the Iraqis onboard - without revealing the true nature of the crisis - then that is what we'll do." Coffman paused for a beat, then said, "The State Department will take care of diplomacy, General. Your job now is to give us options and solutions."

She watched Schultz grumble into Moody's ear and wondered what he was saying. She imagined his gravelly voice whispering words of insurrection, words like *earliest opportunity* and *kill-team.* That's how it went for JFK when he went toe-to-toe with the military. Schultz was trouble, Coffman knew that, and she made a mental note to speak to Bob Blake, to discuss an eavesdropping mission on the mutinous Admiral when the Baghdad situation had been resolved.

"As far as the Iraqi administration is concerned, I will talk to President Aswad personally," she told the room, "before those teams touch down in Baghdad. Rest assured, the State Department will provide the necessary diplomatic cover. A statement will be formulated so we're all on the same page." Her eyes settled back on Moody. "So, what are our immediate options?"

"We have aerial reconnaissance assets in Kuwait," Moody began. "They can be on-station in the next hour—"

"You're forgetting the *shamal,*" Coffman reminded him.

Moody grimaced. "Yes, the *shamal.* Dammit."

"If low-altitude reconnaissance is not an option, I would suggest re-tasking one of our Global Hawks." It was the Air Force Chief, Frankel, who spoke. "We have one already operating in the region and they fly high and quiet. It could be on-target in two hours."

"Giving us what, exactly?" Coffman asked him.

"High-resolution thermo-graphic imagery and target acquisition capability. The storm shouldn't cause too much interference, and it will give us real-time snap-shots of ground movements."

Coffman looked at Moody and raised an eyebrow. The Marine Commandant nodded. "It's coverage, at least until the storm clears. After that we can deploy low-level assets."

Coffman nodded her approval. "Then let's make that happen. Now, General Frankel."

She watched the Air Force Chief leave and felt a sudden rush of excitement. She really did own the room and recognised the deferential looks from the surrounding faces. They'd read the opinion polls too; in their minds, she was already President. It wouldn't be long before she was chairing similar meetings in the White House Situation Room.

"What else can we do?" she asked, searching those same faces.

"We can find out how this happened," Schultz snarled. "A US embassy does not suffer a catastrophic comms failure without good reason. My guess? This is a deliberate act."

"I agree, it's highly probable," Coffman told him, "and we'll get to that later. Right now, our sole responsibility is to the people in that embassy and ensuring that terrible virus does not leave the compound." She wagged a finger at the uniforms across the table. "We're all relying on the military to help resolve this situation, quickly and quietly. Let's reconvene in two hours."

"When do we tell the Security Council?" a voice at the other end of the room asked. "If the Resolution needs to be implemented, they'll have to be briefed."

Coffman looked down the table at Nikki Price, the United States Ambassador to the UN. She was referring to the secretive Resolution Sixteen-Sixty, the sealing of Iraq's borders. Coffman thought it ironic that a small, clandestine group of international politicians, military personnel and key United Nations officials were now effectively policing the planet, albeit in the utmost of secrecy. In effect, a global shadow-government had been created, the very thing The Committee had strived for decades to achieve.

Coffman deflected the question to Moody. "General?"

"Let's hold off on informing the UN until we have a better grasp of the situation and those response teams are on the ground."

"Agreed," Coffman echoed.

Chairs were pushed back as people around the table got to their feet. Coffman stood too, rapping her knuckles on the thick mahogany. The murmur of voices ceased immediately.

"And no leaks, period," she warned. "Everything we've discussed in this room - the *Messina* operation, the virus, casualties, the blackout, all of it - must remain a secret. If one word of this gets out, those responsible will find themselves in federal custody. Do I make myself clear?"

More murmurs, more nods, then they were funnelling out through the doors. In less than a minute, Coffman and Mulholland were alone.

"Blame apportioned, responsibility passed, authority stamped," Mulholland beamed. "Great job, Amy."

Coffman stared at the conference room doors. "We're not there yet, Erik. What's the news?"

"Aswad is expecting significant reparations. Hamid quoted a figure. A big one."

"We'll pay it, whatever it is."

"There's more. The President predicts internal difficulties in the months ahead. Troublesome religious leaders who might resist Aswad's progressive programs in favour of a mediaeval caliphate. He would like help with potential troublemakers."

Coffman turned to Mulholland and raised a carefully

plucked eyebrow. "He expects me to rid him of his opposition?"

"You knew this would happen, Amy. You get into bed with these people and they expect to fuck you every once in a while."

Coffman shook her head. "Ungrateful prick. I'm saving his country from annihilation."

"And he's putting you in the White House. Quid pro quo."

Coffman took a calming breath. "You can tell Hamid that his brother can expect the full cooperation of a Coffman administration - after he's delivered on his end."

"I already did," Mulholland said. "They'll come through."

Coffman didn't want to dwell on the outcome if they didn't. "Anything else?"

Mulholland smiled. "I got a call from the Justice Department. Former President Stein has been assaulted. He's recovering in the prison hospital. His injuries are serious but not life-threatening."

Coffman glanced at the wall, at the discoloured square that until recently was occupied by President Stein's official photograph. "The truth is, I'm still struggling with the fact that our former President tried to kill me."

"You. Me. A hundred million other Americans," Mulholland reminded her.

Coffman got up and walked around the table, past the other portraits of former Presidents, until she arrived at the missing frame. She imagined her own hanging there and considered what colour suit she might wear that would pop against the Stars and Stripes.

"I remember the first time I met him, at a fundraiser in Chicago. He told me he'd heard good things, schmoozed my ass off. That sonofabitch was so charismatic, so persuasive, before I knew it I was sitting on his campaign bus thrashing out foreign policy detail alongside a dozen other disciples who'd drunk the Kool-Aid. And boy did we hit that trail hard, freezing our butts in Montana, frying in New Mexico. But we were a team, and Bob Stein was our glorious leader. We would've done anything for him."

Coffman recalled the one and only night she'd spent with Stein in a Mississippi hotel, his tongue lolling up and down her neck like a decorator's brush, his rough hands kneading her tits and ass like bakers' dough, the crude and clumsy dirty talk. And afterwards, the post-coital intimation of a West Wing office, his words dripping like honey in her ear. Coffman cringed at the memory, her fangirl excitement, cooing her own unequivocal devotion as she chewed the President-elect's untrimmed lobe. She'd busted her hump for the man, literally.

She remembered standing on the steps of the Capitol Building, clapping with tear-filled eyes as Stein was sworn in, then choking on the bitter disappointment of her subsequent banishment to the office of Deputy Secretary of State. Yes, Bob Stein had ultimately betrayed his country, but worse than that, he'd betrayed Amy Coffman.

Yet despite his impeachment and detention at ADX Florence - a *Supermax* prison in Colorado - her resentment towards Bob Stein lingered. Sometimes she lay awake at night, wondering how she might've reacted had Bob told her about The Committee's ambitions and invited her to join the ruling elite and reign dominant over what remained of mankind after Angola had swept the globe. No more nations, no more borders, no more elections; every man, woman and child beneath her a citizen - and subject - of a New World Order. She imagined the invitation hanging in the air between them, dangling like ripened fruit, tantalising for all of its potential. And in the darkness of those sleepless nights, Coffman knew what her answer would've been.

Yes.

But the invitation had never come, a fact that still troubled her. Somewhere between that fateful fundraiser and Stein's triumphant ascendancy to the Oval Office, a conversation had taken place, her suitability debated, her loyalty questioned. The result? Amy Coffman couldn't be trusted, period. The thought made her seethe, her anger tempered by the fact that, had she become part of that conspiracy, she'd probably be climbing the walls of an eight by ten concrete box right now.

She turned and faced her Chief of Staff across the conference table. "I thought Bob was a friend, Erik. How could he keep such a lethal secret for so many years? And the Nine Eleven thing? My God, to think those conspiracy nut-jobs were right all along."

Mulholland leaned back in his chair and folded his arms. "You never had doubts about the Nine Eleven Commission report? They spent twice as long and five times as much money investigating Bill Clinton."

"Nine Eleven is ancient history, Erik. Besides, Angola posed a far more serious threat to the world."

"As does this new strain."

"Indeed."

She came back around the table and picked up her Fendi leather handbag. She reached inside its soft green calfskin folds and handed Mulholland a cell phone.

"It's a burner. It has a single number programmed in, which is my burner. I want you back at Rock Creek, giving me updates. I need to know that things are going our way."

Mulholland leaned forward in his chair. "My absence will be noted, Amy. They'll expect me here, by your side."

"I'll tell anyone who asks that you're back-channelling. Hamid will give us cover. And when this is over, I'll make sure you'll get kudos for brokering the Iraq deal."

Mulholland got to his feet. "You're the boss."

"I can't trust anyone else, Erik. Now go. And take a rental."

"Yes, ma'am."

He left the room and Coffman was on her own. Twelve hours, maybe less, and this would be over. She hoped, prayed, it would be so. Then the real work could begin, the funerals, the speeches, the honouring of heroes, the TV specials devoted to the events in Baghdad. And as Secretary of State, Amy Coffman would take every single opportunity to speak directly to the American people in the aftermath of that tragedy. And when the masses thought of bravery, of heroism and sacrifice, it would be Amy Coffman's words, broadcast around the world, that would echo in their hearts.

Those words would find their way into the Presidential debates and resonate with the American people, words that would be subliminally and inextricably linked to Presidential candidate Amy Coffman.

Words that would be remembered when the nation stood in line to vote.

Words that would lift her up and carry her into the Oval Office.

It took Erik Mulholland just under thirty minutes to reach the DOD hub at Rock Creek. He'd taken a rental, just as Coffman had ordered, and parked it in the underground car park like before. Bob Blake was waiting for him and escorted him to an elevator that took them down four levels beneath the surface.

The environmental change was stark. Above ground, the building was barely finished, a lot of bare drywall and windows obscured with protective tape. Below ground, everything was shiny and new, and freshly painted corridors guided them to one of many equipment rooms. The one Blake showed him into was surprisingly small. There were no windows, and the room was warm, artificially heated by the two racks of computer equipment that hummed in the corner. Cabling snaked across the floor to the other side of the room, where two men in civilian clothes sat in front of an array of computer screens. On the wall above them, a large TV screen occupied most of the real estate.

Mulholland steered Blake out of earshot.

"Who are these guys?" Mulholland demanded. "This is a need-to-know deal, Bob."

"What did you think, Erik? It was just going to be you and me and a book of instructions? That's Chuck and Eugene. They were part of the original development team. They know Grand Slam from the inside out."

"Can they be trusted?"

Blake smiled, his teeth stained, his breath tainted with tobacco. "Money buys a lot of silence, Erik. You should know that."

Blake gave him a *good boy* pat on the shoulder and crossed the room. Mulholland followed him and sat down in one of the wheelie chairs, watching Chuck and Eugene sweeping their mice and tapping away at various keyboards. Their monitors displayed a combination of code and graphical interfaces, and Mulholland had no idea what he was looking at. One thing he did notice was a screen filled with CCTV feeds. There wasn't much to see because of the dust storm.

"Is that what I think it is?"

"That's the embassy. Be quiet and let the guys work."

Mulholland fumed. Blake was an intimidating guy, always had been, and it was clear he'd never like Amy's consiglieri. It was the gay thing, Mulholland reasoned, yet the industrialist had pinned his colours to Amy's mast a long time ago and Amy had reciprocated that loyalty. With a President Coffman in the White House, Kroll Industries' stock would see a further, sustained uptick over the coming years. They were all going to become seriously rich, including Mulholland, who'd secretly acquired a sizeable chunk of KI stock some years before. It was that thought that tempered Mulholland's animosity towards the often openly-homophobic Blake.

Maybe one day he'd get the chance to even up the score a little. *Happy birthday, Bob. I wrote you a cheque, so you can get those nasty teeth fixed. Asshole…*

"Our friend needs regular updates," Mulholland told him. He held up his burner. "No signal down here."

Blake held out his hand and Mulholland gave him the cell phone. The burly executive turned it over, then gave it back. He unwound a cable from a mess of them on a nearby desk and plugged one end into a sleek black unit in the server cabinet. He offered the other end to Mulholland.

"Plug your phone into that. You can make calls or send text messages. All encrypted and squirted out through the transmitters up on the surface."

Mulholland plugged in the cable and sent a message - *Ready to go. Stand by for updates.*

It was less than thirty seconds before Coffman texted him back.

Keep them short and pertinent.

Mulholland pointed to the CCTV feeds. "Are we recording those?"

"Of course," Blake growled from his chair.

Chuck, a close-cropped, bearded African-American who looked a little like LeBron James, turned and spoke to Blake. "We're juiced in to all the primary systems, including Grand Slam. We're good to go."

Mulholland felt his heart rate increase. Despite the horror of what he was about to witness he actually felt excited. He reached into his coat pocket and slipped on a pair of glasses. He didn't want to miss anything at all. He realised Blake was looking at him, his eyebrows raised. He was waiting for Mulholland's approval and that pleased the next White House Chief of Staff.

"Do it."

Blake gave Chuck a nod.

"Cut the power."

CHAPTER 10
SHAMAL

Outside, dusk had fallen and Baghdad was getting slammed by rolling yellow clouds sweeping across the city. Visibility was down to a couple of hundred metres, and Bosco could barely make out the perimeter lights that ringed the walls of the compound. Out in the Green Zone, small clusters of light winked and faded as the dust storm swallowed buildings whole. He could almost feel the wind buffeting the Chancery, and tiny grains of sand and dirt whispered against the ballistic glass. The storm was a bad one for sure.

He brought the lights back up and unlocked his security cabinet. Inside the compartmented strongbox were his personal weapons, a Glock 19 and a Colt M4 carbine, plus several boxes of ammunition. It also stored his tactical vest and bug-out bag, a backpack that contained rations, water, medical supplies and other essential items. Bosco never thought he'd have to use it, but now he pulled it out and jammed a box of 5.56mm in there just in case. He clipped the Glock to his belt and put everything else back inside.

On his way out of the room, he zipped up a tan windbreaker and tugged on a black baseball cap emblazoned with the letters *RSO*. He had to get the Chancery locked down for the foreseeable future. That meant deciding on a cut-off. It was a call Bosco didn't want to make.

Downstairs in the atrium, hundreds of people milled around, the sound of their nervous chatter filling the void and echoing around the glass walls. They were being shepherded by Lynch's Marines who were trying to keep the floor clear. Bosco saw they were armed and kitted out in all their tactical gear, and it made him nervous. He was halfway across the atrium when he heard his name called.

"Tom?"

Lynch was walking towards him. He too was geared up, his rifle slung in front of his chest.

"Is the whole tactical thing really necessary, Gunny? Folks are nervous enough."

"SOPs," Lynch replied. "You should know that."

Bosco did know, but it didn't make him feel any safer. If the military *did* make a move, there'd be little any of them could do about it. "How many have you processed?"

Lynch pointed to the growing crowd. "Almost two hundred have arrived since the EAP was broadcast. Including the people already here and the line outside, that's around seven hundred bodies."

Bodies? Why say that?

"I want your guys out on patrol, Gunny. As many as you can spare."

Lynch stared at Bosco from beneath the rim of his helmet. When he spoke he kept his voice low. "You've got to be kidding, Tom. I've lost half my guys to that fucking bug and the remainder are stretched to the max."

Bosco took a step closer, also conscious to keep his voice down. "Duly noted, but I'm giving you a direct order. I want all the Marine detachment out patrolling the compound and watching for stragglers."

Lynch looked at Bosco as if he were a lunatic. "In this

fucking weather? Are you out of your mind? Besides, that goes against regs. It would leave the Chancery exposed."

"My guys will take up the slack. In the meantime, I want you all out there, sweeping the compound. It's not up for discussion, Gunny. Understood?"

Lynch nodded his head. "It's your call, but be advised I strongly disagree with your decision. Leaving the Chancery exposed and without its Marine complement is a tactical mistake."

Bosco nodded. "Also understood. You can make it official when this is over."

"I will," Lynch grumbled.

Bosco entered the security lobby as Lynch trailed behind. Outside the main doors, the screening tent flapped and rippled before the wind. Uninfected arrivals came through the doors, sand-blasted and spluttering, but clearly relieved. As Bosco and Lynch pulled on gloves and paper masks, one of Lynch's Marines approached.

"What is it, Diaz?"

"Sir, we got a report of a disturbance in one of the State blocks. A lot of shouting and screaming, apparently."

"Who made the report?"

"That guy," Diaz said. Bosco followed Diaz's finger. Outside the main doors, a thirty-something man was being buffeted by the wind. He wore shorts, sneakers and a Yale sweatshirt, and he appeared oblivious to the storm.

"I'll speak to him."

Bosco put his hand on the door. Diaz called after him. "He failed the screen."

Bosco hesitated. "Why isn't he on his way to the warehouse?"

"He's refusing to go. He's convinced he's okay."

Bosco studied the guy through the glass. "Someone needs to take him."

"Maybe you should check out that disturbance," Lynch

said. "We can run you over there, drop this guy off at the same time."

Before Bosco could argue the Gunny was firing orders. "Diaz, the RSO would like an escort. Bring a Humvee around front. Corporal Hayes!" Lynch hollered at a tall Marine with glasses policing the new arrivals with a couple of buddies. He doubled over quick time.

"Gunny?"

"Round up the guys. I want everyone out walking the compound."

Bosco cursed silently. Lynch had shanghaied him. He pulled his mask up over his nose and mouth and stepped outside the main door. Immediately he felt the sting of grit against his exposed skin. He snapped his collar up against the wind and approached the guy standing a few feet away. "What's your name?" Bosco shouted.

The guy stared at Bosco with dead eyes. "Brian De Santos."

"Brian, my name is Tom Bosco, Regional Security Officer. I'm going to get you re-screened by the Chief Medical Officer. That sound okay to you?"

"People go in that warehouse, they don't come out," De Santos croaked, his dark hair whipping around his face.

"It'll be fine, trust me."

He heard the whine of a Humvee, and headlights swept across the building. The vehicle screeched to a halt a few meters away.

"Let's go!" Lynch shouted, slapping Bosco on the back.

The RSO climbed in the back and De Santos got in next to him. The Humvee was wide, and Bosco was grateful for the space between them. Up front, Lynch slammed the door. "Let's go, Diaz. And take it easy. We don't want to run anyone over."

"You got it, Gunny."

Diaz ground the gearbox and the vehicle lurched forward,

heading east along Main Street. The buildings on either side were barely visible. Bosco spoke to De Santos.

"Which block did you say you were from?"

"Block Four," De Santos rasped.

"And there was some sort of disturbance?"

"The girl was blind. I tried to help, but she's sick. She's got the bug."

"What girl?"

"Someone pulled her eyes out," De Santos said as he stared out into the storm.

He saw Lynch half turn in his seat. Diaz stared through the windshield as the wipers beat away the dust.

"This girl, where is she now?"

"How the fuck should I know?" De Santos snarled. "With the others. They're all sick."

This was a bad idea, Bosco realised. Lynch gave him a look that said something like, *what the fuck?*

De Santos leaned forward. "I don't feel so good—"

"Stop the vehicle!" Bosco yelled. Diaz slammed on the brakes and De Santos stumbled out of the Humvee, vomiting a stream of yellow bile that sprayed wildly in the wind. Bosco slapped Diaz on the shoulder. "Drive!"

Diaz floored the accelerator and the door slammed shut. Bosco pulled a tac-light off his belt and swept it over the adjacent seat and door. "We're clean," he told the Marines. "Jesus, that was close."

"Slow down," Lynch ordered. He was checking his mirror. Bosco turned around. There was nothing to see, nothing but the shadows of buildings and rolling clouds of dust and sand.

"We're just going to abandon that guy?"

Bosco turned back to Lynch. "You want to swing round and pick him up? The guy's infected, Gunny. I thought we could get him to Hays in time but - well, you saw."

"We can't just leave him on the loose like that."

"Agreed."

Lynch put a call out on the Marine net, warning his patrols. "You realise that one of my guys might have to put him down?"

Bosco looked at Lynch and tried to read his face. It was difficult to know. "Proportionate force, that's what the ambassador said."

"Good luck with that," Lynch snorted. "You've seen them, right? Up in the cage? They're wild fucking animals that want to tear us apart. They're getting smart too," he said, tapping his helmet with a finger. "I'm not losing any more of my guys to this thing. My orders are, you get attacked, you shoot. I'll take the heat for it down the line."

He drilled Bosco with an unblinking stare. After a few seconds, the RSO conceded. "You made your point, Gunny."

"So, what now?" the Marine asked.

"Take me up to the blocks. We need to find out what's going on."

It took them less than ten minutes to crawl through the storm and mount the kerb outside the State apartment blocks.

"Kill the lights," Bosco told Diaz.

The driver complied and they sat in silence for several moments, listening to the low drone of the wind and watching Block Four. A faint light shone from inside and Bosco cranked his window down an inch or so and listened. He heard nothing. He saw nothing. No disturbance.

"What's the plan?" Lynch asked.

Bosco wound up his window. "I'm going to take a look. Wait here."

"You need me to come with?"

Bosco shook his head. "I'll be right back. If what De Santos said is true, we may have to quarantine the building. Just stay here. And keep the lights off. We don't want to attract any attention."

"Roger that."

Bosco pulled a scarf from his pocket and tied it over his

paper mask. He left a narrow slit for his eyes, then bailed out into the storm, slamming the door behind him. He used the lights of the building to guide him, and then the alcove of the main doors appeared ahead. He looked back at the Humvee but he could barely see it.

What was Lynch up to? Could he really be involved in some kind of revolt? Bosco found it difficult to believe. Marines were fiercely loyal, to both Corps and country. They believed in the defence of the constitution, didn't they? Lynch was a professional, and Bosco had always enjoyed a good relationship with him. He didn't seem the type to join some half-baked revolution. And if he was part of the conspiracy, why would he object to leaving De Santos behind? Nothing made sense.

The alcove gave him some shelter from the wind. Like most building doors around the embassy, Block Four's were practically impenetrable without the right access card. Bosco's was dangling around his neck, but he held off swiping into the building. Through the door's small window, the hallway beyond was lost in darkness. Bosco fished a small torch from his pocket. He snapped it on and shone it inside—

Bosco dropped into a crouch, his fingers fumbling for the off-switch. He'd glimpsed something beyond the glass, moving bodies, naked flesh, hair, blood, wild red eyes. Like a vision from hell. Whatever was—

The door rocked as something inside slammed against it. Then he heard a low howling, like animals in pain, competing with the wind. The door shook again. Bosco scrambled out of the alcove, panic snapping at his heels as he imagined the door splintering behind him, the monsters inside pouring out of the building, hunting him down. He tripped and fell, hands and knees scraping the dirt. He pulled himself up and staggered towards the road, dust blinding him, his hands outstretched. His shoes found the kerb, the empty road. He looked left and right.

Lynch was gone.

He reached for his radio.

That was gone too.

And then Bosco saw the most terrifying thing he'd ever seen. Every light he could barely see, on the perimeter wall, in the surrounding buildings, suddenly went out, plunging the compound into a swirling, blinding world of shadows.

Bosco pulled the gun from his belt and started running, back towards the Chancery.

The lights were out, and Veronica Hays switched the computer monitors off. The room was in darkness, and that's how she wanted it. They would have to move the equipment into another room because the light drew them to the window, and that wasn't good.

The door opened behind her, and Young entered the gloomy office. Even the lights in the hall outside had been turned off.

"That's all of them processed."

"Did we get them all in?"

Young shook her head. "Some took off. I radioed Bosco, but he hasn't come back yet."

"Dammit," Hays cursed. "How many is that now?"

"Three hundred and four," Young replied. "We're out of sedatives and scrubs."

Hays removed her white medical tunic and folded it over the back of a chair. She crept towards the window. Young joined her as she cracked the blind.

"What the hell is this thing?" The captain whispered.

Hays folded her arms. It was a comforting gesture, she knew that. Whatever this *thing* was, it both fascinated and terrified her.

She watched them through the blind. Bathed beneath the glare of the overhead lights, the herd was on the move, marching - for want of a better word - counter clockwise around the cage. Uniforms, clerical types, men and women in coveralls, medical scrubs, and the naked ones, smeared in blood and vomit, their arms and legs swinging wildly. Some ran around the outside, pushing others, screaming at the top of their lungs. The noise was incredible, and it chilled Hays to the bone.

"It's happening again," Young pointed. "Nine o'clock, the girl, by the fence."

Hays saw. The girl was young, early thirties, and naked, her body bruised and bloodied. She was lying on the ground, her legs spread, the naked man inside her grunting and gasping as he raped her. But it wasn't rape, Hays knew that now. Like the other women they'd observed, this girl was submissive, allowing his entry, rocking back and forth in unison until the brief and sudden climax. And like the others, the man scrambled to his feet and rejoined the circle, falling into step, pushing and shoving. The girl pulled herself up, and she too staggered back into the crowd. The bizarre group dynamic, the random, brutal sex, were all recent developments. This was something primordial, as if the virus had the power to trigger cognitive regression, to strip away the layers of humanity until all that was left were the basest of instincts. Hays wondered about the animalistic coupling and what such a liaison might produce.

"I think we're in serious trouble," she whispered in the darkness.

"I think you're right," Young echoed. "I'll be glad when those teams—"

The bank of overhead lights blinked out and the cage beyond the window was lost in the darkness.

Then the howling began.

Crouched on the roof, Jon Roth shifted his body and turned his binoculars east, then south, towards the Karada district. Across the Tigris River, between the towering clouds of dust gusting across the city, he could just make out the tiny pinpricks of light. Behind him, the Zone was out, a blanket of darkness wrapped in a blinding storm.

Costello appeared out of the haze. He squeezed in between the air-con units and crouched next to Roth. Like his boss, his head was wrapped in a shemagh, his eyes protected by tactical goggles. And like Roth, Costello also cradled a Heckler & Koch 416 assault rifle.

"The whole building's out," he shouted, voice muffled by his scarf.

"The compound too, *and* the Zone. That's no coincidence." He pointed a gloved finger. "Take a look at the towers."

Costello pulled a mono-scope from his rig and squinted through his goggles. "No one home." He looked to Roth. "We're gonna get hit."

"Looks that way. Is everyone ready?"

Costello grunted confirmation. "Gearing up as we speak. Personal radios are all dialled in. How do you want to play this?"

"We need to conference with Lynch and Bosco. This is their turf, so there'll be a plan. In the meantime, we set up a defensive perimeter around this building, and I want eyes on the roof. Snipers and spotters take the top floor windows, three-sixty-degree coverage."

"What the fuck is happening here, Jon?"

The wind gusted, lashing them with grit and sand. Roth had to shout to make himself heard.

"First, we lose comms, then someone pulls the contractors from the walls and gets to the power grid. We're sitting inside a billion-dollar facility and we can't even turn the lights on or pick up a phone and call home. That's too many coincidences. Someone with serious juice has got a plan for us that we're not aware of. Let's try to disappoint them."

"Roger that," Costello grunted.

"We need to speak to Bosco, ASAP."

"That fucking guy," Costello shouted. "He doesn't have the—"

Gunfire rattled somewhere in the darkness, the sound snatched away by the wind.

"It's starting," Roth said.

FREDDIE CRUZ STOOD IN THE DARK, ROCKING SLOWLY ON HIS heels as the howls rose around him. Earlier, after the blood and rage, the beast had gone to sleep inside him, inside the others, and they'd gathered in the dark, trapped by the surrounding walls. Their numbers were many, and they moved slowly and in silence, soaked in blood and vomit. The smell comforted Freddie, so he'd closed his eyes and welcomed the darkness.

Until the light.

His nostrils registered the shadowy stink beyond the doors, the ripple of disquiet through the throng as the light washed over them. He felt the beast squirm and slither inside him, felt the rage building. He spat blood into the hair of a woman pressed against him, then pulled her out of the way. He clawed a path through the mass of bodies until he reached the doors. He slammed his head against the window, his eyes searching for the stinking shadow. He hammered his fists against the doors. Other hands joined him, beating, scratching and thumping. Freddie screamed, in fury and frustration. He had to escape, be free to roam and kill.

He felt the pressure build behind him as others crowded towards the doors. He heard howls from above, echoing through the halls and stairwells, the stampede of feet that grew louder, the pressure that squeezed his chest. He reached up above the door and clawed at the red light that pulsed there, mocking him, fuelling his frustration. Freddie screamed. The others joined him. Their cries filled the building.

Above him, the light blinked out.

The door flew open and Freddie was swept out into the storm in a tide of screaming, squirming, furious bodies.

"You see him?"

The driver shook his head. "I lost him, Gunny."

Fuck. The figure was barely visible, but it had passed so close to Lynch's window he'd instinctively raised his M27 rifle. He'd ordered Diaz to hit the lights but all they saw was clouds of dust rolling through the high beams. They circled the block to try to reacquire the figure. Friend or foe, Lynch was unsure, but it might have been somebody in trouble. Now they were stationary again, waiting for Bosco.

"Shall I kill the lights, Gunny?"

Lynch shook his head. "Keep them on. Visibility is for shit." The Humvee's engine rattled noisily. Lynch stared into the storm. "Come on," Lynch muttered.

Diaz pushed his face against the window. "You hear that?"

"What?"

"I dunno. Sounded like dogs barking or something." He cracked the window open a couple of inches, his eyes squinting into the darkness.

"Kill the engine," Lynch told him.

The motor rattled and died. The wind gusted and howled, and then there was something else, something that did indeed sound like dogs barking and howling. A lot of dogs.

Diaz shook his head. "What the fuck *is* that?"

Lynch scanned Block Four. "That's coming from inside. Didn't that guy De Santos say that people were—"

Block Four went dark. Lynch twisted in his seat. He couldn't see a single light anywhere.

"We've lost power."

Then they heard the howling again, only this time it was louder, closer.

"Start the fucking engine, Diaz, right now!"

Lynch scrambled into the back seat and wound the window down behind Diaz. The engine turned, rattled for several moments, then died. That's when Lynch saw them. The next words he spoke were calm, measured. "Don't flood it, just turn the key and start that fucking engine."

He could hear Diaz's rapid breathing, the twisting of the key in the ignition, and then he was firing into the screaming wave of infected that was about to crash over the vehicle.

The engine died again. Diaz reached for his gun. A body smashed through his window. Arms reached in, clawing at his face. Diaz screamed. Lynch kept firing until his weapon clicked empty. The first one through his window was a woman, wild-eyed, her clothes ripped, her hair matted with blood and sand. Lynch stamped a boot in her face, reloaded a fresh mag, and then shot her through the forehead. She was dragged backwards and someone else took her place, and Lynch shot him too. The noise was terrifying. Diaz was screaming and swearing in Spanish, then his door flew open and he was dragged out into the storm. Lynch fired another burst and keyed his radio.

"All call signs, this is Red-Alpha-One," he shouted over the growling, snapping mob. "The compound is compromised, multiple infected on the loose. Stay inside. I repeat, stay—"

And then they were crawling over the front seats, pulling at his boots, his rig, tearing at his limbs. Foul-smelling vomit sprayed across his face.

Gunnery Sergeant Lynch yanked the Beretta from his thigh holster, jammed it under his chin and pulled the trigger.

• • •

Hays blinked several times as light spots danced before her eyes.

"Shit," Young cursed as she stumbled into a chair. She felt her way across the room and reached for the light switch.

Hays spun around. "Don't—"

Young had already flipped the switch. Nothing happened.

"Damn, I didn't think," Young said. "Power to the whole building must be out." Then her voice dropped to the faintest of whispers. "Don't move."

Hays' heart began to race. She couldn't make out the soldier's face in the dark, but she could see her eyes, wide with fear. "What is it?"

"They're right outside the window. They're looking at us."

Slowly - so very slowly - Hays turned around. They were pressed against the cage wall like before, but now it seemed like all of them were there, a dark, heaving mass of bodies, staring right at them.

"Where's your radio?" she whispered.

"In the other office," Young answered.

And then Hays saw movement. She saw faces turn, heard shrieks of - what exactly? She inched closer to the window. The herd was now distracted, agitated, and she saw figures at the back of the crowd, peeling away, running across the ware-house, whooping like crazed chimps, the sound of their feet building into a stampede.

"Oh my God," Young trembled. "What's happening?"

Hays knew. She spun around, her skin crawling, her voice shrieking with terror. "The gates to the cage," she screamed, "they're open—"

Young grabbed her arm. "Run!"

They bolted out of the room and along the corridor. Behind them, the screams of the infected filled the air as they poured out of their cage.

Young shouldered the main door open and disappeared into the storm. Hays followed, and then the wind caught her breath and sand stung her face. She faltered, coughing and spluttering. She squinted into the wind, but Young was gone, swallowed up by the storm. All around her the buildings were dark, recognisable only by their silhouettes. She ran north, towards Main Street. She passed the State blocks on her left and heard screaming from inside. The storm gusted and moaned through the concrete canyons, and sand stung her face and eyes.

Hays didn't see the woman and ran into her at full speed. She tumbled to the ground, lacerating her hands and knees. She gasped in pain then sat up, looking for her other shoe, for the woman she'd just cannoned into. She knew it was a woman because she was smaller than Hays and had long hair. She got to her feet, kicking off her other shoe. The other woman lumbered out of the swirling storm and Hays was horrified to see the blood that streamed from her eye sockets.

"Give me your hand, quickly!" Hays yelled above the wind.

The woman lumbered forward and vomited in Hays' face. The doctor spun away, horrified, felt the woman's hands clutching at her shirt. Hays turned around, and in a fit of rage, knocked the woman to the ground.

She turned away, leaving her attacker behind. She sobbed in despair, because she knew she was doomed, knew the virus was already mutating inside her. She ran blindly, saw the tarmac of Main Street beneath her bare feet. She slowed, her head swimming. She threw up, violently, the retch sounding more like a scream. She squatted down and peed, soaking her underwear. Tears rolled down her face as she felt her sanity being stripped away, like roof tiles in a tornado.

She kept moving, crossing Main Street, her limbs suddenly energised, her mind whirling with anger and confusion. And then something shifted inside her, a beast that lurked in a darkness she had never known existed. Its soft whisper filled her head, urging her on. She moved faster, cuffing the sand that clung to the vomit on her lips. She felt her feet slapping against the road, then saw a strip of yellow tape, twirling in the wind. She walked through it, stretching it until it snapped, and then she saw the doorway ahead, a shadowy recess filled with vile, stinking shadows.

"It's Doctor Hays," she heard a voice shout. "Someone call the Major."

Hays headed toward the doorway.

Bosco lurched through the dust and wind, his breath ragged and painful. He was moving too fast for the conditions and he knew it. He could run into a light pole, or a concrete bollard, knock himself out, break an ankle. Suicide.

The screeching drove him on. It was behind him somewhere, out there in the dark, and Bosco knew what it was. The occupants of Block Four, or whatever they had become, were now loose in the compound. The thought of them roaming free made his legs weak and he pushed himself harder, the gun gripped in his right hand, cocked and ready. *Proportionate force be damned*, he thought. If Bosco was confronted by an infected, they'd get two rounds in the chest.

He heard the *tap-tap-tap* of snap hooks and he saw the pale shaft of the flagpole ahead, the Stars & Stripes cracking in the wind above him. The dark mass of the Chancery squatted behind it, and Bosco headed towards its row of polished metal doors.

He pounded on one with his left hand. He peered through the thick glass but the security lobby was shrouded in darkness. Then he saw torches waving and a face appeared at the glass.

"It's Mister Bosco!" confirmed the muffled voice, looking back into the darkness.

"Open the fucking door!" Bosco pounded again, his head twisting left and right. The wind moaned and his mouth was dry. He heard bolts being thrown and then the door was swinging open. Bosco barged through it. Diplomatic Security agents waited on the other side. They wore Fast helmets, tactical vests and cradled their weapons across their chests. All except one. Agent Pat Murphy, a tough Bostonian, had his sidearm drawn.

Bosco leaned over, hands on his knees, trying to catch his breath. "Seal it," he panted, waving an arm at the door.

Murphy asked, "Are you okay, Sir?"

Bosco glanced at Murphy, at the gun in his hand, and was reassured by the agent's apparent willingness to put a round in his boss should the need arise. "Stand down, Pat. I'm fine. Shook up, is all. Lost my radio too."

Murphy holstered his sidearm and handed over a radio handset. "I figured. We've been trying to reach you," he said.

Bosco's heart was still hammering, but now he had bigger problems than his fitness. "We've got a situation. The infected are on the loose out there."

The agent nodded. "Gunny Lynch's last transmission confirmed the same. He said the embassy compound was compromised."

"What d'you mean his *last transmission*?"

"The Gunny is off-air. Sounded like he was getting attacked. Captain Young and Doctor Hays can't be reached either."

Bosco swore. "What about the power?"

"The whole embassy is out," Murphy told him, "and the backup generators failed to kick in. The Chancery has some emergency lighting—"

Bosco's mouth dropped open. "Jesus fucking Christ," he whispered. "Warehouse Seven, it's a secure facility, electronically controlled. If the system detects a sustained power loss, the doors trip to unlock."

"But the infected—"

"Can get out."

Bosco walked to the doors and peered out into the storm. *Mulholland was right, wasn't he?* Lynch had pretty much forced him to leave the Chancery, and then abandoned him outside Block Four, a building that contained who knew how many infected. And the warehouse - the last update Bosco got from Hays put the number of infected at over two hundred and fifty. That meant there were possibly three hundred plus infected out there on the loose. Three hundred homicidal maniacs just like Jackson.

So, if Mulholland was right and the military's goal was to release the virus, they'd succeeded, right? But at what cost?

Lynch was gone, Young and Hays too, plus a bunch of other Marines. Was that part of the plan? Collateral damage, to make this thing look genuine? Yet Lynch had protested about dumping De Santos. Why?

Bosco didn't know what to think. He knew one thing though - he'd rather face an assassin's bullet than a screaming, infected mob.

"Seal the building," he told Murphy, "and post guys on every access door. No one gets in or out, understood?"

Bosco headed into the Chancery, his heart pounding, his hands still shaking.

CHAPTER 11
NAKED DEATH

DOUG WAS LOCKED IN THE INTERVIEW ROOM. HIS COFFEE WAS cold. No one had come to see him in a while. He'd been forgotten, it seemed.

He drummed his fingers on the table, and beneath that table, his leg bounced nervously. He wanted to climb the walls, roar in frustration. If he did, he doubted anyone would hear him because those same walls were covered with grey soundproofing tiles. The only door had a small wired-glass window. He was, in effect, a prisoner, and every so often someone would look in on him with resentful eyes.

His detention was being justified under an espionage clause or some military code he had no knowledge of. The thought of being branded a traitor chilled him, but what froze the blood in his veins was his inability to get to Holly. He couldn't even call Gould. He was going out of his mind.

He stood up and peered through the window. He couldn't see much other than a narrow view of the hallway outside. People passed at regular intervals, most of them Diplomatic Security agents. He felt like banging on the door, protesting his innocence, but that would be a waste of time. No one was interested. His only chance at redemption was for communications to be restored and for Bosco to verify his credentials. At least then he would be one step closer to getting out of Iraq.

He sat back down.

The light overhead flickered and died.

What now?

Doug watched the ceiling, waiting for the juice to come back. It didn't, so he got to his feet, felt his way over to the door. Outside in the hallway, shadows whipped past the window and torch beams swept the walls. Doug glimpsed guns and tactical gear. Minutes passed. He heard orders being hollered, radios chattering.

What the hell's happening?

Doug's stomach churned. First the comms, now the power. If things got out of hand, he could be stuck in Iraq for weeks, maybe months. He had to get out of this room, the embassy, out of the country. And he had to do it fast.

Wait. No power meant what, exactly? A system-wide lock, or unlock? Had to be the latter, purely from a safety perspective. He reached out, put his hand on the door.

It flew open.

Two DS agents stood waiting in the gloom. Unfriendly faces beneath FAST helmets.

"Come with us," one of them ordered.

Hays spat grit from her mouth as dust devils swirled around her.

Her face was scratched, her skin torn, and blood ran freely down her neck, but she felt none of it.

Instead she felt confusion and a growing anger, compounded by the rank odour of the stinker who waved at her from the doorway. This was where they nested, where they ate and shat. She would throw herself amongst them, spill their blood. The beast inside her demanded it.

Hays headed towards the shadow that beckoned her, throwing one leg in front of the other, her back stiff and straight, because all she wanted to do was run, arms flailing, and release the scream that burned her throat.

"Get inside," she heard the stinker yell, and the words sounded familiar. She wanted to attack him, felt a terrible rage building, but instinct told her that the pickings were richer inside.

The shadow stepped aside and she moved past him, the stench of his skin forcing the bile to rise in her throat. She heard voices down a darkened hallway, saw another stinker walking towards her. She moved her bowels and reached between her legs, working her shit-covered fingers across the stinker's mouth as he greeted her. She kept moving, heard him splutter and curse behind her, and by the time she reached the end of the hallway she could hear him vomiting.

Torchlight beckoned her across the threshold. She heard their vile noises, her nostrils assaulted by the fetid stench of their flesh. She stepped into the room. Stinkers everywhere, lurking in the darkness. *Chatter-chatter. Jabber-jabber.*

A shout echoed along the hallway behind her, a name barely remembered. *Hays—*

A torch blinded her.

"Jesus fucking Christ!" she heard one of them scream.

The rage, the madness that consumed every fibre of her being, was overwhelming, and the person that was Veronica Hays finally gave into it.

She worked her gut muscle and sprayed vomit across the nearest shadow, then leapt on another close by, raking his skin with her nails, spewing bile and blood over his face, his neck, the floor.

Crack!

Light danced before her eyes and she felt blood running down her face. She spun around and launched herself at her attacker. Torchlight bounced around the walls. The stinkers yelled and screamed. She ripped the face off another with her broken nails. Bloodlust filled her body with power, speed and a glorious rage. Her arms flailed like chains, her legs given new life as she sprang from shadow to shadow, clawing, spewing, raking flesh, clinging to clothing and equipment as she rode their backs.

Then she heard something else, a musical *zing*, the clatter of metal objects hitting the floor. The screams of the stinkers filled the room, a chorus of grating screeches that morphed into a single word, one that sent them scattering like cockroaches.

Grenade.

ROTH AND COSTELLO LAY FLAT ON THEIR BELLIES AS THE building shook beneath them.

"That was inside," Roth yelled. He barked into his radio. "Dealer Team, this is Hitman One, sitrep, over!"

Both men winced as the Delta net exploded with traffic. Roth sprang to his feet and looked over the parapet. Four storeys below, orange light flickered off the walls of the opposite block.

"We got a fire," he told Costello.

"You hear that?" the Sergeant Major answered, pointing to his ear. "Something about Hays?"

"Let's get below."

They dropped through the hatch and slammed it closed. They yanked down their scarves, flipped their goggles up over their Gentex helmets. Another voice cut in across the chatter.

"Hitman One, Dealer Three-Three. Explosion in the mess room. Doc Hays was infected, got in amongst the guys."

"You still on the second?" Roth asked.

"Affirmative."

"Seal the doors. We're coming down to you."

Costello shook his head. "Hays got infected? What the fuck?"

"Get Young on the radio, find out what happened. Then update Lynch."

"Roger."

"Let's move," Roth ordered.

They descended quietly, gun-barrel torches sweeping the walls and landings. Suppressed gunfire rattled up the stairwell. Building security was compromised, Roth knew. Time to bug out.

On the second floor, he banged on the door to the accommodation wing. "It's Hitman, open up."

The door swung inwards. Delta soldiers lined both sides of the hallway like silent shadows. No one spoke, the only sound the familiar rattle and scrape of guns and gear. Costello peeled away and whispered into his radio.

Roth lowered his weapon and thumbed his tac-light on. "Sound off," he ordered.

"Dealers Twenty-Two through Forty," answered the voice on the radio. It was Drake, one of his snipers. He moved in close, his G-28 marksman rifle slung over his back. "I got spotters at the windows—"

A loud scream from downstairs startled them. It was followed by more gunfire, more shouting, urgent, painful.

"What happened?" Roth asked Drake.

"Hays came out of the storm, passed Meyer on the way in. He didn't pay her any mind, just assumed she was coming to see you. Then he heard a whole bunch of shouting and screaming and the grenades popped off."

Drake dropped his voice a little lower.

"The smoke drove Meyer outside so he covered the door. First guy out was Rosario. He shouted at Meyer to stay back, said the Doc had gone crazy, attacked the guys in the mess room." Drake paused, then said, "He pulled his sidearm and shot himself."

Roth nodded in the dark. "Where's Meyer now?"

"North of us. He's holed up behind a shipping container with a couple of other guys."

Costello appeared out of the dark. "Can't reach Young or Lynch."

Roth said, "Okay, given the tactical situation and the danger to this embassy, we're going to regroup at the Chancery. Everyone set?" Thumbs and whispered *affirmatives* told Roth they were. "Good. Standby."

Roth led Costello into an empty room. He closed the door and re-dialled his radio into the security net.

"What's Bosco's call-sign?"

"Javelin," Costello told him.

Roth thumbed his PTT switch. "Javelin this is Hitman One, over…"

By the time Bosco reached the Executive Suite, he was breathing hard.

He marched through the dimly lit hallways, his torch picking out pale, frightened faces. He fought hard to keep his neutral.

"If your movement isn't necessary, stay in your offices," Bosco yelled. In Ashcroft's outer office his torch swept over two men in green flight suits as they pored over a map spread across a desk. Bosco kept moving.

Inside Ashcroft's office, the Acting Chief of Mission and Bill Jacobs were studying a schematic of the compound. The room was lit by a single battery-powered storm lamp that threw the walls into deep shadow. Both men looked up as Bosco slammed the door behind him.

"Tom! Thank God you're back," Ashcroft stuttered a little too loudly. He was standing behind his desk, sleeves rolled up, tie pulled loose, a damp ring of sweat beneath each arm.

"Lynch and Hays are unreachable," he announced. "Captain Young too. We have to assume they're gone."

Ashcroft held up his hands. "Stop, Tom! Back up a minute. Who's gone? What are you talking about?"

"Gunny Lynch, Captain Young and Doctor Hays. They're almost certainly dead. Or worse."

Ashcroft's eyes widened. "Veronica's dead?"

"How?" Asked Jacobs.

"There's more," Bosco told them. "The infected, they're out of the warehouse. When the power—"

"*Got out?*" Ashcroft's pink face suddenly drained of colour. "There were a couple of hundred people in there."

"Over two hundred and fifty at the last count," Bosco corrected him.

"Jesus Christ," Jacobs muttered. "This changes everything."

Ashcroft stared at his RSO for several silent seconds then dropped into his chair. He dabbed at his neck with a balled-up handkerchief. Bosco thought he might have a heart attack. When Ashcroft spoke, his voice quivered.

"This is it. It's happening, right, Tom? They're going to—"

"We're safe here," Bosco cut in. "We just need to figure things out."

"What do you mean, *it's happening*?" Jacobs asked.

Bosco stared at the CIA chief. He sounded genuine, but the man was Langley, well-schooled in the art of deception.

"Mister Ashcroft is referring to an earlier conversation," Bosco explained. "A *what if* discussion. Forget it."

Jacobs shrugged, then slapped Bosco on the shoulder. "By the way, good call with the EAP. Getting everyone to fall back to the Chancery was a solid move, Tom. You've probably saved a lot of lives."

Bosco's mind raced. *Do you mean that, Bill? Or are you just fucking with me?* "I've given the order to seal the building. I've got my people posted at all access points."

Ashcroft let out a relieved breath. "Thank God."

Jacobs said, "What about Lynch's Marines? They're still out there patrolling, right?"

"We've lost contact with some of them," Bosco confirmed. He'd sent them out there, and if they were dead or infected, that was on him. "The rest have been ordered to seek shelter and stay out of sight. We've got a half dozen more downstairs in the Marine House."

"Okay, well, we need help and we need it fast," Jacobs said. "Time to get this delegation organised and on the road. I propose a low-key transit to the Brit Embassy. The storm outside is still blowing hard so I figure we use a three-vehicle convoy, one for the diplomatic team and two escorts."

"I've assigned the Marines for security," Bosco announced.

Jacobs frowned. "Why? We're in the zone. Your agents can do the job."

"Tom has a point," Ashcroft said. "I'd feel safer if you had a military escort, Bill."

"We could use Delta," Jacobs suggested.

Bosco shook his head. "They've done enough damage. They can sit this one out."

Jacobs' eyes narrowed. "That's a little harsh."

"I have to agree with Tom," Ashcroft nodded. "Delta are not an option right now."

"Yes, but with the Marine Guard depleted—"

"Can we just get it done?" Ashcroft snapped at the CIA man.

Jacobs nodded. "Yes, sir."

"When you get over there, contact State in the first instance," Ashcroft told him. "Speak to Secretary Coffman directly if you can, tell her the infected are loose."

Bosco said, "Why not take Sanderson from Political Affairs along for the trip? He knows the Brits well. He can help grease the wheels."

Ashcroft brightened. "Good idea, Tom. I'll go see him myself."

"And the escort?"

"Marines are gearing up now," Bosco told Jacobs. "I'll organise the vehicles, call you when they're outside the building. We'll use North Exit Two to load everyone aboard."

Jacobs headed for the door. Ashcroft waited until it had closed behind him before he spoke.

"Bringing Sanderson on board was a good move, Tom. Christ knows what Jacobs would've told them." He paused for a moment, then said, "Maybe I should go myself? To be sure?"

Bosco saw Ashcroft's eyes and knew what he was thinking, but abandoning the post wasn't a good idea. "You're safer in this building," Bosco told him. "Sanderson will do the job."

"Wait a minute, there's nothing to stop Jacobs and the Marines taking Sanderson hostage. Or calling State." Ashcroft slammed his hand on the table. "Dammit, Tom, you might've scuppered the only chance we have of getting help!"

Bosco stepped closer to Ashcroft's desk, lowered his voice.

"Once they leave this compound, Jacobs is out of the equation, likewise most of the Marines, and they're not getting back in. My guys outnumber the remainder by three-to-one. Once Jacobs leaves we'll have the tactical advantage." He hesitated for a moment, then said, "If this whole thing is on the level."

Ashcroft came around the desk, stood in front of him. "What d'you mean? What's happened?"

"I don't know," Bosco said, his eyes drifting across the compound schematic. He saw Warehouse Seven, the Chancery, the commissary, where this whole thing had started. It felt like days ago, not hours. "Something feels off. It's not—"

"Javelin, this is Hitman One, over."

Bosco unclipped the radio from his belt. Ashcroft stared at it like it was a live grenade.

"That's Major Roth, right? What does he want?"

"One way to find out." Bosco lifted the radio to his mouth. "Go for Javelin."

BOSCO'S VOICE CRACKLED IN ROTH'S EAR.

"We've got a situation," he told the RSO. After he'd spoken for several moments, he said, "We're falling back to your location."

"The Chancery is sealed," Bosco told him. "No one in or out."

"Have you seen the perimeter walls? The contractors have disappeared. We have no power, no comms. My opinion? We're going to get hit. The ambassador needs protection and my guys can provide it. It's not open for debate."

"Two things," Bosco told him. "One, I'm the RSO, which means you do as you're goddam told, and second, this building is locked down. You find somewhere else to hole up until you hear from me."

"The Chancery is the fallback, right? So, we're coming to you."

"Negative!"

In the darkness of the room, Roth shook his head. "This fucking guy," he muttered, echoing Costello's earlier observation. "What the fuck is he playing at?" He squeezed his PTT switch. "Be advised, we're coming in hot, front entrance. I'll give you a heads-up when we're thirty seconds out. If those doors aren't open, I'll blow them."

"You can't do that!" Bosco snapped. "You risk bringing that infection in here!"

"My guys are clean."

"You don't know that."

"Make sure those doors are open, you hear me? Out."

Roth shook his head, then said to Costello, "Get Drake in here."

As the Sergeant-Major left the room, Roth went to the window. Down below he counted eight bodies, all of them his guys, all immobile, the sand already gathering in the folds of their uniforms. Then a movement caught his eye, a pack of shadows rushing around the side of the building. Roth watched them and felt sick.

They were Delta, and they were all infected. He noticed Hoyer first, the big, blond Californian, smart as hell and funny too. All the guys loved Hoyer. The second thing Roth noticed was Hoyer's missing right arm, severed below the elbow, his clothing and gear shredded, and he dragged his weapon along the floor behind him by a broken strap. The others with him - Grant, Weber, Lewis - they moved the same, hunched against the wind, heads snapping left and right, and Roth realised they were searching for targets. He could hear their animalistic growling even through the thick glass of the window.

He watched them disappear into the darkness and knew he was going to have to end the lives of his own people in order to save the rest of them. The guilt hit him like a punch, and he felt sick to his stomach. He put a hand on the window to steady himself. He'd never considered himself a failure, not until now, but he'd failed his men, this facility, his country, in every way possible.

He straightened up as Costello entered with Drake in tow. Roth met them halfway across the room.

"Fires have taken hold downstairs," Costello reported. "We've got to get out of here."

Roth looked at Drake. "How many long guns do we have left?"

"Three, including me."

"The Humvee is still outside?" Drake nodded. "Okay, I want your snipers set up at the Chancery. And take the three best sharpshooters with you. I want y'all covering our approach. Go!"

Drake wheeled away. Roth turned to Costello. "You hear from Myers?"

"Affirmative."

"Tell him we're going to loop around the building to his position and approach from the east. And Nick..." Costello paused. "When we move, we stop for nothing, you hear me?"

"Fucking A," Costello answered.

BOSCO HURRIED BACK TO HIS OFFICE.

Ashcroft was coming apart, and Bosco had to talk him down and convince him he was safe. Ashcroft had a point though. His agents were no match for Delta in a gunfight, and then there was the additional threat of Roth and his men bringing the virus in with them, despite the Delta commander's assurances. It was all going to hell, but Bosco had a plan. The Chancery was the fallback, yes, but the *real* fallback was the Safe Haven, right beneath their feet. He'd told Ashcroft, but the man didn't seem too keen on the idea of being trapped deep underground. If things got worse, he might yet change his mind.

He slammed the door behind him and emptied his security cabinet, dumping it all on his desk. He pulled on his tac-vest and slotted the carbine magazines in the front pouches. He pushed another magazine into his M4 carbine and dropped the bug-out bag back in his locker. He left it unlocked.

He tugged his windbreaker back on and headed downstairs. The beam of his torch revealed an empty atrium - everyone had been moved to the floors above. *A little less chaos,* Bosco thought. His footsteps echoed on the marble floor.

A detail of Marines packed the gloomy service corridor.

They'd scaled their kit down to tac-vests and fatigue caps and wore goggles and scarves in preparation for the storm that waited for them outside the grey steel North Exit doors. Red chem-light sticks glowed on their tac-vests.

"Make a hole!" one of them barked as Jacobs and Sanderson approached from the opposite direction. Both men wore suits, with dark windbreakers over the top. Sanderson didn't look happy at all. There was a woman with them, one of Sanderson's people, press-ganged into the delegation to smooth things out, Bosco assumed. Like her boss, she looked pretty scared.

"Are we ready? Jacobs asked.

Bosco nodded. "Vehicles are right outside," he said. "Drivers are watching for infected."

"In this storm? We won't see them until they're on top of us," Jacobs warned.

"Vehicles are tight to the building. The Marines will cover you. My guys too." Bosco nodded to the helmeted and heavily-armed agents who flanked the doors. "They'll be waiting for you when you get back. Give us a heads up on channel eight."

Jacobs pulled a tactical scarf over his face. "Okay, let's do this."

Bosco took a step back as the DS agents slung their weapons and released the doors. Dust swirled around the lobby as the Marines left the building, splitting left and right, weapons tucked into their shoulders. The vehicles were parked less than six feet from the doors, three dark-coloured Toyota Land Cruisers. Wind and dirt hammered through their headlights.

"Good luck," Bosco shouted over the storm.

Jacobs and Sanderson ducked outside and the doors swung shut behind them.

"Do not open these doors without my express permission, understood?"

The agents answered in the affirmative and Bosco headed back up to his office. He crossed to the window and snatched up the high-power binoculars that always rested on the ledge. He swept them across the Green Zone but with the storm raging, he couldn't see much at all.

A flare of red light caught his eye and he tipped the lenses down; the convoy had stopped at the main gate. He fingered the focus ring, zeroing in on the nearest guard tower. Then he switched to the only other one he could see.

Roth was right. They were empty.

He lowered the binoculars. Who had the juice to pull security from a US embassy? Northridge had that contract. Did that mean they were siding with the military?

Of course they are, his inner voice mocked, *and the lights in the Zone are out too, which means the Iraqis are in on it.* Bosco felt dizzy. This was some Machiavellian shit-storm that he just couldn't wrap his head around.

Yet someone had to know the truth. Someone on the inside who could tell Tom Bosco exactly what the hell was going on. And he had a good idea who that might be.

There was a knock at the door. Waiting outside was Pat Murphy and another agent. Standing between them, Doug Walker.

Bosco cocked his head. "Step inside, Mister Walker."

THE AIR ON THE SECOND FLOOR WAS HAZY AND STANK OF burning plastic. Some guys were coughing. That kind of noise wouldn't do at all.

Drake came through the door, reported that the exit was clear. Roth took him to one side. "You're going to have to shoot, no question. Don't think, just do it. Everybody's lives depend on it."

"Understood."

"Confirm when you're in position."

Roth turned, saw his men waiting in the darkness. "Listen up. When we hit the main entrance we turn right, then head north past the ball courts. We pick up Meyer and the others, then we head west. We move quickly and quietly. Anyone comes at us, drop them. And don't hesitate; they're not human anymore. Christ knows we'll be doing them a favour."

He tried to pick out their faces in the dark. They were shadows, nothing more, and for a moment he wondered what they were thinking, whether they too held him responsible for all of this. Roth knew one thing for sure - he'd never lead this team again. And that meant saving as many of them as possible.

At the end of the hallway, the room was ablaze, and orange flames roared and cracked across the walls and ceiling. Roth headed for the main door, took a quick look left and right. Nothing. The storm was still blowing hard and Roth was grateful for it. He peeled right and the others followed. They moved fast, found the shipping container, linked up with Meyer and the others.

They waited, crouched in the darkness, as the Humvees roared into life and swung around, lights cutting through the storm, tyres bouncing over kerbs, and then they swung west onto Main Street. A moment later they were lost in the storm.

He slapped Costello on the arm. "Tell Bosco he's got incoming friendlies, two minutes out. Tell him those doors better be open or I'll shoot him myself."

Roth got to his feet as Costello relayed most of the message. "Prepare to move," he said into his radio.

Roth led his men into the swirling, shifting darkness.

THEY CIRCUMNAVIGATED THE SMALL, WINDOWLESS BUILDING IN A snarling, snapping, restless throng.

Freddie Cruz was lost amongst them, pushing and shoving, spraying bile at those who tested him, clawing his way past the weaker ones, trampling over the lame. The building drew him, as it drew the others, and the low-frequency hum filled his belly, comforted him. It tamed the beast inside him, tempered his rage. He trudged on, swaying amongst the throng.

Their numbers were many, much more so than before, and Freddie felt their strength as much as he felt his own. Soon that strength would be tested because the wind carried the whiff of the stinkers lurking somewhere out there in the darkness. And they had to be hunted down, their blood shed, their kind destroyed. But not yet. Not until they had all answered the call, had gathered together as one. Freddie saw some of them as he moved, watched them scamper out of the darkness and throw themselves in amongst the pack. Only when the calls finally went unanswered, when the last of them had joined the throng, would they hunt once more.

Freddie kept moving. The throng moved in a heaving, hissing circle, oblivious to the storm that rolled over their contagious ranks.

CHAPTER 12
HARD STOP

Bill Jacobs sat behind the driver of the second Toyota as it weaved its way through a chicane of concrete security blocks.

The embassy was now behind them, swallowed by the darkness. Up ahead the Toyota's headlights picked out the next security gate, this one manned by Northridge contractors. As they approached the rusted metal wall, it started to slide across the road.

"Rolling back the gate," the Marine riding shotgun announced. His M4 lay across his legs, barrel pointed into the footwell.

Next to Jacobs, Sanderson said, "It's been a while since I was outside of the compound."

"How safe is it out here?" asked the woman sitting by the opposite window. Her name was Anne, and she sounded nervous.

"Safe enough," Jacobs told her. "Especially with this storm blowing through."

"I don't want to go back," Anne said. "Not with those poor people running around."

Jacobs offered her a smile. "It's going to be okay."

Anne glared at Jacobs. "How exactly? There are rumours about that warehouse. Terrible things—"

"Take it easy."

"We should drive straight to the consulate in Basra," Anne declared. "It's not safe at the embassy anymore."

"That's not our call," Sanderson told her. "Just relax, Anne. Please."

Brake lights flared ahead as the lead Toyota bumped over the gate rails. Jacobs stared out of the window as they followed, but he didn't see anyone.

"We're in the channel," the Marine said.

The channel was a hundred-meter strip of sand-blown tarmac bordered by twenty-foot-high concrete blast walls. It was normally lit up like a football field. Now it was a dark no-man's-land, and Jacobs could barely see the vehicle ahead.

"What d'you think knocked out the power?"

It was the Marine again. He talked too much, Jacobs observed. The kid was jumpy. "Let's keep the chatter down."

"Roger that."

But Jacobs felt it too. As a younger man he'd served with the CIA's Special Activities Division in Afghanistan. During that time, he'd seen a lot of action, and he'd developed a strong nose for trouble. That antenna was twitching now.

He leaned over the driver's shoulder. They were crawling, and the Toyota's wipers beat back and forth in a vain attempt to improve visibility. He could just make out the concrete walls on either side of the road. The wind was barrelling around them, whipping dust and sand through the head-lights. All three vehicles were now in the channel, the gates in front and back closed—

He blinked as something wet sprayed across his face.

The driver slumped forward.

Bullets stitched across the windscreen, and the Marine riding shotgun grabbed his own neck as a round passed through it. His headrest exploded in a puff of foam stuffing.

Sanderson screamed as Anne's brains spilled across his lap, then he grunted as a bullet thumped into his chest. Jacobs was already out of the door and drew his body in tight behind the big rear wheel. A hail of rounds peppered the Toyota's thin skin and Jacobs was showered with broken glass. He peered beneath the vehicle but the storm robbed him of any tactical intel. His Glock 23 was already in his hand but he had no target. The Toyota was lit up by the headlights of the one behind, and out of the glare a shadow loomed and hunkered down next to him.

"Ambush," the Marine spat. "Murder holes between the blast walls. All of my guys have been hit. Fucking chemlights. You see any movement up front?"

Jacobs shook his head. "No return fire, nothing. Looks like they're all down too."

The Marine twisted around the back of the vehicle and fired a long burst from his M4. "That should wake up the guys back at the gatehouse."

"Don't bank on it," Jacobs shouted, as return fire cracked off the tarmac around them. "This storm will cover a lot of noise. We've got to use it as cover, get back to the embassy."

Both men cringed as the gunfire intensified, hammering the vehicle. They heard a scream up ahead by the lead Toyota, then it was snatched away by the wind.

"They're using suppressors," the Marine observed. "Can't hear a goddam thing."

"Not ISIS then. Could be a rogue Iraqi group."

"So where the fuck are the contractors?"

"We need to get out of here."

The wind howled and Jacobs spat sand from his mouth. He pulled the Marine in close. "We crawl back the way we came."

"We're in the channel. Gates at both ends. We're trapped." He slapped a hand against the Toyota. "We need to light this baby up. Someone might see the flames."

The gunfire intensified, then stopped. All they could hear now was the wind.

"They're on the move. How much ammo you got?"

"Two clips," Jacobs told him.

"When the wind dies a little, I'm going to loose off half a mag. You do the same."

"Roger that."

A pistol shot rang out and bullets punched the bodywork just above their heads. Jacobs squinted into the wind and thought he glimpsed someone.

"Ours or theirs?" he hissed over his shoulder. The Marine stared back at him with sightless eyes, one of them destroyed by the round that killed him. Jacobs holstered his Glock, pushed the Marine over and grabbed his M4. He scrambled to his feet and ran. If he had to climb that fucking gate, he would.

He'd managed only a few steps when the first bullet hit his left arm, spinning him around. He cursed, dropping the M4, and then the second round hit him in the back and he fell to the ground. He pulled himself to his knees, felt the blood soaking his shirt, and realised the bullet had passed through him. His left arm dangled uselessly by his side, the bone broken, his windcheater ripped. He reached for his Glock. He'd loose off that magazine before they got to him.

Through the dust he saw a pair of desert boots. He crawled towards the dead Marine who was lying on top of his rifle. Jacobs tried to push him off but his strength failed him. He was losing blood, and a lot of it. His head swam with the effort.

They appeared out of the storm, four armed men wearing dark tactical gear, the stalks of their NVGs clearly visible on their helmets. Jacobs tried to lift his Glock but one of them stepped forward and kicked him over on his back. The gun skittered out of sight. Jacobs flinched as one of them fired two rounds into the dead Marine. They were taking no prisoners, and suddenly everything made sense.

Vann Jackson had brought something terrible into the embassy, and somebody somewhere had decided that the risk was too great. No one was getting out of that compound. Their attackers weren't ISIS, or a rogue Iraqi element. They were Northridge contractors, and like all contractors they carried out the orders of whoever was paying them.

One of them stood over him, his face wrapped in a Nomex death-skull mask, his eyes hidden behind his night-vision optics.

"I'm not infected," Jacobs wheezed.

The man twisted his head. "I can't hear you," he said in heavily-accented English.

Jacobs yelled as loud as he could. "I don't have the virus!"

"I don't care," the man shouted against the wind.

He felt hands grab his wrists and ankles and he was lifted off the ground. The wind stung his eyes as he was carried like a dead buck between two hunters. More hands grabbed him, and then he was being dumped into the back of the Toyota he'd vacated only minutes before. He twisted his head as his breath rattled in his chest. He was lying on top of Sanderson and the woman, Anne. He was dying, he knew that, but he wasn't scared. He'd had plenty of close shaves during his career. Death had finally caught up with him, that was all.

His head lolled to one side and he saw Death climb behind the wheel. He heard doors slamming and felt the vehicle begin to move.

Then his eyes closed and he felt nothing at all.

Doug stood in the middle of Bosco's private office.

It was carpeted, well appointed, and a battery lamp on a coffee table threw a pale light across the room. The windows overlooked the Green Zone, but Doug couldn't see a thing.

"Delta are on their way," he heard Bosco mutter. "Get down to the security lobby and let them in." He closed the door and offered Doug a seat.

"Thanks, but I've been sitting down all day."

"Sit."

It wasn't a request. Bosco was wearing his tactical gear and had an M4 carbine slung across his chest. He cut a pretty intimidating figure, Doug thought, so he sat down. The RSO perched himself on the edge of his desk, uncomfortably close to Doug.

"Time to level with me, Walker. What's the plan? What happens next?"

Doug stared at Bosco. Despite the shadows, he could see the anger in the RSO's face. "Excuse me?"

"You cut the comms. You're working with them."

"With who?"

"The military."

"Sure. I work for the DOD."

Bosco pulled a pistol and jammed it into Doug's chest. "Don't be a fucking smartass," he hissed, pushing the barrel deeper.

For a split second, Doug thought he was going to die. Bosco's mouth was twisted in anger.

"I'll shoot you dead, right now, in this office, if you don't level with me. I'll tell everyone you went for my gun, that I was forced to defend myself. And they'll believe me because I'm the Regional Security Officer and you're a piece-of-shit contractor who deliberately sabotaged my embassy. So, start talking, because I'm all out of time *and* patience."

Very slowly, Doug raised his hands. Bosco meant what he said, he could see it in the man's eyes. He tried to keep his voice as calm as possible.

"Mister Bosco, please listen to me. Whatever happened in The Hub was not the result of anything I did. Yes, I'm a defence contractor, and have been for a long time, but I don't know what you're talking—"

"Bullshit! That virus is loose. That was the plan, right? What's next?"

Doug saw Bosco's finger curl around the trigger, watched his knuckles whiten.

"You've got five seconds, Walker. Four—"

"I don't know what you're talking about," Doug pleaded, his hands still raised. "You've got it all wrong. The only reason I'm out here frying my ass off is—"

"Three seconds."

"I killed my wife. I killed her, okay?"

Bosco's eyes narrowed. "What the hell are you—?"

"A couple of years ago I had an affair at work. My wife, she took it real hard, started drinking—"

"Shut the fuck up!" Bosco shook his head, pressed the gun harder. "I don't care if—"

"Wait! My daughter Holly, she was just a kid. She came home from school, found her mom dead on the couch. She'd OD'd on booze and pills, choked on her own vomit. My daughter couldn't cope, blamed me. She started drinking too, using drugs. She dropped out of school, started living on the streets. Because of me."

Doug stared up at Bosco. His voice trembled, but not because he might get shot.

"I did something unforgivable, and I ended up ruining two innocent, precious lives because I was selfish and stupid. I can't do anything about my wife - and that'll haunt me to my dying day - but I've got a shot at reaching my daughter. That's the reason I'm here, Mister Bosco, the reason I take the hardship postings; they pay for the investigators who are looking for her."

Doug felt the pressure of the gun ease a little. He held Bosco's icy glare.

"I got a call, before all this shit happened. They've found

her, after two long years, but she's in a bad way and she's mixed up with some dangerous people. I've got to get home, Mister Bosco. That's all I care about. Whatever you think I've done, whatever it is you think I'm involved in, you're dead wrong. My daughter is lost to me. She's lost to the world and I have to find her, bring her home. She's all I've got."

Doug saw the vicious glint in Bosco's eyes fade a little. The RSO straightened up. He pulled the gun from Doug's chest and sat back on the edge of his desk. Whatever was going on, it had the RSO contemplating murder. Then he spoke, his eyes focussed somewhere over Doug's head.

"I've worked for the State Department for much of my adult life, and it hasn't always been easy. It's cost me two marriages, two good ladies who deserved more than what I was selling. Thankfully there were never any kids because, well, it just never worked out that way. The job came first. Always the job."

"I hear that," Doug said.

"Now? I have no clue what is happening or who to trust. And there's a very real chance that a lot of people might die, and that includes you and me."

Doug watched him holster his pistol and breathed a quiet sigh of relief. He sat forward in his chair.

"It's Tom, right?" Bosco nodded. "Well, Tom, in those situations, in the absence of reliable intel, I trust my gut. Do what's right. Whatever happens after that, at least my conscience is clear."

The RSO gave Doug a long stare. "Fuck it, maybe I will get my name on that wall after all." He stood up, waved Doug to his feet. "Okay, Walker, I'm going to give you the opportunity to prove me wrong."

Doug let out a grateful breath. "Anything I can do to help. Just say the word."

Bosco said nothing. Instead he crossed the room and held the door open. "Let's go say hello to your Delta buddies."

"They're not my—"

"Let's go."

Bosco walked away and Doug hurried after him. The gloomy hallway outside was busy with people hurrying back and forth. They parted like the Red Sea for Bosco. Alone on the stairwell, Bosco said, "You should know, the infected got out of the warehouse. There're hundreds of them out there in the storm."

Doug heard that terrible scream again, saw the crazy guy pummelling the girl. He felt his stomach churn. "Jesus fucking Christ! How?"

"Doesn't matter. And there's no help coming. We're on our own."

Doug grabbed Bosco by the arm. "Wait, what? What d'you mean?"

"It's complicated. In short, we're in a deep, dark hole and there's no way out. So, we're going to sit tight and hope events elsewhere go our way." He shook his arm free. "Let's move."

Down in the atrium, Doug saw a group of shadowy, helmeted figures moving quickly towards them. Heavily-armed figures. A voice said, "You're Bosco, right?"

Bosco stopped short. "Correct."

The figures encircled them. Torches were held low, bearded faces cast into shadow. Serious faces. The voice spoke again.

"The windows on the first floor, east facing. We need access to them, right now."

Doug was a weapons geek, and even in the gloom, he saw that three of the men carried HK G-28 Marksmen Rifles with high-power scopes mounted on the top rails. The other guys carried a combination of M-110 Sharpshooters and HK-416 assault rifles. They wore tac-vests front-loaded with translucent magazines and a bunch of other kit that Doug barely recognised, but all of them wore compact ballistic helmets with battery packs and panoramic NVGs. Their equipment was personalised, state-of-the-art stuff. These guys were the real deal.

"Follow me," Bosco said, leading them back across the atrium towards the stairs.

Doug hurried after them. The first-floor offices were large shadowy spaces filled with people sitting against the walls or standing around battery lamps in small groups, talking quietly. Everyone stopped talking when Bosco and the Delta boys marched into the room.

"Give us some help here," Bosco ordered as he began dragging tables and chairs away from the east-facing windows. "The rest of you, find somewhere else. This room is off-limits."

Eager hands went to work, dragging tables and wheeling chairs away from the windows. Bosco broke the emergency seals and the wind blasted dust and sand around the room. By the time he was ushering Doug outside, there were eight Delta operators positioned at four windows, all of them covering the ground below with night scopes.

On the stairs Bosco said, "We're going up to see the ambassador. Don't talk unless he speaks to you directly, okay?"

Like the rest of the Chancery, the Executive Suite was lit by blue emergency lights. When they got to Ashcroft's office, it was filled with some very worried-looking admin types. Three of them wore aviator uniforms, and all of them were huddled around the embassy chief, talking low. The chatter ceased when Bosco entered the room.

Ashcroft told the group, "Give us a moment, please."

When the door closed behind the last of them, Ashcroft jabbed a finger at Doug. "What's he doing here?"

Bosco didn't answer that question. Instead he asked, "What's the deal with the chopper crew?"

Ashcroft cleared his throat. "I want them prepared, in case we need to leave in a hurry."

"You can't leave. You're the Acting Head of Mission, and there are over seven hundred people in this building who are looking to you for leadership."

"Don't lecture me!" Ashcroft snapped.

Bosco pointed toward the window. "Besides, you can't fly in that. It's suicide."

"You're a pilot now?" Ashcroft dropped into the chair behind his desk. His fingers tapped his lifeless keyboard, then he shoved it aside. Papers tumbled to the floor. "Besides, is it any worse than staying here?"

"Delta just arrived. The rest are on their way over."

Ashcroft's mouth dropped open. "Are you stupid, Tom? Coffman said they can't be trusted."

"Secretary Coffman?" Doug blurted. He felt his face redden as Ashcroft glared at him.

"We didn't have a choice," Bosco reminded him.

Ashcroft stared at his desk and muttered, "We're sitting ducks, goddammit. They could come up here, kill us all."

Doug thought he'd misheard. "What?"

Ashcroft pointed at Doug and said to Bosco, "Why is he here? Get him out of this office."

"No," Bosco said. "He can help us."

"How, for Chrissakes?"

Bosco didn't answer straight away. Doug watched him walk to the window and stare out into the darkness. After a few moments, he said, "Maybe we're getting played here, David."

"What?" Ashcroft got out of his chair and joined Bosco at the window. "What d'you mean?"

Bosco's eyes were fixed on the world outside. "It all started with Walker," he said quietly, cocking his head in Doug's direction. "The Hub reboots and we lose all comms. Then we lose power, mains *and* backup, and not just in this facility. The Zone is out too. Does that mean the Iraqis are in on this thing?" Bosco snapped his fingers. "And just like that, Northridge pull security from the walls." He turned to face Ashcroft. "Who has that kind of influence?"

"The military of course!" Ashcroft sounded exasperated, as if he were talking to a child. "You heard what they said. There's a coup in progress—"

"Wait, a what?" Doug cut in. This situation was getting crazier by the second.

"Keep quiet!" Ashcroft yelled at him.

Doug zipped it, kept his ears open instead. Ashcroft glared at him a moment longer then turned back to Bosco.

"As improbable as all this seems, we have to trust in our leaders, Tom. The chain of command is all we have."

Bosco finally turned to face him. "If they wanted this thing to spread, why didn't they take Jackson and drive him out of the embassy? Dump him in Sadr City? That's a million people right there, densely populated, poor sanitation - the virus would've spread like wildfire. They could've done that without either of us knowing about it."

"I don't know if—"

"Sure they could."

Doug couldn't help himself. "Wait a minute. They want the virus to *spread*?"

"So we've been told," nodded Bosco.

Ashcroft grabbed the RSO's arm. "Enough, Tom! This is classified. He's a goddam saboteur!"

Bosco shook him off. "And what if we're wrong, David!" He pushed past Ashcroft and stood in front of Doug. "Take a seat and let me tell you exactly what's happening here."

"Tom!" Ashcroft protested.

But Bosco ignored him, and for the next few minutes Doug listened from the sofa. When he was finished, Doug remained seated. He wasn't sure if his legs would support him if he tried to stand.

Finally, he said, "Well, that Mulholland guy is right about one thing - that virus has to stay behind these walls."

"And what if Mulholland is right about everything else, Tom?" It was Ashcroft, still standing by the window.

"We'll know soon enough," Bosco told him. "Bill should be with the Brits by now. If he's on the level, he'll radio us from the main gate when he returns."

"And if he's not?"

Bosco shrugged. "Then one of two things will happen - Delta will either shoot us or expose us to the infection."

Ashcroft failed to mask his horror as he stared at his security chief. "How can you be so blasé about this?"

"Because I don't believe it'll come to that."

"You don't know that!"

Bosco checked his watch. "The next hour is crucial. I suggest you remain here, David, in this office. You have my guys outside, and I'm on the radio. Let's just take a breath, wait it out."

Ashcroft's face was twisted with anger, frustration. And fear. "We could be signing our death warrants!"

"Or help could already be on its way. In the meantime, I'm going down to the Safe Haven, to prep it, just in case."

Ashcroft shook his head. "I won't go down in that dungeon, Tom."

"Let's hope it doesn't come to that," Bosco replied. He got to his feet. "Let's go."

Doug stood, his legs still feeling shaky, and followed Bosco from the room.

CHAPTER 13
EYE SPY

Roth led what remained of his Delta team north, to the security wall that ran parallel to the deserted Kindi Street.

They moved through the storm as fast as the conditions would safely allow, heads swivelling left and right, sharp eyes behind tactical goggles sweeping the ground ahead and to the sides, leap-frogging each other as they covered their six.

Roth led them away from the open ground of the embassy, preferring instead to keep to the boundary walls where the chances of encountering either friend or foe were much slimmer. So he hoped.

He saw a cluster of vehicles ahead - cars, minivans and pickups - their bodywork and glass obscured by sand. Roth raised his hand and brought the team to a halt. The silent command rippled down the line behind him. They stood guns up, barrels pointing out into the storm.

Roth swept the parking lot through his scope. Somewhere out there were the infected, hundreds of them, and the storm gave them perfect cover. The thought made Roth's skin crawl but his personal safety was no longer a concern. All that mattered now was saving as many people as possible. Still, he thought it strange that they hadn't seen anyone yet. Hays had mentioned something about cognitive function and group dynamics, and Roth was concerned about butting heads with a pack. In this weather, that kind of contact could be lethal.

Roth saw Costello right behind him, waiting for the next order. He gave him the signal - *travelling*. He wedged his rifle tight to his shoulder and moved ahead, alternating between squinting through his scope and watching over his gun barrel. They weaved slowly through the abandoned vehicles, dust and sand swirling around them. A minivan appeared out of the haze, tyres and windshield choked with sand. He passed close to the front grill, twisted his body to cover his left flank—

He caught a glimpse of hair trailing in the wind, a face streaked with crusted blood, hands reaching for his face—

Roth fired twice and the woman dropped to the ground. She lay dead at his feet, her legs folded beneath her, two tightly grouped impact holes in the tunic of her medical scrubs. His heart hammered - she'd almost got the jump on him. She was about his age, her skin blotched with those weird broken veins

Costello tapped his shoulder, gestured with a gloved hand. Roth saw them too, vague shadows a few meters ahead. He brought his gun up. He could hear them snarling and barking like animals, but he was unsure how many there were. At least three, maybe more, drifting in and out of the fog, bumping and scraping against abandoned vehicles.

Roth gave the corpse a final glance. The wind plucked at her hair and sand was already soaking up the blood pooling beneath her body. He gave the signal to turn around, saw his guys melting back into the storm. *Two rounds gone,* he reminded himself. He'd always counted his expended rounds. Back at Bragg, he had a rep for knowing exactly how many he had left in his mag at any given time. It was a skill that had earned him a lot of gambled bucks. Now he had twenty-eight rounds left. He hoped he'd have the same amount by the time they got to the Chancery.

He felt Costello's gloved hand tap his shoulder.

He moved backwards for a few steps, still watching the hazy figures ahead, his finger resting on his trigger.

Then he turned and followed the others.

THE WINDS THAT HAD BATTERED BAGHDAD FOR SEVERAL HOURS slowly eased. The clouds that had swept across the city in towering waves gradually dissolved and stars were once again visible in the night sky.

Inside the embassy compound, dust devils twirled their last dance and evaporated into nothing. Sand drifted, then lay still with a final, dying hiss. The yellow, shifting fog that had wrapped itself around the most expensive slice of diplomatic real estate in the world began to clear.

Outside the Chancery, Old Glory managed a final, tired flutter then lay still against its pole. Buildings reappeared as the horizon unfurled. Yet the embassy remained a city of shadows, bordered by the slow-moving Tigris on one side and the empty, lightless Green Zone on the other. The United States embassy was a black island in a sea of darkness.

The storm had passed.

The carnage was about to begin.

"GRAND SLAM STATUS?"

"Locked and loaded."

"Stand by," Blake ordered.

Erik Mulholland dragged his chair closer to Chuck and Eugene and peered over their shoulders. What they had achieved already was impressive enough - cutting off a diplomatic facility from the world while taking control of its systems - but now they were about to kick things up a gear.

Mulholland was impressed, but he was also a little scared. He realised at that very moment that Blake was about to commit murder for Amy Coffman, and that made Mulholland an accomplice. He snatched a quick glance at the Kroll executive, saw him pacing the floor behind him, muttering into a satellite phone. Mulholland heard him end the call and say, "It's airborne. Try the feed."

"Coming online now," Chuck announced, watching the TV display.

Mulholland saw a fuzzy storm of interference on the screen, followed by a crystal-clear, high-definition aerial view of what he could only assume was the compound in Baghdad.

"Is that the embassy?"

Blake ignored him, spoke to the technician. "Are we recording?"

Chuck hooked a thumb over his shoulder. "Backing up to the drive in the rack."

Mulholland watched the feed, a look-down view that was slowly tracking across the roof of a large building. The picture was sharp enough to see the detail of the air-conditioning units. "That's a drone, right?"

"Just launched from the Northridge compound. Super quiet blades, low-light camera and pretty much invisible against the night sky," Blake told him. He laid a hand on Eugene's shoulder. "Status?"

"Assuming flight control now." Eugene had a remote cradled in his hands, like an X-Box or PlayStation controller. He twisted it and thumbed some buttons. The distant drone changed altitude, direction. "She's ours," Eugene confirmed.

"Give me a circumnavigation of the facility."

Mulholland was captivated by the feed. The compound looked eerily deserted as the drone drifted across the distant embassy. He saw the Chancery, the consulate building, the commissary, parking lots, warehouses, the Black Hawk squatting on its pad. Then he saw bodies, lots of them lying between buildings, some in groups, others scattered individually. The body count was already rising.

"You seeing this?" Blake asked him. He had a smile on his face as if he was watching Monday Night Football. Mulholland hated football. He decided he hated Bob Blake even more.

"We've got a fire." Eugene reported.

Blake stood behind him. "What building is that?"

"That's the old school," Chuck told him. "Military Liaison took it over a while back."

Mulholland saw the flames glowing white on the screen. The fire was a big one, the smoke drifting beneath the camera lens in thick clouds. Then he noticed something else, an odd movement at the very edge of the screen. He stood up. "What's that?"

Blake saw it too, got to his feet, his chair rolling backwards. "Holy shit, is that what I think it is?"

Mulholland nodded, speechless. Finally, he said, "It's them, the infected ones. Jesus Christ, what the hell are they doing?"

"Pull up a schematic of the compound," Blake ordered.

Mulholland's eyes were riveted to the screen. The images were macabre. He saw people moving around a building at the far end of the compound, hundreds of them, their bodies densely packed. It reminded Mulholland of Mecca where pilgrims circumnavigated the *Karbala* in their thousands. But this was very different.

On the outer edges of the shifting, heaving ring, he saw figures, mostly clothed, others naked, running around the outer edges, arms waving wildly. He saw others stagger and fall, saw them trampled beneath the crowd. The building they circumnavigated was small, about the size of a Winnebago, yet they were pressed against its walls as if they were trying to crush it. It was the strangest site Mulholland had ever seen.

"It's a Grand Slam node," Blake explained.

Mulholland, spooked by the feed, recalibrated. "What? What does that mean?"

"The building is drawing power."

"Maybe they're attracted by the voltage," Chuck theorised, "or maybe the residual heat of the building."

"Hey, take a look at these guys." It was Eugene, and he'd flown the drone lower, hovering above a group of infected just outside the ring. There were several of them, gathered around a couple who were fucking. The woman was on all fours, and when one man finished another dropped to his knees and mounted her.

Blake laughed. "Jesus, that broad likes to party."

"They're laying a train on her ass," Chuck grinned.

Mulholland couldn't decide what was more disgusting, the spectacle on the screen or Blake's reaction.

"Show's over," the executive chuckled. "We need to draw them away from that structure, get them moving west." He pointed at a management console. "Let's fire up one of those babies. That might draw them."

"Fire what?" asked Mulholland.

Blake dismissed him with a wave of his hand. "Sit back and relax, Erik. The show's about to begin."

Mulholland obeyed, his stomach churning. He'd been shaken by what he'd already seen. He was pretty sure that what he was about to see was going to be far worse.

They took cover in the shadow of the commissary wall.

To the east, orange light danced somewhere in the storm. Despite the buffeting wind, Roth could hear the muted roar of the fire that was consuming their accommodation block. As he quietly mourned the bodies that must still be in there, something else died...

The wind.

Roth turned and looked along the wall. Every few seconds another operator appeared as the dust that had wrapped them in its opaque embrace melted away. He craned his neck and saw stars above. Now they were back in business.

He took a quick peek out onto Main Street and saw the embassy slowly reveal itself as the storm left Baghdad behind. He pulled the scarf from his nose and mouth and dragged the goggles up over his helmet. To the west, the Chancery was roughly three hundred meters away. Directly across the road to the south, the State Department blocks lay abandoned and wrapped in darkness. It was difficult to see anything east. A hundred and fifty meters away the fire raged and thick smoke rolled across Main Street. Two floors of their building had already been consumed, and Roth heard the pop of glass as window frames twisted and buckled—

Boom!

Roth ducked as an explosion ripped out the southern wall of the burning building. Debris rained down around them, and then the floors above the fire collapsed in an avalanche of rubble that sent clouds of dust billowing across Main Street.

They waited for the dust to settle. The fire threw orange light across Main Street, plunging everything else into shadow. There was no moon, but ambient light from the city gave them something to work with. Roth thumbed his radio. "We're moving in sixty seconds, straight up Main Street to the Chancery. Stay sharp and watch for targets. The shooters will give us cover if we need it. Prepare to move."

Roth wondered where the infected were. Out there somewhere, but he could hear nothing but the roar of the fire. He knew movement was risky, especially now that the storm had cleared, but staying still was riskier. Besides, he had to get his men to safety. He raised his hand.

It was time to go.

• • •

Freddie Cruz pushed and shoved his way through the others, trying to get closer, but he was finding it impossible. The building spoke to him, its vibrations warming his chest and calming the rage. He tugged his arm out from the press of bodies and tried to touch it, but he wasn't close enough and the pack was too dense. He screamed in frustration. Others around him screamed too.

Something had changed, he realised. The blinding, choking winds had stopped and now his eyes could see everything. He saw that the pack had grown. He saw the surrounding landscape, familiar yet foreign, dark but not threatening. He saw the insect that hovered above them, thought he could reach up and grab it, but it was out of reach. He clawed at it one more time, then ignored it.

Somewhere behind him there was a loud rumble that shook the ground beneath his bare feet. Freddie tried to see what it was but the throng carried him forward around the building. He shuffled with them, distracted by the rumble and by the sudden chorus of whoops and howls. He felt the beast inside him shift, uncoil itself. It hissed angrily. Freddie felt that anger too, saw others peeling away from the outer edges of the pack and disappear into the darkness. Freddie was desperate to join them, to join the hunt. He pushed and shoved, the excitement loosening his bowels. Filth ran down his legs.

The pack thinned and suddenly he had room to swing his arms and legs. Others stumbled against him and he pushed them away, toothless gums spitting bile and blood in their faces. Then he was free.

Excitement rippled through his body. The ground opened up before him and Freddie broke into a run. The pack unwound itself from the building and followed, their feet pounding the ground beneath them, their cries building, the sound of their fury echoing across the dark landscape before them.

Freddie screamed too.

ROTH LED THEM OUT OF THE SHADOWS AND CROSSED THE OPEN ground towards Main Street. There was enough ambient light to operate with the naked eye, something all of his guys were used to, and tactically their NVGs were a little restrictive. Right now, they needed eyes in the back of their heads.

Roth pulled a Gerber from his vest and cut the security tape that surrounded the commissary. They filed out onto Main Street, moving as quietly as possible. The Chancery was three hundred metres away, a straight shot. *A few more minutes, that's all they needed.*

Their formation was loose and staggered, their weapons trained outwards, giving them an all-round defensive posture. They passed between the commissary and the State Department blocks, moving like ghosts through a canyon of darkness. Red-dot optics probed shadows and doorways. A hundred and fifty metres ahead the ground opened up. That's where Roth wanted to be. In the meantime, he moved slow and quiet, red-dotting the black corners and dead ground between the buildings.

He stepped out of the column and waved his men through, keeping a sharp eye on their six. Costello stopped by his side.

"You hear that?" he whispered.

"Hold position," Roth ordered over the radio. His team crouched on the road, eyes and gun barrels sweeping the terrain. Roth cocked his head.

"What is that?"

"It's coming from the east." Costello lifted his rifle, checked his optics. "I've got nothing."

But Roth could feel it through his Merrells. A faint tremor. "Another structural collapse, maybe?"

Looking east, Roth couldn't see much beyond the flames

of the burning building. The explosion had punched out the ground-floor wall, bringing down several tons of rubble and blocking Main Street.

Then, in the darkness beyond, Roth thought he saw something.

Movement.

"Give me your scope." Costello pulled it from his vest and passed it to him. Roth held it to his eye.

And swore.

They spilled over the rubble like a wave, hundreds of people, men, women, clothed, naked, all scrambling amongst the debris, drawn by the flames. Roth watched them as they clawed at the air, at each other, a horde that pushed and shoved and screamed like animals. The noise was chilling. Roth felt the hairs on his neck stand on end.

"Nobody move," he whispered across the radio net. "Delta Three-Three, Hitman One, are you seeing this?"

"Roger," came Drake's reply. "We can hear them too. You're deep in the ink so hold your position."

Roth did the calculation. The infected were maybe a hundred and fifty metres away, most of them transfixed by the flames, but it wasn't them he was worried about. It was the others who'd pushed on, probing ahead, their bodies hunched, arms held wide, like apes. *More like cavemen*, Roth realised. They scuttled forward, then stopped. Scuttle, stop, scuttle, stop. Getting closer, peering into the dark.

Right at Roth and his team.

"Nobody. Fucking. Move," he repeated.

CHUCK IS PROBABLY NOT YOUR REAL NAME, MULHOLLAND decided, watching the technician tapping away at his keyboard. *You're a hired gun. A contractor. Mercenary. No principles, no ethics. It's all about the bottom line, right Chuck?*

Mulholland felt uneasy. He wasn't especially familiar with

the defence sector. To him, it was a secretive world of black budgets and private armies, a multi-trillion-dollar industry controlled by a small group of powerful individuals with little political oversight. Since his arrival at Rock Creek, Mulholland had come to the conclusion that it was more than that - it had become the *Military-Industrial Complex* that Eisenhower had warned of all those years ago, and he was troubled by how insignificant he felt.

Because it was Bob Blake who wielded the power in this room. In Blake's world, a thousand American lives meant nothing. Mulholland had always assumed that Amy controlled men like him, but now he wasn't so sure. Maybe Blake was keeping his powder dry until Amy was in the White House. That was a deeply troubling thought, but entirely plausible, Mulholland believed. He decided then and there that any references to Blakes' teeth - comedic or otherwise - were off the table, period.

His eyes flicked to the TV monitor. The flames from the building glowed white. The mob was a mass of pale figures too, and even though he was watching a soundless feed, he could almost feel the energy in that seething, shifting mass of bodies. A stark contrast to the statues that were staggered along the road a short distance away. *Soldiers,* Mulholland guessed. *Why were they just standing there?*

"Who are those guys?" Mulholland asked.

"Military," Blake answered. "Watching the herd, I imagine."

"They're so close."

"It's night, and there's no power. Probably sitting in the dark."

That made sense. Still, they must be pretty scared. He studied the white blobs, saw one or two of them move a little. The evolving battlefield of twenty-first-century warfare, Mulholland mused, the action monitored from a variety of God-like surveillance platforms, the orders given from comfortable control rooms hundreds, if not thousands, of miles away. Like the one he was in now, where lives could be taken with the press of a games console button.

War was becoming a video game, and a century from now, Earth's battlefields would probably be populated with robots and autonomous machinery, and mass casualties would be a thing of the past. So that evolving technology could be a good thing, but right now there were human beings down in that embassy and Mulholland wouldn't swap places with any of them for all the money in the world.

Chuck tapped a few more keys, then looked at Blake, finger hovering over his mouse button.

"Ready to launch."

Blake nodded. "Do it."

ROTH'S HEAD TWISTED AROUND AS THE *BOOM* ECHOED ACROSS the embassy. He saw a trail of sparks shoot up into the night sky and he cringed because he knew what was coming.

He heard the *pop* somewhere high above, and then the parachute flare burst into life, bathing the ground below in a ghostly white light. Night turned to day. Roth felt as naked as a newborn.

"Hold," he whispered into his radio. His lips and eyeballs were the only parts of his body that moved. Everything else was frozen. He watched the outliers, the infected that were closest to them, saw them freeze beneath the light, their necks craning upwards as they watched the flare drift across the embassy.

Except the closest one. He was looking right at Roth.

Busted.

The man was naked, and his chest appeared to be covered in blood, his legs in something else. He took three or four quick steps towards them, then stopped. He tilted his head back and screamed, the sound so primal it frightened Roth.

Behind him, the mob turned as one, then scrambled down the rubble, drawn to his terrible cry.

The naked man charged, bare feet slapping against the tarmac. Roth fired two rounds in quick succession and the man fell headlong to the ground. The mob charged towards them.

"Move!" Roth yelled to the others. "Run! Go!"

Delta bolted for the Chancery. Roth's next words were punctuated by rapid breathing as he radioed Drake at the Chancery.

"Dealer Three-Three, we are incoming. Get them goddam doors open!"

The noise behind him was like nothing Roth had ever heard before. It was a screeching, wailing, animalistic crescendo that was amplified by the surrounding buildings. He risked a quick glance over his shoulder. He wasn't moving fast enough. Then he heard Drakes' voice in his ear.

"Going to whittle the front runners down some."

Roth didn't see a muzzle flash from the windows of the Chancery but he heard the supersonic passage of high-calibre rounds ripping the air a few feet above his helmet. He heard the impacts behind him, the wet slap of lead impacting flesh and bone, the sprawl of bodies as they hit the ground.

"Target down. Switching. Target down," was all he could hear through his headset as Drake and his shooters tried to improve the odds.

He saw the Delta front-runners clear the shadows. The flare was drifting low now, its dying light casting long shadows across the ground to Roth's left. He saw the Black Hawk on its pad, the ambassador's private residence, its façade flickering like a silent movie as the flare sputtered and died nearby.

Darkness returned.

Targets turned to half-glimpsed shadows, closing in from all sides. The noise was incredible. Screams, gunfire, rounds zipping past, the howling thunder of the chasing horde, ejected brass ringing off the tarmac. Chaos.

Everything became a blur. He heard savage growling, pounding boots at his ten o'clock. The infected Marine bore down on him so fast that Roth barely got his shots off. He'd lost count of his rounds, he realised. That was a first.

The Chancery was getting closer. So were the infected. Roth daren't look back. His breath was ragged. He pushed himself harder, determined to catch Costello ahead of him.

He saw a red light dancing. Someone was directing them towards the doors of the Chancery. There was still a hundred metres to go.

Roth wasn't going to make it.

"Prepare to deploy AP measures," Blake ordered.

Chuck responded in the affirmative. Mulholland barely heard them, his eyes glued to the TV screen, to the tableau of death that was unfolding at the embassy six thousand miles away. The infected were closing in from all sides. It was like watching a modern day Little Big Horn. It was awful. Mulholland couldn't bear to watch, yet neither could he drag himself away.

"They're not going to make it," he whispered.

"That's the plan," Blake scowled. He slapped Chuck on the shoulder.

"Deploy."

Roth couldn't run any faster. He could hear them right behind him and his skin crawled. He couldn't hear the snipers' guns. Too close, too many targets. His front runners were almost at the flagpole. Some of them might make it. Roth knew he wouldn't—

Phut-Phut-Phut-

He heard a drum-roll of compressed air, saw an object shoot out of the ground—

"Cover!"

He hit the tarmac as a ripple of sharp explosions detonated overhead. The pressure wave rolled over him and then he was back on his feet, bringing his gun to bear. His ears rang. Around him, carnage, the mob's momentum stalled by the directional mines that had scythed through their front ranks. The wounded still crawled towards him, dragging punctured bodies and shredded limbs. Others lay still, skewered with shrapnel, their bodies piled on top of one another. Roth ran for the Chancery.

He swore as he leapt over the bloodied corpses of his own people. Ahead, Costello was dragging a wounded operator towards the building. Behind him, the mob trampled their dead and wounded and kept coming. Diplomatic Security agents screamed at Delta from the Chancery doors, firing their M4s in controlled bursts.

And then Roth was inside, tumbling to the floor as the agents bundled in behind them. He heard the doors slam shut, the dead bolts rammed into place—

Boom!

The wave hit, shaking the building. Roth scrambled backwards across the floor. Ten feet away the mob crushed themselves against the doors, their faces twisted with rage, the glass smeared with blood and vomit.

You did that, said the voice inside him.

"Evacuate the lobby!" Roth ordered.

And then he was helping the wounded into the atrium. Behind him, the agents secured the inner doors.

The thundering fury of the mob echoed throughout the building.

"Misfire!"

It was Chuck, and he was stabbing his keyboard with an angry finger.

"What happened?" Blake was staring at the screen, waiting for the smoke to clear. When it did, the carnage wasn't as extensive as the Kroll executive had hoped. "Shit! They got away. What happened?"

Chuck shook his head. "Node malfunction. Only a third of the munitions detonated."

"Run a status check."

Mulholland stared at Blake, saw his face etched with something that resembled concern, though not for the scores of butchered, immobile white figures on the TV.

"Is there a problem?"

Blake scratched at his jowls. "Partial system malfunction. Not unexpected, but we need to carry out some more tests."

Mulholland studied the drone feed. On the screen, the Chancery was under siege by hundreds of infected. Behind them, dozens more were crawling along the road towards the Chancery, attempting to join the fight. Many of them trailed shattered, missing limbs. It was one of the most bizarre and horrifying scenes that Mulholland had ever witnessed. He wanted it gone, wanted it all erased, wiped clean.

"Please tell me that everything is going to work as planned."

"We'll know in a couple of minutes," Blake responded.

Mulholland sat back down and folded his arms. This was Amy's plan, and Amy's plans never failed. If they did, she always had a backup.

But not today. This was a one-time deal, all or nothing. He took the phone out of his pocket and checked the display. No calls, no messages. Amy would expect an update soon.

Mulholland desperately wanted to give her good news.

CHAPTER 14
THEY LIVE AND BREACH

IN A VIDEO-CONFERENCE ROOM ON THE SIXTH FLOOR OF THE Harry S. Truman building, Amy Coffman sat at the table and tuned out the fevered debate around her.

She was used to being in control but right now fate was in the driving seat, and that was causing her a great deal of anxiety. Foreign governments were expressing deep concern about their embassies in Baghdad. Outside the building, TV crews were gathering as cell-phone footage of flares, flames and gunfire in Baghdad circulated on social media. That wasn't unexpected. In fact, Coffman welcomed it, but the cause of her anxiety was not the breaking news but Mulholland's earlier phone call. There were problems with Grand Slam. Now she was waiting for an update, but in the meantime, she had her own part to play. All eyes would be on Amy Coffman now.

The meeting room was jammed to capacity. Coffman was flanked by her Deputies and Under Secretaries from Political and Public Affairs, International Security and Foreign Assistance. Alongside them were their own deputies and representatives from other agencies. All eyes were focussed on the video wall in front of them. The feeds were being broadcast from the Congressional Crisis Committee, the US Justice Department, the Federal Bureau of Investigation, the Senate Joint Committee Leaders and the Pentagon. That screen had Moody's face front and centre, and Coffman thought the lines around his eyes looked a little deeper, the skin a shade paler. She wondered if the General had health issues. She heard him talking and refocussed.

"The footage from Baghdad is deeply disturbing," Moody told the room. "We need to get eyes on without direct physical intervention. The Global Hawk gave us something, but now the storm has passed we can get improved, real-time coverage. To that end, a Gray Eagle UAV has been launched from Al Salem Air Base in Kuwait. We'll need you, Madame Secretary, to liaise with the Iraqi administration."

Coffman scratched a note on a pad and nodded. "I'll take care of it, General. Now, talk to me about communications."

Moody shook his head. "Still down. The NSA are working the problem, but with the Green Zone suffering its own power outage, this is starting to look more like sabotage."

Coffman made another note. "What are we talking about here? Some kind of disruption programme? Russian involvement, perhaps?"

She heard the whispers around the room. It wouldn't hurt to stir up the pot a little, and Russia was such an easy target these days.

On the screen, Moody looked perplexed. "I'm not sure this has anything to do with Moscow. The Iraqis might—"

"President Aswad is an ally of the United States," Coffman shot back. "In any case, our primary goal is to get our people to safety and ensure this biological weapon doesn't spread. What are we doing about that, General Moody?"

"We don't know if it is a weapon," snapped Admiral Schultz. He was at Moody's elbow again, and where the Marine's face expressed genuine concern, Schultz just looked pissed off. He wasn't used to being dictated to, especially by a female politician. She imagined him in the den of his Springfield home, a cell phone pressed to his ear while bouncing a favourite grandchild on his knee. She pictured him cooing and smiling while he discussed *taking care of the cunt problem.* She wondered if Schultz had been passed over by The Committee too, which might explain his belligerence. Maybe they had more in common than she imagined. Something to consider for the future, perhaps.

Moody was still talking. Coffman silenced him with a raised finger as Karen Baranski, her Operations Centre chief, leaned into her ear.

"You have a call," she whispered, handing Coffman her burner. There was only one other person who had that number. She got to her feet.

"General, I have to take this. Please excuse me."

Coffman stepped out of the room. Across the hallway was another secure meeting room. She swiped the lock and waited for the door to close behind her. She crossed to the furthest corner of the room and took the call off hold.

"Give me good news, Erik."

"The Grand Slam failure was partial. They've lost some nodes but the core components are intact. Blake says we're good to go."

Coffman closed her eyes and let out a relieved breath. The nightmare vision of a courtroom appearance, of shackled wrists and ankles, receded. "How does it look over there?"

"Frankly? Pretty fucking horrifying."

"We'll need footage, to sell our story to the American people."

"Blake is taking care of it."

"Good. Where are they now? The survivors?"

"Most of them are in the Chancery. A few Marines are holed up in the gatehouse, and there might be others hiding around the facility, but all the eggs are pretty much in one basket."

"Then get on with it. President Aswad called me a short time ago; the Baghdad drums are beating and he's concerned about security." She lowered her voice, injected her customary sweetness. "Please tell Bob it's time to end this thing." As her finger hovered to end the call, she heard Mulholland's voice.

"Amy, wait."

"What is it?"

"You have to see this thing to believe it. It's absolutely terrifying…"

He stopped talking. Coffman detected a tone, something she'd never heard before. Erik was frightened. She could hear him breathing, heard some other voices in the background. "Erik? Are you there?"

"What you said to Hamid, about the nuclear option—"

"You know that wasn't—"

"Amy, if this thing gets out it might be the only way of stopping it."

Coffman was momentarily speechless. Her fiercely liberal Chief of Staff had just tabled the notion of dropping a nuke on an Iraqi city of seven million inhabitants. "It's that bad?"

"It's much worse," Mulholland whispered.

Coffman shrugged. "So, we're doing the right thing. Just make sure you get that footage."

"Yes, ma'am."

Coffman ended the call. Things were back on track and Erik had confirmed the severity of the crisis, albeit a little dramatically, and as she crossed the room, she felt a new surge of confidence.

She trusted herself implicitly, her instincts, her alliances. The Aswads had delivered, as would Bob Blake, and the whispers about General Moody were already circulating. Coffman would ensure those whispers became so much more until the arrogant prick was buried under the weight of his own culpability. The White House beckoned, and nothing was going to stop Amy Coffman from achieving her goal.

Back in the conference room, she retook her seat, handing the burner to Karen. She scratched a few random notes on her pad while she waited for the chatter to die down. When it did, she addressed Moody and his Pentagon cronies.

"General, how long before your surveillance aircraft is over Baghdad?"

Moody looked off-screen for a moment, then said, "Ninety minutes, Madame Secretary."

Perfect.

THEY WERE THIRTY FEET BENEATH THE CHANCERY AND HEADING deeper underground.

Bosco led the way, twisting down the concrete stairwell. With every step, it got deeper and darker. Emergency lighting faded as battery power drained.

They'd spent the last twenty minutes in The Hub where Doug had tried and failed to connect to the outside world by using a laptop and terminal commands. Nothing was getting past the firewalls it seemed. Bosco had called it quits, and now Doug followed him, as did the Diplomatic Security agent who trailed after them both. Bosco and the agent were armed. Doug wasn't, and he felt naked because of it.

They reached another set of security doors on Sub-Level Two. Bosco pushed one open and Doug followed. It was much darker down here, and most of the emergency lights had died. Bosco gave Doug a torch from a box on the wall and he waved it around.

They were at a junction of three concrete corridors, each roughly ten meters long. At the end of each one was a grey steel door, like a bank vault. Doug thought about orientation and concluded they headed north, west and south. Bosco walked straight ahead, into the western corridor. He rapped his knuckles on thick steel.

"This is the Safe Haven. If things get desperate, people will be directed down here."

He pulled a flat piece of metal from his tac-vest and reached up to the ceiling. "Give me some light up here, would you?" Doug held the beam steady as Bosco pushed the key into a barely visible insertion point. The steel door groaned inwards and Doug followed Bosco over the threshold.

Lights flickered on overhead. The room was basic - rough concrete walls and rows of blue plastic chairs set back-to-back. There was a chemical toilet and a small kitchenette at the other end of the room. Bosco opened and closed cupboard doors as he took inventory of dried foods and bottled water. He ran the sink taps, his finger under the water.

"Okay, we're all set."

"Where's the power coming from?" Doug asked.

"Solar converters on the roof. There's some storage battery power too but it's limited. The Safe Haven isn't designed for extended stays, but the door is pretty much impenetrable and it'll provide some protection until help arrives."

"Nothing's impenetrable," Doug said, looking around the room. "Exactly how many people can you fit in here?"

"Fifty. Every additional person impacts the air quality."

Doug pointed to the ceiling. "There are seven hundred people up there."

"Safe Haven is for high-ranking personnel only." He saw Doug's face and said, "Hey, I don't make the rules. Let's pray it doesn't come to that."

As Bosco tried to walk around him, Doug caught his arm. He kept his voice low. "If it does, you think maybe I could..."

"No contractors," Bosco told him. "I'm sorry."

"Understood." Doug nodded, shame burning his cheeks. He hoped Bosco didn't think of him as some kind of weasel coward but that's probably how it looked. Doug didn't care about his own life. If he had to trade it for his daughter's he wouldn't hesitate, but he was Holly's only hope. If he died out here, no one else was going to try to find her, rescue her from herself, care for her, only Doug. So, if things went from bad to worse and the Safe Haven wasn't an option, he'd have to hole up somewhere else.

Bosco ordered them outside and left the Haven door open. Back at the junction, Doug swung his torch beam along the other corridors. "What's in those other rooms?"

The RSO shrugged. "Not part of my orientation. Let's go."

Feet pounded the stairwell outside the doors and Agent Murphy appeared. He was breathing hard. Beneath his black helmet, his face was beaded with sweat. "Couldn't reach you on the net this far down," Murphy panted.

"What is it?"

"Delta are here but they nearly didn't make it. A bunch of claymores exploded outside the Chancery, killed half of them—"

"Wait, back up, Pat. What the hell are you talking about?"

"They were ambushed. We saw it from the windows."

"Claymores?" Bosco echoed, clearly struggling with the intel.

"There's more..." Doug saw a twitch of fear behind Murphy's eyes. "The Chancery is under siege."

"Siege?"

Murphy nodded. "The infected are at the doors, trying to break them down. People are starting to panic."

"How many?"

"All of them," Murphy said. "Hundreds."

"Is Jacobs back yet?"

The agent shook his head. "No word since they left. The Marines at the main gate thought they heard shots fired but they couldn't swear to it because of the storm. They've got the gatehouse locked down and they're keeping a low profile. Infected are nosing around their building."

"Tell them those gates stay closed, got it?"

"Yes, sir."

Bosco took the stairs two at a time. Doug followed him up into the atrium where they were met by a handful of armed agents. Thunder rumbled through the building.

"That's them. The infected," Murphy told them.

The sound rattled Doug. "Will those doors hold?"

Murphy shrugged in the dark. "They're supposed to be able to withstand a sustained, non-ballistic attack for forty-five minutes."

The man didn't sound too confident, Doug thought.

Delta were in a huddle near the main staircase. Two of their number were on the floor receiving medical treatment. Heads turned as Bosco's group approached them. Doug held back but kept his ears open.

"Major Roth?" Bosco began. "You guys okay? I just—"

Roth took three steps and got into Bosco's face. He jabbed him in the chest. "Who launched that flare?"

"Wait, what flare?"

"The storm blew through. We got caught out in the open. Someone saw it and fired a flare from the roof of this building. Who was it?"

Bosco shook his head. "I don't know—"

"Don't fucking lie to me, Bosco." Roth drew his pistol from a holster on his chest rig. He did it slow and deliberate and held the gun by his thigh.

Doug saw the anger in the shadows of Roth's face. The man wanted revenge, and Doug realised he was looking at what was left of the Delta team. Forty-odd guys down to what, a dozen? No wonder Roth had murder in his eyes.

Bosco held up his hands. "Major, I have no knowledge of what happened or who is responsible. I've only just heard it from one of my team."

Doug noticed that Delta had spread out in a half-circle behind their boss, facing off against Bosco and his agents in the dark of the atrium. The tension escalated fast. Doug thought a wrong word or movement might just trigger a gunfight. Roth jabbed his finger into Bosco's tac-vest.

"Find out who did it and bring them to me. Now."

More DS agents pounded into the atrium, weapons gripped in their hands. Delta gun barrels raised up and met them. Bosco marched towards the agents, waving his arms.

"Stand down, stand down!" Bosco called Murphy over. "Pat, get the guys out of here. I want them hitting the floors. Keep people away from the windows and try putting a lid on that panic. Move!"

Murphy led the DS agents out of the atrium. Now there was only Doug, Bosco and the Delta operators. Bosco was the first to speak. If he was scared, he wasn't showing it.

"I'm sorry about your guys, Major, really I am. Why don't you tell me exactly what happened?"

Roth did. Even in the dark, Doug could see the confusion on Bosco's face.

"I did not authorise any such countermeasures. Fact is, I never knew they existed, not until Agent Murphy told me."

"Bullshit," Roth spat.

"You're going to have to take my word on that. Besides, we may not have a lot of time to argue about it." Bosco pointed towards the security lobby. Beyond, the thunderous rage of the infected rumbled through the atrium.

Roth said nothing. He stared at Bosco for several, long moments. "If I find out you're lying—"

"Lying?" Bosco snorted. "You think *I'm* being dishonest?"

Roth's eyes narrowed. "What's that supposed to mean?"

"What's your *real* mission here, Major? You want this virus to spread, right? Why? What's the end game?"

Now Roth looked genuinely confused. "End game?"

"The infected are loose. Mission accomplished, Major. So, what's next? Take us prisoner? Shoot us?"

Roth stared at the RSO as if the guy were crazy. "Have you lost your fucking mind, Bosco?"

"There's no need for bloodshed. No one is going to resist. I'm ordering my people to lay down their weapons. It's over." Bosco unslung his carbine and offered it to the Delta commander. "Here. Take it."

No one said anything for several moments. Roth's eyes flicked between Bosco and the gun. Even Doug could see the man was genuinely baffled. Finally, Roth said, "I have absolutely no fucking clue what you're talking about."

Bosco rattled his carbine. "Take it, for Chrissakes. You've won."

Roth holstered his pistol. "I don't want your gun, and no one is laying down their weapons."

Bosco stared at the soldier for several, long seconds, then re-slung his rifle. "That's what I figured."

Roth was still confused. "I think you'd better fill me in."

Bosco did. When he finished, the Delta commander looked angrier than ever. "Now we're traitors? Motherfucking politicians."

"We're getting played here."

"Where does Langley stand in all of this?"

"Bill Jacobs led a delegation to the Brit embassy, to try and re-establish comms. He hasn't returned. The rest of his people are dismantling their offices."

"So, it's just us."

"Affirmative."

"Maybe not." Shadowy faces turned towards Doug. "Maybe it's not just us," he told them.

"Explain," Roth ordered.

"I've worked a lot of classified contracts, okay? I heard rumours about this place a while back. Nothing specific, but some people mentioned exotic defence systems, autonomous stuff. Maybe—"

"The claymores," Roth realised. "You think—"

"Wait, that's impossible." It was Bosco this time. "I'm the RSO. If there was some kind of advanced defence system, I'd know about it."

"I worked a contract at Raven Rock," Doug told them. Blank faces stared back at him. "Site R?" Still nothing. "Really? Okay, well it's a Pentagon relocation facility in Pennsylvania. It has a six-mile underground tunnel that connects it to Camp David. You know how many people working at either location knew about it? A handful."

"Point taken," Bosco said.

"You can't tell anyone that, by the way. That's classified."

"You said you hadn't been here that long," Roth reminded Bosco. "Is there a chance you haven't been fully briefed?"

Bosco frowned, stroked his chin. "It's possible."

"That's my point," Doug said. "Maybe someone, somewhere, has got a hand in this game. The comms blackout, the power outage—my guess? Someone's flipping switches."

"Who?" Roth asked. "Coffman? This Mulholland guy? They're politicians. They're not going to get their hands dirty."

"Someone else, then. Someone who has access to the DISA networks, the satellites."

"You're talking NSA," Roth growled. "You're telling me they're in on this too?"

Doug shrugged. "Who knows, but they own the infrastructure."

"They're watching too. The CCTV—"

"The power's out," Bosco countered.

Roth wasn't convinced. "They knew when to fire that flare, when to trigger the claymores. That was coordinated. Someone has eyes on us."

"Probably a drone."

It was the guy with the porn moustache. No one said a word. The thunder sounded much louder. Roth turned to Drake.

"Take a couple of guys up to the roof. See if you can see anything."

Bosco told them how to get there. Drake and two other shadows disappeared up the stairs. Doug spoke next.

"The claymores, they'd need power, cabling. It's got to lead back inside—"

"The doors, down in the sub-basement," Bosco realised.

"What doors?" Roth asked. Bosco explained. "So open them," the Major told him.

"I don't have any access, and they're solid steel."

Roth slapped the porn guy on the shoulder. "Costello here can crack anything."

Costello nodded. "Just show me the way."

Roth cocked his head towards the security lobby. "We should have a plan, for when those main doors give way."

"Agreed," Bosco said. "There's a lot of manpower in this building. Give them something to do. Pile furniture in the security lobby as high as you can, then barricade the inner doors."

As Bosco turned to leave, Roth caught his arm. "When this is over, someone's going to pay."

"We don't know for sure if—"

"My men are dead. Murdered."

Bosco lowered his voice but Doug heard every word. "I stand by what I said, Major. This is your fault. If Jackson had been—"

Roth held up his hand. "You're right, and that's something I'm going to have to live with for the rest of my life, but it doesn't change the fact that whoever's behind this has to be held to account."

Bosco nodded. "Let's worry about that later, okay? Just get that lobby secured."

Doug followed Bosco and Costello. As they passed the main staircase, Bosco peeled away.

"Walker, escort the Sergeant-Major downstairs. Do what you have to do. I've got to talk to the ambassador."

"Roger that," Doug said. He led him into Service Corridor A, torchlight sweeping the darkness.

BOSCO RAN UPSTAIRS TO THE TOP FLOOR. WHEN HE GOT TO THE Executive Suite reception there were twenty plus people having a heated discussion by torchlight. A lot of shrill voices and pointing fingers. They turned as one when Bosco strode into the room.

"That's enough," he shouted. Most of the faces he knew. All of them were either angry, frightened or desperate. And in most cases, all three.

"Somebody needs to tell us what the hell is going on."

It was Mary Dubose, the embassy's Administration Officer, a smart, capable woman in her mid-forties. Dubose had been in Baghdad longer than Bosco. He'd need her onside.

"We've got a critical situation here," he told the room, "but we'll all be safe as long as—"

"Are you fucking kidding?" an angry voice retorted. It was Vish Patel, one of the Commercial Attaché team. "Have you seen them out there? They're going to get in here and they're going to kill us all!"

The room broke out into a desperate chorus of frightened voices.

"Are they evacuating us?"

"Why isn't anyone telling us anything?"

"We're going to die here—"

"Enough!" Bosco shouted, and this time he really had to yell. The voices faded. He tried to make as much eye contact as possible.

"Right now, we're on our own. The State Department, the Pentagon, they'll be pulling out all the stops, mobilising assets to reestablish contact, mount a rescue. That'll mean evacuation." He pointed at Dubose. "Mary, I'll need you to initiate burn procedures. All classified materials to go into the incinerator down in the Post Room. Start burning everything. Vish?"

Patel looked startled. His eyes were like saucers. "What?"

"Round up as many able-bodied people as possible. We're going to barricade the security lobby with anything we can get our hands on. The main doors will hold, but we need to be prepared, just in case."

"And if they do get in? What then?"

"We get down to the Safe Haven. You'll be fine, don't worry." He clapped his hands together. "Let's move, people."

The crowd broke up. As Dubose turned away, Bosco caught her by the elbow. "Mary, walk with me. We need to talk to the ambassador."

Dubose hesitated. "I thought you knew."

"Knew what?"

"Mister Ashcroft has gone."

Bosco thought he'd misheard. "What do you mean, gone?"

"He left the building with a couple of agents. Tubman was one of them, I think. And the helicopter crew."

Shit! "Okay, focus on the burn, Mary. Destroy as much as you can."

IT TOOK BOSCO A MATTER OF SECONDS TO REACH ASHCROFT'S office. He came across another staff huddle, PAs this time, most of whom were either crying or consoling.

"All of you, initiate burn procedures, right now!" He barged into Ashcroft's private office. It was empty and there were papers strewn across the floor. Ashcroft's wall safe lay open, bare. Bosco kicked the door closed and dialled his radio into the security channel.

"Tubman, this is Javelin, receiving, over?"

The reply came back almost immediately. "Go for Tubman."

"What's your location?"

When Tubman spoke again, he was almost whispering. "Ambassador's residence. He ordered me and Smitty to provide security, said you'd cleared it. Did the same with the two Marines who drove us over there."

Bosco cursed. "Where's the ambassador now?"

"Waiting by the front door. The pilots snuck out to the chopper. They're carrying out pre-flight checks. We're about to leave."

"Put him on the radio, right now."

Bosco went to the window and looked out towards the ambassador's residence. The building was close to the helipad, designed that way for eventualities just like this one. The helipad itself looked deserted, the Black Hawk squatting in the darkness. Bosco saw the battery cart on the pad next to the aircraft, the discarded engine plugs. Any minute now those turbines would fire up and the infected would have a new target.

"Tom, are you there?"

It was Ashcroft in his ear.

"Go ahead."

"I'm sorry, Tom, but somebody has to do something. Jacobs isn't coming back, is he? What do you expect me to do, just wait until we're all infected?"

"Don't do this, David. Help is on its way—"

Ashcroft's voice crackled angrily. "Don't bullshit me, Tom! No one is coming, you said so yourself!" There was another burst of static, then Ashcroft said, "We're going to fly to Basra, to the consulate. I'll contact State, send help. Good luck, Tom."

And then he was gone.

Bosco stared at the distant helicopter. Maybe Ashcroft had a point. The consulate was well within the Black Hawk's range and once there he'd be able to contact State. Unless this thing was bigger than just Baghdad. What then? So many unknowns.

He could radio Ashcroft back, tell him he was doing the right thing, or tell him he was committing career suicide, as well as endangering the lives of the people with him.

Or he could give them a fighting chance.

"Tubman, Javelin."

Bosco waited. There was no response.

"Tubman, this is Javelin. If you can hear me, I'm putting shooters in the Chancery windows, try and improve your odds a little. Tell the ambassador to stay put until you hear from me, understood?"

The response was immediate. "Received."

Bosco sprinted from the room.

David Ashcroft had never been so scared in all of his life. Throughout his career, he'd actively sought the elusive Foreign Service assignment that would shape his future, so when Secretary Coffman had offered him Baghdad he'd leapt at the opportunity. Baghdad was a career-changer, a quasi-military outpost in one of the world's most dangerous countries. A stint there would see his star rise, and this particular brief had been like music to Ashcroft's ears - *we just need you to take care of the place, David. Steer the ship until things return to normal. There will be some JSOC activity but Bill Jacobs is dealing with that. Nothing for you to worry about.*

Easy.

But Baghdad had turned into a nightmare and Ashcroft's only priority now was to leave. He knew he was acting against protocol, that his actions were not those expected of a United States Ambassador, but he wasn't going to die like Chris Stevens in Benghazi all those years ago, at the hands of a vicious mob. Worse still, an infected mob.

No, he wanted to live. That's why he'd lied to the agents, to the Marines. There was only so much room on the helicopter, he'd told them, and he needed men with guns around him, not diplomats.

"What the hell are they doing?" Ashcroft hissed. He was sitting in the back of the Humvees, squeezed between the DS agents, watching the faint movement of the pilots in the cockpit of the Black Hawk.

"They're making sure we get a fast lift-off," the Marine riding shotgun whispered. "Just watch the flanks. One of them fuckers creeps up on us, we're toast."

Ashcroft turned and looked out of the window. The embassy was still a world of shadows. Anything could be lurking out there. Shooters in the Chancery would cover them as they left, Tubman had explained a few minutes ago. That gave Ashcroft little peace of mind. What if a stray bullet hit one of the engines? Or worse, one of the pilots? *The aircraft is armour plated,* the Marine driver had explained. Ashcroft wasn't convinced.

Then he heard it. The unmistakable, glorious whine of the helicopter's engines. *Alleluia!*

The driver fired up the Humvee. "This is it."

The agents on either side of Ashcroft tensed, gun barrels poking out of the windows. Then he saw it, a red beam of hope waving at them from the cockpit window.

"There's the signal!" Ashcroft screamed. "Go, goddammit! Go!"

"Hang on!"

The driver crunched the Humvee into gear and roared towards the helicopter as its mighty blades began to chop the air.

"We've got movement," Chuck said, pointing at the monitor above him.

Mulholland saw the spinning rotor blades, watched the Humvee racing towards the aircraft like a toy car.

"Fifty bucks that's a VIP making a run for it," Chuck said.

"A hundred they don't make it," Eugene countered. Chuck slapped the outstretched palm. Mulholland wanted to bash their heads together.

He watched the Humvee closing in on the helipad. *If Ashcroft or Bosco is aboard that chopper, if they get out, that's a problem…*

Blake pointed to the screen. "Here they come."

"My God," whispered Eugene. "Look at those fuckers."

Mulholland imagined himself inside that helicopter, watching the crowd stampeding towards them, a wailing, screaming infected horde that threatened to rip them to pieces. He shivered, felt his skin crawl.

"It's going to be close," Blake said. "Chuck, let's bring up the lights a little."

Chuck smiled. "You got it."

Drake and his snipers were on the roof. The rest of Delta were at the windows on the first floor of the Chancery. Roth stood behind them, lowlight binoculars pressed to his eyes as he watched the Black Hawk winding up, the roar of the engines building quickly, pounding the surrounding buildings.

Come on, come on, he whispered, willing the rotors to go faster, knowing the pilots would be coaxing as much power as they could in a fraction of the time it would normally take. Roth knew it was going to be close.

"Clip the frontrunners!" Roth ordered over the radio.

A volley of shots rang out and he watched four or five bodies hit the road. His guys were some of the best shooters in the world but there were too many targets and not enough time.

And they are still people, Roth thought. *Friends, colleagues, brothers. I can't just open up on them, not if there's a chance for a cure. I have to keep the body count down, save as many lives as possible.*

"They're not going to make it," Bosco said beside him.

"It'll be close." Roth looked down. Ten feet below, hundreds of arms reached up for him, clawing the air, hissing, screaming. Some pounded the doors, trying to get to the guys barricading the lobby. He heard the pitch of the Black Hawk's engines increase, and his hopes soared—

Pop - pop - pop!

Roth looked skyward, knew what was coming.

One after the other the flares exploded overhead.

Below them, Broadway and Main Street, the parking lot, the Ambassador's residence, the Black Hawk, the whole goddam embassy was suddenly bathed in white, searing light. Night had turned to day.

The noise of the Black Hawk filled the building.

The anguished roar of the infected rose up to meet it.

"You hear that?"

In the northern tunnel, Costello had his ear pressed against the steel hatch.

Doug was close by, on his knees, cleaning the detonators and cutting the det cord as per the Sergeant-Major's instructions.

"Hear what?"

"Not sure," Costello frowned. "It's real faint, but I think I can hear a bunch of beeping, like a computer." He gave Doug a look. "Maybe we shouldn't blow this one, huh?"

Doug shrugged. "We've got no power, no lights, no comms, no cavalry coming and no way out of here. Fuck it, blow the bitch."

"What did you say your name was?"

"Doug Walker."

Costello grinned beneath his moustache. "I like you, Walker. Pass me up that block of C-4."

Freddie Cruz cursed the wind.

It battered his naked body, flailed it with grit and dirt, but still he staggered towards it, struggling against its power, conscious of the lifeblood that leaked from the hole in his side. He'd been so close to the prey that ran from them, but then something had punched through his body and Freddie had staggered into the darkness, wounded.

He knew his strength was fading, could feel the weakness slowing his place, making it harder to breathe. Soon he would have no breath and he would stop moving. He ground the shards of his broken teeth in fury. He had to shed more blood before the weakness spread.

He stood in the shadows and watched the massive black beast beating the air, whipping up the wind that lashed his skin. It made him angry. The hole in his side made him angry. His fading strength made him angry. It was time for one final attack, to seek out the stinkers and rip the skin from their bodies before it was too late.

He saw them ahead, cowering inside the belly of the beast. Freddie Cruz was going to kill them all.

The agents bundled Ashcroft out of the Humvee, screamed at him to get aboard, opening fire as they went. Ashcroft needed no encouragement. He ran the final few yards and scrambled inside Black Hawk, throwing himself on a bench seat and desperately yanking the safety belts across his lap.

The noise was tremendous, the roar of the mob almost as loud as the engines. He could see them through the cockpit window, through the side door to his left, racing towards them. He saw the Humvee roar away in a cloud of dust. Tubman climbed in next to him.

"Where are they going?" Ashcroft shouted.

Tubman was changing the magazine on his weapon. "They wouldn't leave!" the agent yelled above the noise. "They're going to draw them away!"

Ashcroft watched the jeep bounce over the open ground towards the mob, then turn hard left at the last second. The Humvee kept going, veering left and right, the infected chasing after it like some kind of bizarre Pied Piper scene.

"Get us off the ground!" Ashcroft screamed. Both agents were firing non-stop as the front runners of the mob closed in. Twenty meters. Fifteen. Ten. There were too many of them.

Then he felt the helicopter shift, felt the skids leave the earth. *Thank God!*

He saw a movement to his right, a glimpse of something pale bursting from the shadows, scampering towards the aircraft, leaping…

The engines screamed.

Ashcroft screamed.

Then the toothless, blood-soaked creature was ripping at Ashcroft's face and neck, infected blood and saliva spraying across his nose and mouth.

"No! Stop! Please, God! No—"

Ashcroft thrashed his head from side to side, tried to fight the thing off, but then he dropped his arms, let the creature rake his skin and gouge his eyes. His own blood ran freely from multiple wounds, from his punctured eyeball. Ashcroft wanted to die quickly. He knew he was already infected.

The helicopter roared upwards and banked hard over, and the creature wrapped itself around Ashcroft, its skin wet and stinking. Ashcroft vomited over them both. He saw the agents still firing their weapons, even as they tumbled out of the aircraft.

The creature let go and hurled himself into the cockpit. Ashcroft felt it then, a growing rage, an uncontrollable urge to do bloody violence to someone, anyone. He tore at his seatbelt, bucked his body, swore in a voice that his failing mind barely recognised.

The seatbelt broke free.

David Ashcroft was no more.

What replaced him threw itself into the carnage of the cockpit.

Bosco yelled, pointing. "Jesus Christ, look!"

Roth shoved him towards the door. "Everybody move!"

He took one last quick glance at the helicopter, saw it thunder over the heads of the infected as it dropped from the sky, its engines screaming. Roth sprinted across the office, hurdling desks and chairs, bundling through the door and out into the hallway beyond.

Outside the Chancery, the Black Hawk hit the ground in a shower of sparks and a screech of metal and hurtled towards the main doors, its rotor blades still running at full speed. It hit the building at seventy miles an hour and exploded, the shockwave punching through ballistic glass and reinforced steel. A ball of orange flame rolled up over the building and into the night sky as debris rained down for hundreds of meters. The structure already weakened, the floors above the point of impact groaned and collapsed in an avalanche of steel, concrete, and screaming bodies.

"Holy shit!"

"That's a hundred bucks you owe me."

Chuck was beaming a bright white smile. Eugene grinned

too. Mulholland thought they were going to high-five each other, but Eugene was too busy piloting the drone as he captured the carnage below. Mulholland couldn't quite comprehend what he was seeing. He knew it was all real, but he felt so detached from the violence that he had to remind himself he wasn't watching a video game.

He felt relief too. Whoever was in that helicopter was gone. Whoever was left inside that building, they had to go too.

"What's happening?" The smoke on the screen was thick and Eugene was flying blind. A moment later and the drone was operating in clear air.

"Looks like those pilots did the job for us," Blake chuckled, his arms folded across his chest.

"What do you mean?"

Blake pointed to the monitor. "Look there, at the impact zone. The doors are gone. The Chancery is wide open."

Mulholland saw the gaping hole, the dust, the rubble and the bodies that had been hurled across Main Street and Broadway. He saw the horde gathering, heading back towards the Chancery, probing the dust and smoke, towards the huge gash in the side of the building. It was almost too perfect.

"Is Grand Slam ready? Are we good to go?"

Blake smiled. "Relax, Erik. The system is armed. All we need to do is start the countdown."

Mulholland stepped a little closer to the monitor. He saw the infected funnelling towards the hole in the Chancery, saw the smoke beginning to clear. On reflection, it helped him to frame everything he was seeing as some kind of video game. The reality, *the experience*, would be too horrific to contemplate.

"Wait until they're all inside," Mulholland told him.

CHAPTER 15
TOUCHDOWN

The first victims were the people still alive and trapped in the rubble.

Bodies crushed and torn open, their pitiful moans drew the snarling pack towards them. Escape was impossible. When the infected surged out of the haze and attacked them, death was a welcome release.

They trampled the dead and clambered over the rubble. Falling dust showered them as they probed the Chancery, their breathing rapid, hearts pounding, an uncontrollable fury driving them forward. Through the smoke and flames more injured cried for help, trapped by twisted metal and skewered by splinters of wood. Some tried to crawl away over piles of shattered furniture but the infected moved too fast. The lucky ones died. The others turned.

The infected surged forward, spilling over the wreckage like a wave, pushing deeper into the lobby. The walls narrowed as they squeezed into the security corridor. They surged against the heavy doors, their path blocked. The pack leaders sniffed the air and barked at each other, their ability to communicate evolving with each passing hour, each subsequent mutation.

The smell was stronger than it had ever been, more powerful than the black smoke that filled the air. It was a foul stench and it leaked through the minuscule gaps around the doors. It stoked their anger. They howled in furious anticipation.

They'd found the stinkers' lair.

"Wait…"

Drake kept the low-light binoculars pressed against his eyes and on-target. Meyer and Scott were also searching the night sky. He needed them to locate the drone fast.

"You see it?"

"Wait…got it! Drifting north, ten o'clock."

"Locked on," confirmed Scott.

"Stand by."

Drake brought his G-28 rifle to bear, resting the bipod on the air-con unit in front of him. Things had got real crazy these last few minutes - first the Black Hawk crash then the breach. The infected were pouring into the building below them, but the smoke and flames had added texture to the night sky and Drake had finally caught the briefest glimpse of something moving in his peripheral vision. There *was* a drone. Costello had been right, the Major too. Someone, somewhere, was cooking their shit. Time to let them know that the jig was up.

He nestled the rifle into his shoulder, brought the Vortex scope to his eye. "Talk to me, guys."

"Target holding steady at ten o'clock. Keeping out of the smoke."

"Aim point, Annexe, top-floor, third window from the south corner."

"On target," confirmed Drake.

"Check your vertical."

Drake tilted his barrel up slowly, searching the night sky through the low-light optics until—

"Target acquired," he told them. It hovered somewhere in the darkness between the consulate and the Chancery, its black body reflecting a small wedge of orange firelight. It bounced gently on the night air, multiple rotors whirring silently. Watching. Reporting…

"Firing."

Drake squeezed the first shot off, the recoil bumping his shoulder.

"Miss," Meyer reported.

"No shit." Drake settled back in, dialled back the scope's power ring. The drone was clearer now, still relatively stationary. He had to hit it before its pilot became aware of the threat.

"Firing."

The rifle kicked, the suppressed report like a quiet blast of compressed air. The 7.62mm bullet travelled through the air at a velocity of two-and-a-half-thousand feet per second, drilling through the body of the drone and shattering its plastic heart.

It dropped from the sky like a stone.

"Flight controls are not responding," Eugene reported.

"Dammit," snapped Blake, staring at a close-up view of the tarmac somewhere on Main Street. The drone's camera zoomed in and out robotically.

Eugene threw the remote control onto the desk. "Still got picture but she's out of operation."

"Is this a problem?" Mulholland asked Blake. The Kroll boss shook his head.

"We're still good."

"That's not what I meant. Someone took it out, right?"

Blake shrugged. "We don't know that."

"Your friend Chuck saw movement on the roof. If they took out the drone, they know somebody's watching."

"Could be anyone," Blake said. "Anyway, it's moot. Grand Slam is armed. We've got the CCTV footage backed up and everyone is in the Chancery. It's all about the timing now."

Mulholland folded his arms and began pacing the room. He was glad the drone was dead - its footage was sickening, the crash, the infected attacking the injured outside the Chancery, pouring into the building unmolested. He didn't want to think about those inside, what they were seeing, hearing. The panic, the unbridled terror, would be unimaginable. A vision of Hell, in all its dark, mind-bending horror. Only Grand Slam could save them now.

"Finish it, Bob, for God's sake."

Blake gave Chuck a silent nod. The technician tapped his mouse a couple of times and sat back in his chair.

"Here we go."

Deep in its lair, the spider received a new command.

Normally, this type of instruction would involve both mechanical and human interaction but the earlier software update meant that the system no longer required such restrictive processes. Grand Slam now possessed fully autonomous capability.

The command was of the mode-selection variety, and the remote instruction authorised Grand Slam to initiate *Alamo*. Named after the famous Texas battle, *Alamo* was a Grand Slam defence mode designed to counter not only a perimeter breach and subsequent ground attack, but also the loss of the entire embassy after an emergency evacuation. The original software design incorporated restricted arcs of fire and the strategic deployment of anti-personnel munitions, culminating in the triggering of a weapon of last resort - *Touchdown*.

Now that *Alamo* had been selected, *Touchdown* would initiate shortly thereafter.

A final systems check confirmed that some nodes were still unresponsive; the anti-personnel munitions could not be deployed. Everything else was functional.

Alamo went to work.

Up at ground level, explosive bolts detonated on several structures dotted at strategic locations across the embassy. Side panels blew off to reveal the *Watchmen*, a series of Close-In Weapons Systems located at road junctions, overwatch positions and the open ground between strategic buildings. The two-meter-high *Watchmen* twisted on their servo-assisted swivel mountings, their microwave ground radars searching for targets for their M134 Gatlin guns. Launch tubes at the base of each *Watchman* fired round after round of smoke grenades that clattered across the ground and spewed thick white smoke. On the roof of the Chancery, flares began to fire off, one every ten seconds. Soon the ground below was a confusion of swirling smoke and flickering white light, of shadows and autonomous killing machines. It wasn't long before the first *Watchman* found a target.

Located at the overwatch point in the far north-eastern corner of the compound, the *Watchman's* ground radar detected movement, a small group of infected prowling around the main gate. Instantly the barrels ran up to speed and the weapon opened fire at a rate of three thousand rounds per minute, its ripping sound echoing across the embassy, its 7.62mm tracer rounds lighting up the night like lasers and chopping the infected into bloody chunks in a matter of seconds. With no moving targets the weapon ceased fire and continued its radar sweep, smoke drifting from its barrels.

Elsewhere, other *Watchmen* engaged their own targets. Two Marines who'd been cut off by the infected saw the smoke and took their chances. They broke cover from their hiding place and ran for the ambassador's recently-vacated residence. As they sprinted across the helipad, a *Watchman* located on the eastern corner of the consulate building detected their movement and opened fire, the targeting computer guiding the rounds as they stitched their way across the asphalt before cutting the Marines down. Stray tracers cannoned off walls and buildings, ricocheting into the sky. The sound of the guns rippled across Baghdad.

Drawn by the sound, wounded and disabled infected dragged themselves out of the shadows in search of victims. The *Watchmen* saw them too and ripped their broken bodies to pieces in a storm of high-velocity rounds. The compound had become a hundred and four acres of killing fields.

Deep underground, Grand Slam was preparing to initiate *Touchdown*. There was no longer any need for twisted keys and manually entered codes. Grand Slam was taking care of its own business. It sent electronic signals across hundreds of miles of cabling to the specially constructed access chambers buried beneath every significant building across the embassy. The chambers were made of thick plastic, were watertight and varied in size, but all were packed with neatly arranged blocks of Composition B, a mixture of TNT and RDX that would ensure the total destruction of the building above, leaving behind chunks of rubble no bigger than a baseball.

Touchdown was the ultimate burn procedure, a weapon of last resort that would ensure - in the event of catastrophe and abandonment - that the US embassy could offer nothing of any value to its captors.

The electronic signals were confirmed. The detonators were primed. All that was required now was an electronic charge and a pressure wave.

Grand Slam squatted in the dark, chirping quietly. It was master of its own destiny, the decider of its own fate, and the decision to self-annihilate had already been taken.

The countdown had begun.

. . .

ROTH POUNDED DOWN THE STAIRCASE AND INTO THE ATRIUM.

Delta followed and fanned out across the marble floor, weapons pointed towards the security lobby doors. The air was hazy with dust, and the sound of collapsing masonry rumbled through the building. There were other sounds too - shouting, crying, feet pounding on the floors above. Panic, Roth knew.

He heard more footsteps charging down the stairs behind him. Bosco appeared with several agents in tow.

"The building is breached," he panted. "We've got to get everyone—"

Roth held a finger to his lips, silencing Bosco. With that same finger, he pointed at the large white double doors across the atrium. The doors that led to the security lobby. They were creaking as if holding back a great force.

Bosco understood. "You didn't have time to barricade them." It wasn't a question, but Roth shook his head anyway.

Bosco pointed across the lobby. "Service corridor A leads down to the Safe Haven. I'm going to try and round up as many—"

"There's no time. You need to go, right now."

"I can't. There are hundreds of people upstairs—"

The roar filled the atrium, a deafening, bone-chilling howling that did not resemble anything human.

The security doors crashed open.

The horde spilled out of the darkness and charged towards them. Delta and the agents opened fire. Infected tumbled, tripping others behind. Bullets cut them down but Roth knew it would never be enough. They kept coming, a sea of bloody, infected faces filling the atrium, swarming across the marble floor and the Great Seal of the United States.

There was no plan for this. It was only about survival now.

"Run!"

The explosion shook the building deep below ground.

Dust filled the tunnels, adding to the degraded air quality caused by Costello's own controlled detonations. Doug and the Delta soldier coughed and hacked as they cleared their lungs. Visibility was down to less than five meters.

"That was some hit," Costello spluttered. "Felt like a missile strike."

Doug spat on the ground and cuffed his mouth, "You think?"

"The way this day is panning out, anything is possible. Go check the southern hatch."

Doug's torch cut through the dust that swirled around the tunnel. When he got to the steel door, he saw it twisted off its hinges. *Nice work,* he thought. Costello knew his shit. He stumbled on large chunks of concrete and kicked them to one side with his Nikes. Beyond the door, the air was still hazy but clearing fast. Doug stepped inside. The tunnel stretched away into total darkness. Doug hesitated, turned back.

Costello was still in the northern tunnel.

"All good?"

"Take a look." Costello pointed his torch at the door. It was scorched but completely intact.

"Did you use the same amount of—" Doug saw Costello's withering look. "Sure you did."

The Sergeant-Major ran a hand over the smooth metal. "Must be twice as thick. Some of the surrounding concrete has come away though. Gimme some light here."

Costello worked his fingers at a point above the door where the concrete had fractured. He pulled his knife out, widened the crack.

"I can work a little C-4 in there. Pass me the goods."

It took a couple of minutes for Costello to shape a charge and prime it. They took shelter on the landing above. "Fire in the hole," he warned Doug. The *boom* rumbled up the stairwell, shaking the concrete floor beneath them and filling the tunnels with more dust.

When it cleared a little, they saw the fracture was now a gaping hole, but the concrete must've been at least three feet thick. The C-4 had punched through, but the hole was only big enough to squeeze a hand through.

"Boost me up," Doug told Costello. The soldier linked his fingers and Doug stood on them and reached up to the hole. He couldn't see much, but he could hear the quiet hum of machinery. Not mechanical, electrical. Computers. Then a light winked several times, a sharp red pulse that threw a little illumination against the walls beyond the hole. Doug saw it then, the huge black spider that squatted in its dark cage. He shone his torch inside.

"Hurry the fuck up," snapped Costello.

"There's something in there."

"Let me see."

They swapped places. Costello's boots dug into Doug's fingers. The man was heavy with all his kit and equipment. Then he hopped down.

"What the fuck is it?"

"Must be the defence system," Doug realised. "What else could it be? It's drawing power too."

"Where from?"

"Christ knows. Help me back up." Costello gave him another boost and Doug took several pictures with his smartphone. "Someone will know what this thing does."

"What's behind door number three?"

Doug led him across the landing and they stepped around the twisted metal. His torch probed the long, subterranean passage. "Goes a long way. Dark as hell too."

Costello leaned over Doug's shoulder. He heard a snap in the dark and the tunnel lights began blinking on, far into the distance.

He grinned at Doug. "Some technician, huh?"

"Must be a power spur that no one knows about."

"Someone knows," Costello said, his grin fading. "Come on, let's see what's down there."

They set off running.

Roth's boots pounded the marble floor. He heard a scream behind him. One of his guys. He swore with rage and frustration.

While his body exploded with physical energy, his thoughts remained clear, calm, analytical, a gift that had guaranteed his rise through the ranks at Fort Bragg. Death screamed and snapped at his heels, yet all Roth thought about were options. The main staircase was right in front of them, a bank of useless elevators to the left. If they took the stairs, it might slow them a fraction. To the right of the staircase was an admin corridor that led to the post room and other clerical offices. Roth knew there were civilians in there, burning documents in the embassy's incinerator. To the left of the useless elevators was Service Corridor A, and Roth wasn't going to lead the infected there, not if they wanted to get to the Safe Haven. It had to be the stairs.

"Stairs!" he yelled to his team, and everyone veered right and sprinted hard. They took them two at a time, boots squeaking on the slick surface as they rounded the switchback, turning to fire, chopping down the front runners. Bosco paused on the first-floor landing. He pointed to the ceiling.

"Top floor, Executive Suite, there's an emergency escape staircase in Ashcroft's office. Follow me!"

The Delta operators kept going and didn't look back.

Roth yelled into his radio. "Drake, get off that roof! Wait for us in the Ambo's office!"

He took a look over his shoulder. Behind him, the infected swarmed up the stairs like a biblical plague.

DOUG SLOWED AS HE APPROACHED THE DOOR AT THE FAR END OF the tunnel. It resembled a bulkhead door, grey, with heavy handles.

"Is that an airtight door?" The Delta operator was barely breathing after their extended sprint. Doug panted, shook his head.

"I don't think so."

There were locking handles top and bottom. Costello grabbed the top one. "Okay, let's crack this bitch."

Doug grabbed the other. They moved easily, and Doug stepped out of the way as the heavy door swung towards them. Costello pushed past him, his rifle jammed into his shoulder, the barrel torch carving through the darkness ahead. Doug followed. The smell hit his nostrils, the sound all too familiar.

"I'll be damned."

BOSCO SCRAMBLED UP THE STAIRS, YELLING AT THE TOP OF HIS voice. "Everybody, get to the Executive Suite! Go!"

As he passed each landing he saw dozens of people running along the hallways, crying, shouting, panicking. He glimpsed others who stood frozen like statues, men and women, their faces ashen, their minds seized by terror. Neither flight or fight - just total shutdown. There was no time to stop, no time to plead with them, shake them from their suicidal reverie. So Bosco didn't stop, didn't look back, because what followed was only death.

Some answered the call, grasped the lifeline that Bosco

was offering, and by the time he reached the fourth floor he had managed to gather at least twenty others.

The screams of the infected and the rattle of Delta's guns chased them out of the stairwell. Bosco sprinted down the dark hallway to Ashcroft's office, the survivors behind him, Delta bringing up the rear. Bosco charged through the panicked herd in the outer office and kicked Ashcroft's door open. To the right of his desk was the ambassador's private bathroom, a large, well-appointed facility with a walk-in shower, toilet and sink. To the right of the toilet was a floor-to-ceiling mirror built into the wall. At shoulder height were two small silver caps. Bosco placed his hands over them and pushed as hard as he could.

The mirror moved backwards six inches and then swung to the left on silent hinges. Bosco stepped inside, waved his torch. A small landing led to a very narrow staircase. Rough concrete walls and steps led down into total darkness. He listened for a moment, but all he could hear was the thick silence of dead air.

He ran back out to the main office, started directing people into Ashcroft's bathroom.

"Everybody inside, now! The staircase will take you down to the security corridor on the ground floor. Go, quickly!"

Bosco saw a young guy he knew worked in the Political Affairs department. He was trying to push his way past a couple of very distressed ladies. Bosco grabbed him by the arm and yanked him out of the line.

"What's your name?"

"Diaz."

The kid was terrified, his eyes like saucers, his shirt damp with sweat. "Listen to me, Diaz, I want you to round up as many people as you can on this floor. Tell them if they want to live they'd better join you, comprende?"

The kid clearly didn't so Bosco shoved him out into the

hallway. "If you don't come back with at least a dozen people I'm going to handcuff you to your desk. Move!"

Bosco saw the line snaking fast into Ashcroft's bathroom. He did a quick headcount. Forty people, maybe more. Diaz returned a few minutes later. There were four others with him. Bosco yanked him by the arm as he tried to push past.

"That's it? Four?"

Diaz shook himself free. "They're all I could find. I'm not going to die like the others."

Bosco watched him disappear into the bathroom. Four was better than nothing. He headed out into the hallway. Delta were halfway down, spread from wall to wall like a firing squad, guns trained on the stairway doors. He slapped Roth on the shoulder.

"We're good to go. Ashcroft's office, private bathroom." Bosco turned to leave, then realised Delta weren't moving. They stayed locked in position, watching, waiting. That's when Bosco realised.

"Where are they?"

Roth half turned and said, "Can't you hear? Richer pickings on the other floors."

Bosco heard it then, the thunderous stampede, the crash of furniture and glass, the terrible wailing and screaming, the sound of the desperate, of the panicked and the doomed.

"God help them," he whispered. "We should go, before they get up here."

Roth shook his head. "There might be stragglers."

They watched the doors for another minute, then another. The screams and cries for help faded to nothing. Roth finally conceded. "Nick, follow Mister Bosco. Get everyone downstairs."

Bosco ran ahead, guiding them into Ashcroft's office. He lingered in the doorway, watching the distant stairwell. Roth waited beside him, his assault rifle pointed down the hall. Strange, tortured howls drifted up from the floors below.

Bosco knew the sound would haunt him for the rest of his days.

"You think they'll find a cure for this thing?"

Bosco glanced at Roth. The soldier's face was drawn, his eyes red-rimmed with dust and exhaustion and maybe something else. He felt a flash of sympathy, then reminded himself that this was Roth's fault. He talked about making others pay but Bosco knew it would be Roth who'd be facing a military tribunal - if they ever got out of here.

"I don't know," Bosco finally answered. "I doubt any of them will recover from the damage done to their minds."

"That's what I thought."

Roth tensed as the stairwell doors burst open. Not survivors, Bosco saw. Infected - seven, eight, a dozen, spreading out across the reception area, hunched shadows that hissed and snapped their jaws in the dark. Bosco's heart sank as one of them stepped into the fading wash of an emergency light. *Mary Dubose*. Blood ran freely down her face, her shirt was ripped and her shoes were missing. She lifted her legs robotically as if she were discovering them for the first time. She peered into the dark of the hallway, head twisting left and right. Searching for prey.

"We have to go," Bosco whispered.

The Major nodded. They eased back into the office, closing the door behind them. Bosco locked the bathroom door and pushed the mirror back into place. He followed Roth down the narrow staircase.

SOME DIED IN ABSOLUTE TERROR. SOME DIED PLEADING FOR mercy, for God to save them, but God wasn't listening. Some died like heroes, fighting to save friends and colleagues. Most didn't die at all and joined the growing ranks of the infected.

They spilled out across every floor, chasing down the runners, ripping away the makeshift barricades, seeking out fresh victims hiding in every office, in every bathroom stall, in stationery cupboards and cowering beneath desks. They were dragged, mauled, gored, bitten, vomited over, blinded, crushed underfoot. A handful died of heart attacks. Others took matters into their own hands.

A small group of men and women, trapped in their office on the third floor, begged the Diplomatic Security agent to shoot them before the infected broke in. When he didn't - *couldn't* - comply, they knocked him to the ground and took his guns. Eight of them lay dead by the time the office door splintered and the infected got to them. The DS agent was mobbed. Ninety seconds later he charged out of the office, searching for his first victim.

And so it went, from floor to floor, room to room, the infected sweeping through the Chancery like a swarm of diseased locusts until the territory had been conquered and the pack had tripled in size. Guttural barks and yelps rang out around the building, of victory and dominance over another species. They swarmed back down the stairs and gathered in the atrium, where their cries thundered back at them, feeding the frenzied atmosphere. Then they began to move, forming a circle once more, clawing, pushing, shoving, always forward, always in motion, quelling the anger, strengthening the bond between them.

They filled the atrium.

They were one.

His name was Jordan Sweet and he was a twenty-six-year-old Lance-Corporal from Jefferson City, Missouri. Sweet had already served eight months of a three-year tour in the Marine Security Guard. Baghdad was his first posting in the MSG. He was pretty sure it wasn't going to be his last.

Because Jordan Sweet was a lucky guy. At twelve years old, he'd walked away from a car wreck that killed his uncle and two cousins. In high school, he'd met the love of his life, Erin, who'd gifted him with two fine sons, and that made him the luckiest son of a bitch in the world. He'd been shot twice in Iraq, both of them flesh wounds, and the IED in eastern Afghanistan that killed the two guys either side of him left Sweet with nary a scratch. He'd even been screened for the virus after complaining of a headache, and that had *really* frightened him. He'd reported to the warehouse but they'd sent him away again. *Lucky guy,* the Doc had said.

And she was right. Jordan Sweet *was* a lucky mother-fucker and right now that luck was still holding.

He was in a small maintenance room with a dozen other people, most of them DS agents, and they'd all bundled into the room when the infected had poured into the atrium. They'd listened to the stampede of death, the cries of pain and horror, and now they could hear a thunderous stamping and howling from right outside the doors. It was weird and terrifying all at the same time.

Jordan gathered everyone to the far side of the room. They huddled by the pipes and lifeless fuse boxes, torch-lit faces and frightened whispers in the dark.

"What the fuck are they doing out there?"

"Who knows? Some weird shit," Jordan told them. "What we need to do is get down to the Safe Haven."

"How?" one of the agents hissed. "There's hundreds of those things right outside."

"Service Corridor A is a straight shot across the atrium. There are two sets of security doors before we get to the base-ment stairwell. We get in there, bolt the doors behind us as we go."

"There's twelve of us," another agent whispered. "The front-runners might make it but by the time the last man leaves this room they'll be all over us."

"Trapped underground? Fuck that," muttered a big guy in maintenance overalls. "There's an emergency exit halfway along that corridor. We use that to make a run for the utility building behind the Chancery. They'll never get inside the plant room and we've got a kitchen back there, food, water. What d'ya say?"

"Sounds like a plan," whispered another agent.

"Safe Haven is the official fallback," Jordan told them. "Besides, you don't know what's out there."

The DS agent next to Jordan rattled his M4. "We've got the firepower. We'll shoot our way through."

"I say we wait here," argued another voice.

The voices got louder. Jordan had to raise his a little. "Shut the fuck up!"

"You're not in charge here," the big guy told him.

"Go ahead then," Jordan snapped. "Keep flapping your gums and see if it don't bring those things to our door."

The maintenance guy glared at him then turned to the others. "Who's up for joining me?"

Several hands were raised. Jordan shook his head. "Your choice, but we still need to get into that corridor. I suggest we knock off our torches and open both the doors as quietly as possible. We pick our moment then go on my signal. I'm heading to the Safe Haven. Anyone wants to come with, follow me."

The huddle broke up. There was a chance that someone had gone before them, sealed the security doors further down the corridor, but that was a chance he had to take. He couldn't stay in this room forever and besides, Marines didn't hide.

Time to move, Jordo.

He removed his helmet because he didn't need the distraction when he ran. He checked his M4 rifle - full mag, safety off - and gestured for the others to do the same. Everyone was locked and loaded.

Jordan put a finger to his lips and very, very slowly, moved to the maintenance room door. He opened one of them, sneaked a peek, and caught a glimpse of the infected. The sight chilled his blood.

Twenty meters away a huge circle of shadowy figures was moving round and round in the dark. They grunted and wheezed and made a bunch of other weird sounds and it creeped Jordan out. *What the fuck?* He couldn't see the whole circle but they were packed together like a crowd at the Arrowhead Stadium. Jordan Sweet was officially shit scared.

He eased open the other door and looked across the atrium to where Service Corridor A beckoned. Again, about twenty meters, which meant a forty-meter head start, give or take. Doable.

He gathered everyone together. Heads huddled in the dark.

"They're in some kind of trance. I say we move right now, calmly and quietly before—"

"No!"

"Shit!"

Jordan spun around, saw the maintenance guy sprinting across the atrium. *Motherfucker.*

"Go!" someone yelled, and everybody bolted.

They bundled for the doorway, pushing and shoving in a blind panic. Jordan glanced to his right as he hit the atrium. A chorus of screams rose up from the herd of infected and they turned as one, thundering across the marble floor. Jordan sprinted, lifting his knees, chin tucked low, just like coach had taught him in school. He overtook a couple of agents, the roar of the infected snapping at his boots. Ahead, he saw the maintenance guy slam the door behind him. Jordan was almost there. Ten meters, five…*please God, let them be open.*

He hit them hard and they flew inward. The agents spilled in behind him. He kept going. Up ahead the maintenance guy turned hard left into another corridor. Jordan snatched a glimpse as he ran past, saw the emergency exit doors lying wide open, the overalls disappearing into the darkness.

Jordan pounded towards the next set of doors. He heard a scream behind him, shots fired. The tail-enders had been caught. Jordan didn't look back, just kept running, the sounds of hellish pursuit filling the corridor. The next set of doors were right ahead. Jordan prayed again, implored baby Jesus to save his ass. He stiffened his arm and the door flew open. He wheeled around.

Hell followed.

No DS agents, just a corridor filled with infected, all pushing and shoving, grunting and clawing, heading towards him. Jordan lifted his M4 and emptied all thirty rounds into the mob. Bodies fell, tripping the mass of bodies behind, slowing them. Jordan slammed the door shut. It was thick steel and he dropped the bolts with sweaty fingers. He backed away, clipped in a fresh magazine, chambered a round. The doors were thick, the bolts long and heavy. They shuddered as the infected crashed into them, but they held. Jordan ran for the stairs.

He headed down past The Hub, flying around the landings. He heard the thunder from above, felt it deep inside his chest. Then he heard noises from below. He spun around another landing—

—And was blinded by a dozen torches. He skidded to a halt and held up his hands.

"Don't shoot! It's me, Sweet! I'm okay!"

"Turn around. Slowly."

Sweet obeyed, blinking as the torch beams swept across his face, his body.

"I'm okay, I swear."

"He's clean," said a voice in the darkness.

"He's one lucky son of a bitch," said another.

Jordan Sweet grinned.

Fucking A.

· · ·

THE RADAR SPUN TIRELESSLY, SWEEPING THE GROUND FOR THREE-hundred-and-sixty degrees. The *Watchman* had no eyes so it couldn't see that the smoke had finally cleared, that the last of the flares had drifted to earth and extinguished themselves in the Tigris River. It could only detect movement, and movement meant targets.

Like the ones that had just emerged from inside a distant structure and were now moving across open ground. There was a single target ahead of the others, then a larger group of returns. Behind those, a much larger, fast-moving cluster. The ground radar painted them as the *Watchman's* electronic Gatling gun ran up to speed and opened fire. It tracked left to right in a stream of red tracer, cutting down the single target first, then the smaller group, then finally went to work on the cluster. It fired continuously, its rounds chopping the targets to pieces. The radar swept again, finding more targets emerging from the structure. It locked onto the source, the doorway where scores of targets spilled out onto open ground. Tracer rounds glowed like lasers, lighting up the dark. The weapon kept firing until its magazine of four thousand rounds ran dry.

The *Watchman* twisted on its mount one final time then stopped. The power whined and died. Smoking gun barrels drooped.

It had served its purpose.

DOUG HELD A GAUZE PAD AGAINST HIS SPLIT LIP AS HE WATCHED Bosco pounding on the Safe Haven door. He checked the pad again; the bleeding was negligible. He tossed it away.

"Diaz, open the door, right now! Diaz!"

There was no answer from inside. When Bosco and Roth had arrived, Doug filled them in on what had happened.

Doug and Costello had been halfway down the southern tunnel when they'd heard the distant booming, the desperate cries for help. They'd run back to the lobby and Doug had cracked the door. It slammed into his face as the survivors from the fourth floor had barged it open and swarmed into the basement.

One of them, a guy called Diaz, had demanded to know where the Safe Haven was. A bleeding Doug had pointed the way and the civilians had scrambled inside. As Costello fished in his kit for a gauze pad, Doug became aware of the frantic whispers, and before either of them could react, Diaz had slammed the door shut. Doug and Costello had tried and failed. Bosco wasn't giving up.

"Diaz, listen to me. You're not safe in there, none of you. Open the door!" He pounded on the thick grey steel with his fist but there was no reply. "Dammit," the RSO cursed. "They could die in there."

"Unless we move, we're all going to die." It was Roth this time. He pointed to the ceiling. "Those doors up there won't hold. We can't help them."

"We can't leave them either."

Roth's eyes narrowed. "You think that's what I want? We don't have any choice. If no one survives, this whole thing will be buried and the truth will never come out. We can't let—"

Boom.

Doug looked to the ceiling. It was the infected, still attacking the service corridor doors. But something had changed. The constant, irregular thunder had stopped, replaced by a steady, rhythmic beat.

Boom. Boom. Boom.

Bosco and the Delta operators were listening too.

"They're working it out," Roth whispered.

Bosco ran back to the Safe Haven door. "Diaz, if you don't want to come out of there, fine, but at least give others a choice. If anyone wants to leave, let them, okay?"

Doug saw a shadow fall across the spy hole. A muffled voice from inside shouted, "Get away from the door."

Bosco moved back towards the lobby. Heavy bolts were thrown and the door creaked open. A gaggle of men and women scrambled out and then the door slammed closed behind them. Doug heard the locking handles squealing into position.

The new arrivals were a sorry-looking bunch, cut and bruised, torn clothes, tear-streaked faces. Bosco smiled, genuinely relieved.

"Okay, good, you're all going to be fine."

One of them, a woman in her fifties with straggly grey hair and ripped tights, stepped forward.

"What are we going to do now? Mister Diaz isn't going to let us back in. He thinks the infection will get in there if he lets anyone else in."

"Follow me," Bosco said. He led the group towards the twisted steel door. He pushed it back to reveal the tunnel beyond. It stretched far into the distance.

"Get down there as fast as you can. There are soldiers waiting for you. Do what they say and you'll be just fine."

Tired, terrified eyes stared down the empty concrete tunnel.

"What's down there?" the woman asked.

"Life," Bosco said gently. He smiled, and silent tears ran down the woman's face. She nodded several times and headed into the tunnel. The others followed.

Doug watched them go, then he heard a low whistle behind him.

"Come take a look at this."

It was Costello, standing on a chair at the impenetrable northern door. He'd used the last of the plastique to punch out another chunk of concrete above the door. It wasn't wide enough to get a body through but it was certainly enough for a gun barrel and a grenade. Costello had tried both. Neither had bothered the spider that lurked in its lair.

Costello jumped down. "It's doing something."

Bosco nodded at Doug. "You're the expert. Take a look."

Doug obliged. He squeezed his face into the narrow concrete fissure as far as he could. The view inside the room was a little less restricted but he still only had a partial view of the system that lurked behind the steel mesh cage. Costello was right, though; it was chattering away, beeping and bleeping, its processor lights winking like crazy in the darkness. There was something else too, on the display unit, but Doug couldn't make out what it was. Again, he pulled his smartphone from his pocket and took a picture. He hopped down and opened up the image, zooming in with finger and thumb.

"Holy shit."

He held up the phone for the others to see. They gathered round, eyes narrowing.

Bosco frowned. "Is that a system clock or something?"

"It's a timer," Roth realised.

Doug nodded. "And it's counting down." He looked at the photo again. The digital display read: 04:19.

"We have less than four minutes," Costello warned, setting a timer on his own watch.

"Until what?" Bosco looked baffled.

"Until something fucking bad happens." Roth keyed his radio. "Drake, how long?" The sniper's reply came back a moment later. "Work faster," he told him. "We're travelling to you right now. Be ready."

Bosco ran for the Safe Haven door. "Last chance, Diaz!" he yelled, thumping the metal. "Don't be a fool, open the goddam door!" He waited for five, ten seconds. Doug felt like screaming at him. Delta were already on the move. Roth yelled at Bosco.

"We're out of time! Let's go!"

Boom! Boom! Boom!

Then a crash, a rumble of thunder that shook the walls. Dust filled the air.

"They're inside!" Roth yanked Bosco away from the door. "Go!" He pointed at Doug and Sweet. "Seal those doors!"

Doug and the Marine scrambled across the lobby. They threw the bolts top and bottom as feet pounded the stairs above them, getting louder, closer. The howls and screams made Doug's skin crawl.

"Move!" Roth roared from the tunnel entrance.

Sweet turned and ran. Doug realised he was the last man left in the lobby. His Nikes slipped on the dusty concrete and then he was running.

There were no words of encouragement, no yelling, no cursing. It was an orderly, terrified retreat. Heads bobbed and guns and equipment rattled as everyone sprinted single file down the narrow tunnel. Safety was a hundred meters away, ninety, eighty. Doug cringed as he heard wood splintering and metal screeching. He looked behind him, just in time to see the doors give way and a mountain of bodies pile into the lobby, others scrambling over them, searching this way and that for fresh blood. Then they saw Doug.

A terrible wailing filled the tunnel. The thunder grew louder behind them. Ahead, the steel door swung inwards. A moment later and everyone was piling through.

A Delta operator holding an M320 grenade launcher pulled Doug out of the way. He saw him drop a 40mm round into the loading tube and flip it closed.

"Fire in the hole!"

Doug crouched by the wall and covered his ears. He heard the hollow *phut* of the round being fired and a couple of seconds later the explosion rocked the walls. Doug risked a quick look. A hundred meters back down the tunnel, black smoke, blood and carnage. Yelps of pain. The soldier fired another round. Doug cringed. Another explosion, another chorus of painful, furious screams.

"Get in!"

It was Roth, waving his arm at Doug. Behind him, engines burbled beneath the low ceiling and water slapped against concrete walls. Doug was still in shock; not because of the grenades but what he and Costello had discovered at the end of that long tunnel.

What the hell?

Did you know about this?

If I did, d'you think I might've mentioned it?

Roth wasn't surprised. Bosco had been offended. The only RSO in history who was clueless about his own embassy. Doug felt sorry for him.

The tunnel led all the way from beneath the Chancery to the southern perimeter wall where Doug and Costello had discovered a freshwater dock. And four black Zodiac RIBs. A storeroom with ammunition and emergency supplies.

A shot at surviving.

But on inspection, only two of the RIBs were operational. The other two had engine problems and were taking on water. Now they were forced to cram everyone into the two remaining boats. The civilians were split between the two, huddled in the middle, their frightened faces glimpsed by waving torches. At the far end of the dock, another operator was cranking the wheel of a well-disguised gate. It opened out into the embassy lagoon, a large, wedge-shaped stretch of water that acted as a security buffer between the walls of the embassy and the Tigris River.

And they had less than three minutes to get there.

"We've got a problem." It was the guy with the grenade launcher. He was watching the tunnel. "They're massing for another charge and I got two rounds left."

Roth yelled at the guy cranking the handle. "Get that fucking gate open!"

"It's stuck!" The operator shot back. "Rusted or something."

Doug ran down the dock to help him. The wheel probably hadn't been serviced in a while. Doug gripped it, strained his muscles to turn it. Then Bosco barged in between them, got his own hands on the flaking metal.

"After three - one, two, three!"

The wheel budged an inch. The gate moved up a little.

"Again!"

Doug gritted his teeth. He could hear the rising howls of the infected filling the dock, reverberating off the low walls. The bone-chilling crescendo gave him strength. He heaved, his back and shoulders straining. All three of them grunted and gasped and suddenly the wheel spun free and the gate started to rise.

"I'll take it from here!" the operator said. "Pick me up as you go past."

Doug and Bosco ran back to the boats. Up ahead, Roth was on the dock, stuffing mags into his rig, catching grenades as the other operators threw them to him. He saw Doug and Bosco and waved them into the RIBs.

"Get in!" he ordered.

"What the fuck are you doing?" Bosco said.

Roth jerked a thumb over his shoulder. "The door locks from the other side. Someone has to throw those handles."

"Barricade it," Bosco said.

Roth shook his head. "There's no time."

Everyone flinched as two more explosions rocked the tunnel. "I'm out!" the guy with the launcher announced. He jumped into the nearest boat.

"Go!" Roth ordered, stuffing grenades into his vest and pockets.

"Don't be crazy!" Doug yelled at him. He turned on Costello who was at the wheel of the nearest boat. "What the fuck's wrong with you? You can't let him do this!"

Costello wouldn't answer. Roth stood ready, locked and loaded. "Get them home safe, Nick." And then he was gone, through the bulkhead door. It slammed shut behind him, and Doug heard the locking handles thump home. He felt impotent and shaken by a sudden, incredible sadness.

"Ninety seconds," Costello warned. "Cast off."

Bosco shoved Doug aboard. Ropes were untied and the engines roared then settled. The RIBs peeled away from the dock and headed out through the gate and into the security lagoon. Doug looked up at the stars in the sky. They'd escaped the embassy, but it wasn't over yet. Costello increased power.

"You see that?" one of the operators shouted over the roar of the engines.

Doug looked ahead, saw two red lights either side of a dark tunnel. They were almost on top of it when Costello cut back the power. The tunnel was low, about fifteen metres long and stank of rotting vegetation. The sound of the engines rumbled off the low ceiling as the RIBs drifted through. A hinged and barred gate blocked the other end but it was unlocked and Bosco yanked it open. Costello coaxed the RIB through a dense patch of reeds and finally, they were out onto the Tigris itself.

Costello swung the boat to the south. As the other RIB came alongside, Costello opened up the engines and the nose lifted out of the water.

Doug hung on to the steering console. He turned around and saw the perimeter walls of the embassy, the smoke rising beyond. He glanced at his own watch.

Time was up.

ROTH JAMMED THE LOCKING HANDLES AS HARD AS HE COULD AND wheeled around. Fifty meters away the tunnel was thick with smoke and dust. Bodies were piled up, two or three high and ten deep. A carpet of bodies, peppered with shrapnel. Some of them were still alive, hands clawing amongst the pile, bloodied faces twisting in agony and rage. The noise, the screams and wails, of fury and pain, were more than Roth could bear.

And still they advanced, a mass of hissing, snarling creatures that squeezed between the concrete walls, trampling across the injured and the dead, in ragged combat uniforms and filthy suits, in vomit-stained overalls and bloody chef's whites. Some were young, some not, but all of them had only one objective—to rip Jon Roth to pieces.

The door might stop them, but then again it might not. They might get into the dock, the water. Roth might be one of them, and Roth was a good swimmer. He might be the one who makes it to the other side, who carries the virus into Baghdad. That was unthinkable.

He'd tried to save as many as possible but now his mission was to make sure the infected didn't leave the embassy.

One by one he pulled grenades from his pockets and lobbed them down the tunnel, crouching as they exploded. They slowed the advance but the sheer weight of numbers drove the others forward. He took a knee and laid eight magazines on the ground in front of him. He brought his HK-416 up into his shoulder and opened fire, aiming for heads, hoping and praying the misery would end for those he'd doomed. He believed his own misery might be eternal, and he wondered who or what waited for him on the other side. Roth had never been much of a churchgoer but he respected those who were and had always been quietly intrigued by their faith in something so intangible. Pretty soon he'd find out if they were right or not.

He kept firing, stemming the flow, rattling through his magazines. His round-counting days were over, that was for sure. He'd miss Bragg, his Delta brothers, his friends and family, but nothing was forever. He hoped he'd be remembered, with a smile and with respect.

And be forgiven.

They closed in, twenty meters, fifteen, ten. His last magazine clicked empty. He stood up, dropping the HK to the ground. He pulled his pistol, emptied it into the faces that were so close now. They reached out for him.

The sonic wave rushed down the tunnel, shattering his eardrums.

The wall of white fire behind it consumed everything.

THE SKY OVER CENTRAL BAGHDAD TURNED FROM NIGHT TO DAY.

The light mushroomed, blinding in its intensity, a terrestrial supernova that was seen for several kilometres. Milliseconds later a series of enormous explosions rocked the city, shaking buildings and shattering windows for over a kilometre. Inside the embassy grounds, buildings disintegrated one after the other, sending debris rocketing into the dark skies. The sudden and terrifying bombardment sent people rushing from their beds to their shattered windows. Many wished they hadn't.

The explosive chamber beneath the Safe Haven was the largest of them all. There were other, smaller voids scattered strategically throughout the central core of the building, and all of them were packed with Composition B and connected to Grand Slam. The *Touchdown* sequence was almost complete. The Chancery's pressure trigger was the last to be fired.

It was the spider's final, suicidal act.

Detonating…

Another ripple of searing white pulses lit up the Baghdad sky, and then the Chancery building blew out sideways, floor by floor in rapid succession. As the building collapsed the explosive chamber beneath detonated, obliterating what was left of the falling structure and propelling its remains up and out across the city in a white-hot eruption that was so loud, glass and eardrums were shattered all over the city.

The shockwave rippled out across Baghdad, a wall of sound and pressure that shook everything so violently that many inhabitants believed the capital had been hit by a nuclear weapon.

As the smoke cleared and word spread, that fear turned to relief, then disbelief.

CHAPTER 16
BLACKJACK

For the survivors out on the Tigris, the sensory assaults of light and noise were terrifying. When the Chancery blew, people screamed.

Doug shielded his eyes as the sky turned from black to a blinding, searing white. He saw the shock-wave punch out the southern perimeter wall and hurtle across the Tigris, whipping the reeds and palm trees on the opposite bank like a sudden and powerful tornado. As the white pulse faded, pieces of the embassy began hitting the water around them like a concrete rainstorm. Doug hung on as Costello steered the boat beneath the Al Jadriyah bridge. The other RIB followed and the engines were cut. They heard the screech of braking cars as debris slammed into the road above them.

The boats drifted silently in the darkness. Everyone was watching the spectacle behind them. The civilians sobbed quietly and Doug felt close to tears himself. He wondered what had become of Freddie and hoped that the guy was no longer in pain. Nor anyone who'd been touched by the infection.

The rainstorm eased. Above them on the bridge, Doug

heard the excited shouts of Iraqis. Somewhere on dry land, AK-47s were fired into the night sky.

"Everybody, stay down. Keep still and quiet," Costello whispered in the dark. "We've got to put distance between us and the city."

Doug noticed that Costello and the other operators were now wearing their NVGs. That made him feel a little more comfortable. The river was black, the riverbanks a world of shadows. The last thing they needed was an accident. Or worse, trouble.

Engines rumbled and the RIBs eased out from under the bridge. As they rounded a bend in the river, the smouldering remains of the embassy slipped out of sight.

Doug sat with his back against the steering console. He closed his eyes and let the cool night air wash over him.

FINALLY, GATEKEEPER COULD RELAX.

He'd spent the last few hours locked in tense discussions with his colleagues and superiors as they'd worked the Baghdad problem. He'd faked deep concern while being quietly amused by the clumsy attempts of those around him to resolve the situation. But it hadn't been a barrel of laughs *all* day.

When senior management had realised that Baghdad was off the network, all hell had broken loose. Dozens of uniforms and guns had descended on the network centre, and Gatekeeper's heart had hammered like a rabbit's for several hours. He'd offered his own contributions and potential solutions, but it slowly became clear that his colleagues were no nearer to finding out the actual cause of the failure. After the storm had passed, he knew that his digital footprints had been buried by a blizzard of electronic activity. Only then did his heart rate return to normal.

When the opportunity presented itself he deleted the code

and severed the links to Rock Creek. He copied over activity logs with pre-prepared decoys and reset switches and routers with NSA-approved configurations. A short while ago, Baghdad had popped back up on the network. All he needed now was for one of his colleagues to make the connection and claim the credit.

As if on cue, the door to the network lab flew open and a technician hurried in. People shot to their feet. Everyone was exhausted, and even Gatekeeper felt pretty beat - being a saboteur was stressful work - but suddenly there was a fresh energy in the room. The technician was beaming and waving a printout like he was holding a winning Powerball ticket.

"Baghdad is back online!" he babbled excitedly. "Traffic is routing all the way to the Green Zone exchange!"

Gatekeeper joined the others as they crowded around the triumphant technician. He offered his own congratulations and patted the man on the shoulder. As people drifted back to their desks and the global digital network map glowed green once more, Gatekeeper turned his thoughts to the future. The final tranche of dough would soon hit the Cayman's account. The twins would be set, his folks too, and the bitch bought off. Financially he could relax.

Although now he had a bigger problem, one that had caused him many a sleepless night since they'd first dangled that big, fat juicy carrot.

The VIP Grand Deluxe Package at the Borgata in Atlantic City or the *High-Roller Executive Experience* at the Bellagio in Vegas? It was a tough choice.

Gatekeeper smiled behind his computer screens. It was a decision he'd have to make real soon.

"DEAR GOD IN HEAVEN."

Coffman whispered the words as she watched the Gray

Eagle surveillance feed being broadcast from fifteen hundred feet above the Iraqi capital.

The State Department Operations Centre was full to capacity and Coffman had prepared herself to perform a little, to exaggerate her facial expressions and dial up the emotion. The official photographs would be all the more dramatic for it, however, acting skills were no longer required. Her shock was real.

The Grey Eagle had been late to the party but what it was now sending back was as disturbing as the videos that were going viral on the Internet. Coffman had seen the shaky, hand-held cell phone footage, the blinding explosions, the shock waves, the broken windows. She'd heard the screams and cries of terror. It was dramatic and disturbing, and no doubt in the coming days, broadcast-quality media would also become available for public consumption. All of it would lend weight to her narrative, but what she was looking at now was hard to believe.

The Gray Eagle was sending back high-definition, low-light video of what used to be the United States embassy in Baghdad. That facility had ceased to exist, replaced by a series of craters in the ground, one of which looked as deep as a coal mine. Someone told her that was the location of the Chancery building. Coffman knew it to be so, but she was still finding it difficult to process. The devastation was total.

Bob Blake had sold her on *Grand Slam* but she'd underestimated its destructive power. The consulate building was gone as well as most of the storage warehouses. The Ambassador and Deputy Chief of Mission residences were just smoking holes in the ground. One of the State Department accommodation blocks had toppled into the one behind it but the rest of them looked relatively unscathed. There were other, smaller craters dotted all over the compound, and the scene reminded Coffman of the aftermath of a bombing run.

But the destruction wasn't just confined to the embassy.

The crystal clarity of the video revealed extensive damage to buildings right across the Green Zone. There were reports that many people had been injured, and several killed. Central Baghdad was a sea of emergency lights.

Coffman took a sip of water to soothe her dry throat. Her Military Liaison team was compiling a preliminary damage assessment and Coffman had already scheduled a call with the Iraqi president. She suspected he would be as shocked as she was, and the assurances of reparations would no doubt be repeated during their call. Coffman would make sure that the Iraqis got everything they wanted and more. They had played their part and played it well, and Amy Coffman always rewarded loyalty.

She saw Erik hovering close by and she led him from the room. They didn't speak until the door to her private office had closed behind them.

"Well?"

Mulholland flopped in a chair opposite her desk. "Gatekeeper has restored all the links and Bob has broken down the control room at Rock Creek. So far the whole thing has gone undetected."

Coffman stared at her Chief of Staff and cocked her head. "What's the matter, Erik? You seem a little rattled."

He glared at her with bloodshot eyes. "If you'd seen what I have, you'd be rattled too."

Coffman pulled a chair close to him and sat down. "What you've witnessed, that terrible virus - it justifies our actions, Erik. You see that now, don't you?"

Mulholland ran a tired hand through his thick grey hair. "I'm not so sure, Amy. A lot of people died. A lot of Americans. They died horribly, and that's on us."

Coffman took one of Erik's hands in her own. They were soft, the nails manicured, and she wondered if sending him to Rock Creek had been a step too far. Erik was no stranger to playing hardball of course. He'd exploited weakness many times, had destroyed careers and marriages, had blackmailed and bullied. One time he'd arranged to have an Assembly-man's arms broken, but this was something else, and Erik was clearly bending beneath the weight of culpability. She squeezed his hand.

"Then look at it another way. Imagine if we hadn't made our move. That we did what was expected of us. That virus would still have spread. Yes, the outbreak teams would have been mobilised such sooner but would that've helped any of those who were infected? And what if that infection got out? If Baghdad became a city of monsters? Maybe that nuclear option we spun to Hamid might've become a reality. You see what I'm saying, Erik? What we did probably *saved* lives."

Mulholland nodded slowly. He still couldn't bring himself to make eye contact and that worried Coffman. She squeezed his hand.

"Look at me, Erik." He did, the stare vacant, exhausted. "It's been a stressful time for all of us but it's not over. There are loose ends to take care of, the possibility of survivors—"

"Fuck!" Mulholland snatched his hand away and jumped to his feet. "Grand Slam blew away some of the embassy walls. There might be one of those creatures running around the Green Zone right now!"

Coffman stood in front of him. She took his hands and this time she squeezed his fingers hard. "Do you think I'm stupid, Erik? Do you?"

Mulholland shook his head. "Of course I don't."

"Good, because President Aswad is already aware of that risk. The embassy has been surrounded by Iraqi Special Forces. Every inch of the perimeter is under surveillance, and if anything moves, it will be engaged, in the assumption that any survivors must be infected. I've given Aswad guarantees that the United States will view any such deaths as justified. He has a right to protect his country, Erik. We would do exactly the same. And when we release the video footage, the world will understand."

She coaxed him back into his seat and poured two large bourbons. She gave one to Mulholland and watched him down it in one hit. She took the empty glass and gave him the other. She poured herself one and sat next to him. Mulholland tipped back another mouthful and nodded.

"You're right, Amy. I'm just a little strung out. I think I might have PTSD." He tried to smile at his own joke but she could see he was struggling.

"Go back to your office, Erik. Get a couple of hours sleep and a change of clothes. The next few hours are important but the next few days and weeks are going to be absolutely crucial. I'll need you at the very top of your game, Erik. Are you hearing me?"

Mulholland downed the rest of his bourbon and got to his feet. "Loud and clear. Wake me if you need me, okay?"

Coffman watched him go. *He'll be fine,* she assured herself, and in the meantime, she had Karen Baranski to fill the gap. She finished her own drink and headed back to the Operation Centre.

There was much work to be done, statements to be drafted, assurances to be made. She would talk about the loss of American lives and her determination to find out what happened. Grieving families would be her priority. She made a note to purchase a few more black outfits. They would certainly be needed in the coming months.

The Operations Centre was a hive of fevered activity. Coffman stood in the middle of it all, centre stage. The curtain was up now, the players gathered around her, the audience waiting in rapt attention.

Amy Coffman was going to give them the performance of her life.

• • •

THE RIBS POWERED ALONG THE TIGRIS RIVER. THE SLUGGISH waterway was taking them ever southward, leaving the teeming - and now very awake - heart of Baghdad far behind them. They cruised unnoticed past the sprawling industrial estates and factories crowding the riverbanks to the south of the city.

As the miles ticked by, the smokestacks gave way to rural communities and farmland until eventually, the surrounding terrain stretched out into darkness. Stars littered the night sky. Doug welcomed the change of scenery and the quiet peace of the Iraqi countryside where the only witnesses to their passage were river birds. Yet it was too soon to relax.

He heard Costello issuing orders into his radio as he piloted the boat. Draped over the rubber flanks, operators swept the darkness with their NVGs. So far they hadn't encountered any Iraqi patrols, and no one was even sure if traffic along the Tigris was actually monitored but they guessed it would be. The war was over of course, and the Iraqis were now considered allies, but two boatloads of Americans travelling without authority, some of whom were heavily armed Delta Force operators, might not sit too well with the locals.

Doug checked his watch and realised that the dawn wasn't far away. He heard Costello saying much the same thing over the radio. They were stopping.

The boat veered towards a dark channel, separated from the Tigris by an island of thick reeds. The RIB nosed into the cut, quickly followed by the other boat. The gap was narrow, and the boats brushed against towering reeds. There was a sandy riverbank on their right, and Costello cut the engine and drifted into the shallows. Operators eased into the water and onto shore. Costello signalled to the rest of them - *stay in the boats*.

Doug watched the operators spread out across the sand and move up a shallow incline towards a bank that overlooked the river. There was no moon and they were soon lost in the darkness.

Huddled in front of Doug, the survivors from the Chancery sat in morose silence, their heads hung low, each alone with their thoughts, processing their own terrible experiences. Doug took a headcount; seven survivors including himself. In the other boat, six, plus Bosco and the Marine, Sweet. Costello and his operators brought their numbers to twenty-one.

Twenty-one.

Doug felt nauseous at the thought of the people who didn't make it. He also felt something else, a sudden vibration on his thigh. He snatched the phone out of his pocket, saw the signal bars creep up, the *Asia Cell* network logo—

He hopped out onto the bank, keeping low as he dialled the pre-programmed number. He crouched down on the sand, listening to the distant ring, the glorious click of the answered call.

"Rick, it's Doug Walker."

"Hi, this is Rick Gould. I can't take your call right now but—"

Doug cursed and tried again. A shadow loomed over him.

"Shut that fucking thing off," Costello hissed in the dark.

But Doug was desperate. "It's an emergency, my daughter—"

"Shut it off, right now."

Doug felt angry and foolish and desperate all at once, but he knew Costello was right. "My bad," he said.

The Delta operator bobbed his head, the stalks of his NVGs inspecting Doug like a giant insect. "We're not out of this, yet, *capiche?* We got a long way to go. No comms until I say."

"You got it."

Doug powered down the phone and pocketed it. At least Rick would see the missed call. He'd call back, leave a message. Next time Doug fired up that cell he'd have news, either way. He prayed it would be good.

Delta came back down the slope and took a knee around Costello. Doug saw Bosco and Sweet climb out of the other boat and join the huddle.

"What have we got?" asked the Sergeant-Major, his voice barely above a whisper.

"A causeway road running along the top of the bank. A hundred meters beyond that there's a settlement, a couple of dozen houses, pretty affluent; satellite dishes, fancy cars, pickups. Nothing big enough to take all of us though."

"Shit." Costello glanced at the luminous green glow of his watch. "It'll be sunup in an hour. We need to be off the river by then."

"We could liberate a couple of vehicles." Doug recognised Drake, not by his shadowy face but by the G-28 rifle cradled across his legs. "We pick a house, take what we need. We could be a hundred miles away before breakfast."

"I don't like it," Bosco whispered. "We can't harm civilians."

"They'll know where we're going anyway," Doug chipped in. "They'll block all the roads between here and Kuwait."

Costello turned to him and said, "Who says we're driving to Kuwait?"

"So how—?"

An operator came running back down the slope. "Vehicle approaching," he warned.

Everyone got their bellies into the sand. A couple of operators split left and right and disappeared into the darkness. The rest of Delta spread out, weapons pointing up towards the bank. Doug heard it then, the rattle of a diesel engine. Headlamps swept across the bank above, and then Doug saw it, a white Nissan pickup with a light cluster on the roof. It looked pretty beat-up, and it was cruising parallel to the river, slow and deliberate. A patrol. As it drove past, Doug noticed some sort of official crest on the door. As long as they weren't too observant they'd probably pass on by—

The Nissan's brakes squealed and it stopped directly above them. The engine idled as the front passenger door creaked open, and suddenly there was a figure at the top of the bank. Doug saw the glow of a cigarette in the dark, a baseball cap on the man's head. He heard the distinctive sound of liquid hitting the sand and realised he was taking a piss.

No one moved. Doug caught Bosco's eye and the RSO pulled a face. *Of all the goddam luck.* The cop, or whoever he was, was shaking and zipping up. Doug waited for him to slam the door.

And waited.

Another door opened, then another. Voices now, talking over the idling engine. Maybe they'd—

The powerful beams swept across the water once, twice, then settled on the terrified chicks huddled in their rubber nests.

Red dots swarmed all over the Iraqis as Delta moved towards them. Costello was hissing in Arabic. Doug could hear him but all he could see were shadows and the bright beams of the headlamps.

The men began shouting. Doug heard a weapon being cocked. Bosco crawled over to him and whispered, "Get back in the boat." Over Bosco's shoulder, he saw the helmet-less Sweet on his knee, covering Delta with his M4. The Iraqis were shouting now, Costello too. It was about to get real ugly.

An AK thundered, shattering the peace of the countryside. River birds exploded from the reeds. Suppressed rounds rattled off the Nissan. More shouts, breaking glass, bodies hitting the dirt. Suddenly the Nissan roared and accelerated away in a cloud of dust. Delta came back down the bank. Two of them were dragging a wounded comrade between them.

Not wounded, Doug realised.

Down to twenty now.

Somewhere up on the road, the Nissan had hit his lights and sirens. The noise sounded deafening.

"Let's move," Costello ordered.

Doug and Bosco helped lift the dead operator aboard the boat. The civilians huddled closer together as the corpse was laid next to them. Powerful diesel engines roared, and Doug hung on as Costello pulled away from the bank and headed out onto the river. There was no attempt to be covert. Now it was all about distance.

"Time to make that call!" Costello yelled at Doug above the roar of the twin outboards. "Dial a number then hand me the phone!"

Costello shouted out a multi-digit number. Doug punched it in then handed the phone to Costello who clamped it to his ear. When it connected, he shouted, "Ident Code Niner-Seven-One-One-Bravo! Standing by!" Costello banked the boat around a large bend in the river. Wildfowl scattered left and right as the wind whipped through the RIB. The engine noise was dangerously loud. Costello was yelling into the phone.

"JSOC authorisation Yankee-Bravo-Seven-Seven-Two. Emergency transmission. Immediate extraction required for twenty plus personnel including US civilians. Be advised enemy close. Acknowledge!" Costello nodded and shouted, "Affirmative! Deploying emergency beacon, Ident Mike-India-Lima-Four-Two-One-Seven!"

Costello dangled a radio in Doug's face. "Switch that on. It's your responsibility now."

Doug looped the sling over his neck and fumbled with it in the dark. Not a radio. There was no keypad, just a couple of rubberised buttons and a small display. Doug thumbed it on and the tiny LCD screen lit up. Doug unfolded the antennae.

Searching…

Scrolling numbers whizzed through the display. Then:

Transmitting.

Doug gave him the thumbs up. Costello returned the gesture. He pocketed Doug's phone then focussed on the dark waters ahead. He saw Doug's expression and said, "They're gonna call me back. Don't lose that transmitter."

Doug gave him another thumb.

The boat banked continuously, following the river. The Tigris ran all the way to Basrah but it twisted wildly this far north. For every mile south, they had to travel at least the same distance east or west. Doug looked behind, saw the other boat a few metres away skipping across their foamy wake. And beyond that, lights.

A column of vehicles barrelling along the causeway road.

"We've got company," Doug told Costello.

The operator tapped his earpiece. "I know."

The boat swept around a long bend for over a minute. In the distance, Doug saw the sky lit up. *Baghdad.*

"We're headed north," he shouted over the wind.

Costello nodded. "Then it banks south again, narrows too. The trucks will get ahead of us and wait."

"Who are they?"

"Federal police. More like paramilitaries. We could try to explain things but after what just happened I'm guessing they're not in the listening mood. My guys could take care of it but with you people here—"

"I've served," Doug protested. "I know my way around weapons and small unit tactics."

Costello smiled grimly beneath his NVG stalks. "Appreciate the enthusiasm but there are other lives to consider. Help me with that, okay?"

Doug nodded. "Understood."

"Take a seat. We're going to make a hard turn to the south then get off the river."

"And go where?"

"Too many questions," Costello told him. "Just do what I tell you."

Doug watched the distant headlights behind them. They were heading off at a right angle, racing ahead of them. Costello glanced at the other boat and made a circle with his finger. Then he jammed the throttles to the stops.

The engines roared and Doug cringed. They were doing some serious knots and he could barely see twenty meters ahead. *Thank the Lord for night vision.*

The boats carved through the black waters and Doug felt the boat gradually banking to the right. Through streaming eyes, he saw the occasional light onshore, some close, some distant. And crop fields, lots of them. Trees crowded the banks as they headed due south again.

After a few more minutes of high-speed manoeuvring, Costello slowed the boat. Dark waters hissed and foamed as they decelerated. They drifted in the middle of the river, the surrounding banks thick with palm groves. Night birds called and one or two flapped fast and low across the water. Tranquillity reclaimed the night.

Costello was muttering into his radio. A couple of the operators went to work on their dead buddy, stripping off his gear and weapons. One of them laid a hand on the corpse's chest and bowed his head in prayer.

The boats turned into the left bank and stopped in the reeds. Delta went ashore first. Doug waited then followed, quickly joined by Bosco and Sweet from the other boat. They crouched beneath the towering palms and began a whispered conference.

"What's happening?" Bosco asked.

Doug explained about the Feds. "We're getting extracted," he said, holding up the transmitter.

"Thank Christ."

"Fucking A." Sweet was watching the shadows beneath the trees, his M4 held low. "We're probably breaking all kinds of laws just by being here."

"That's not what worries me," Bosco said. "It's the Iraqis."

Doug leaned closer. "What about them?"

"Consider their position," Bosco whispered, making sure the civilians nearby couldn't hear him. "Let's assume they know about the virus. Doubtful, but just hear me out. If the tables were turned, if the US government discovered that two boatloads of potentially-infected Iraqis were cruising down the Potomac, what would we do?"

"Apache their asses," muttered Sweet.

"Exactly."

"So, what's to stop our own people doing it?" Doug speculated. "Didn't you say the State Department were culpable in all this?"

"Maybe, I don't know." Bosco shifted his carbine across his knees. "I'm so fucking tired I don't know what to think anymore."

"Heads up," Sweet warned.

Costello was headed through the trees towards them. He took a knee, rifle held loosely across his chest.

"I'm going to move everyone up to the tree line." He pointed gloved fingers at Doug and Bosco. "My guys are busy so you two need to bring Meyer ashore, okay?"

Doug frowned. "Meyer?" And then he realised. "Sure, of course."

"Appreciate that. Sweet, you've got their six."

"Aye, aye," the Marine whispered.

After the civilians had disembarked, Doug and Bosco manhandled Meyer onto the bank. He was heavier than Doug imagined, even after his rig and weapons had been stripped off. They carried him through the trees to the edge of the clearing.

"Help me hide him," Costello said. They found a deep thicket a short distance away and left Meyer beneath it, disguising the body as best they could with a ground sheet and foliage. When they'd finished, Doug thought it would be almost impossible to see but the insects would soon give

Meyer's position away. Costello noted the grid reference with his wrist GPS.

"Rest easy, brother," he whispered. "We'll be back to get you."

They followed Costello back to the tree line. Beyond, flat fields stretched away as far as the night would let them see. Some were sown with dark lines of crops, others bare and pale beneath the clear sky. Somewhere distant a dog barked.

"Listen up," Costello said. "When the embassy blew, they launched a helo from Kuwait, just in case an airlift was required. It's inbound now, but we need to get the beacon to the extraction point because they might only get one shot. And be advised, there's a lot of angry chatter on the Iraqi airwaves, so if you want to see home again, do exactly as I say, got it?"

Heads nodded in the dark. Sweet said, "Roger that."

Costello pointed across the fields.

"The others are out there already. We're heading after them, east for two clicks, then south. Middle of nowhere country. Space out and keep up. Use your eyes and ears, and no noise." He tapped Bosco's carbine with his finger. "Put your safety on."

"It is."

"Keep it that way unless I say otherwise. Sweet? We good?"

The Marine raised his thumb.

"Okay, let's move."

And then Costello was gone, out into the field. Doug followed, then Bosco. Further back, Sweet trailed them all. They kept to the border of the field where small scrub bushes marked its boundary. Costello was further ahead and would stop periodically to scan the horizon. Then he'd disappear into the dark again.

As Doug trudged on through the fields, his eyes grew accustomed to the night, his ears to the sounds of the sleeping countryside. A gentle breeze was blowing from the south, and a billion stars winked overhead. Far to the east, the sky had turned from black to a deep blue. Dawn was racing towards them, the helicopter too. It was going to be tight. So was getting to Holly in time. He prayed that Rick had taken matters into his own hands and snatched her, but he doubted it. Rick was a pro. He'd wait for Doug.

He stumbled, his Nikes kicking up dust. The adrenaline was leaving his system, replaced by creeping exhaustion. Doug was a fit guy, and he wondered how the civilians ahead of them were coping. *Survival is the greatest motivator*, he knew. It was certainly working for him.

He kept his eye on the horizon. Silhouettes became visible against the lightening sky. Then he saw Costello ahead, standing on a hard-packed dirt road, his NVGs sweeping the flat landscape. As Doug approached, Costello held up a hand - *wait*.

Doug was going to take a knee but he wasn't sure if he could get up again. Bosco appeared out of the dark, then Sweet.

"What's happening?" The RSO whispered. Costello crossed the road and pointed.

"See that outbuilding, Walker?"

It wasn't hard to spot, a single whitewashed structure with a straw roof tucked in the corner of a barren-looking field. "Got it."

"I need you and that transponder about fifty metres in front of it."

Before any of them could move, Delta jogged out of the darkness. They had a dangerous energy about them. Something was happening.

"What is it?" hissed Bosco.

Costello pointed to the north. Doug saw them, small pinpricks of light a couple of klicks away, moving parallel to their position. And moving fast.

"Our friends are back," Costello warned, "and everyone is too beat to run. If they head this way, we're going to have to stop them."

"How long?"

"Chopper is ten minutes out. Those trucks could be here in five if they make a right turn. Walker, move," he said, cocking his head. "Make sure that antenna is fully extended."

Doug ran across the road and out into the field. He saw the outbuilding a short distance away then movement in the surrounding shadows. The other survivors.

Bosco jogged out of the dark, breathing hard. The tac-vest and carbine looked like they were dragging him down. He looked over his shoulder.

"Let's pray those Iraqis haven't called up air support."

"They have to, right?"

"If they do, they'll probably wait until sunup."

"We'll be fine," Doug said, but he wasn't fooling anyone. He was scared, scared of not making it, not getting home. Scared of failing his daughter one more time. Maybe for the last time.

"Think we're going to make it?" Bosco whispered.

"I was just thinking the same—"

Doug's heart sank.

Light washed over the field. He spun around, saw the distant trucks heading their way. *No!*

Sweet came sprinting out of the darkness. "Take this!" he said, handing Doug a small plastic unit with white stencilling.

"What is it?"

"IR signalling beacon. Chopper's coming out of the south-west. That way!" he pointed.

"I'll round up the others," Bosco said and took off into the darkness.

"What about the trucks?"

"Snipers will take out the engine blocks. Hajis will have to hump a couple of hundred metres if we're lucky. Keep that beacon pointed south-west!"

And Sweet disappeared too. Doug held the beacon, pointed the invisible pulse out into the darkness. The sky was darker there, and the chopper would have no lights. He'd have to rely on—

"Walker!"

It was Bosco, leading the civilians into the field.

"Stay behind me!" Doug said. "And get everyone down. There might be incoming."

As if on cue, the sound of suppressed gunfire stuttered over the field. Doug prayed those Special Forces snipers were as good as he'd heard.

"That thing working?" Bosco asked. Doug could hear the note of fear in the RSO's voice. He felt it too.

"Christ knows. I'm so far out of my comfort zone I'm hanging—*fuck!*"

The bullet cracked overhead. Doug and Bosco hit the dirt. In the darkness, one of the civilians started crying.

"Quiet!" Bosco barked at them. Then he stared out at the horizon. Slowly he raised his arm. "What's that?"

Doug saw it too. Then he heard it. Hope soared. He turned the IR beacon towards the bulging black dot.

"Come on, baby!"

The dot got very big, very fast, and then it was banking overhead, a huge Chinook, the sound of its twin turboshaft engines incredible. Doug felt like cheering. He watched it carve through the air in an impossibly tight arc and head straight for him. It flared and settled on the ground twenty metres away, its huge rotors whipping dirt and chaff into eye-stinging clouds.

Doug's filthy polo and chinos were plastered to his body. Bosco yelled at the civilians and bullied them towards the rear ramp.

Doug turned and ran back to the dirt road, keeping low.

He crawled the last ten metres, searching for Costello and his team. Gunfire rang out across the fields. Bullets zipped and cracked around him. He forced himself lower.

"Costello!" he yelled above the noise.

He saw a figure run towards him and crouch by his side. Doug looked up at Costello as if he were crazy. "Get down for Chrissakes!"

"They can't shoot for shit," Costello told him. "Trouble is there's about eighty of them."

"Everyone's aboard. We've got to go, right now!"

Costello keyed his PTT switch. "We're Oscar-Mike. Someone tell the Jarhead." He slapped Doug on the shoulder and said, "Go. Don't stop."

And then Doug was running across the field, doubled over. He heard another round zip by and then the noise of the Chinook drowned everything else. He glanced at the cockpit as he ran past, saw the pilots calmly sitting in their seats, NVGs on, hitting switches and glancing out through the windshield like they were on a Sunday drive. They were also wearing bio-filter masks.

Above his head, the huge rotors beat the air. Bosco waited by the ramp. He was bathed in the dull red wash of the helicopter's interior light and held his carbine ready. The wind battered his hair, his filthy shirt and windbreaker.

"Where are they?" he shouted in Doug's ear.

"Right behind me!"

"Get inside!"

A helmeted crewman in a chemical suit and mask waved from the ramp. He directed him inside and Doug collapsed onto the bench seat, breathing hard. The civilians were seated up towards the cockpit, frightened faces either side of the grey fuselage. Another masked airman manned an M240 machine gun at the shoulder window. Doug looked past him but he couldn't see shit outside. Sweat poured off him and his heart hammered. Then Bosco was scrambling aboard, followed by Sweet, then Delta. Costello stepped aboard last and slapped the airman on the shoulder.

The engines roared and the aircraft lifted off the ground in a storm of chaff. It spun a hundred and eighty degrees, the ramp lifting with a piercing whine of hydraulics. Sweet smiled as he stood over Doug and held on to the grab rail as the nose dipped and the aircraft picked up speed. Doug blinked and wiped a hand across his face.

Blood.

Sweet pitched forward and hit the floor. Doug dropped to his knees.

"Sweet! What's wrong?"

Bosco stumbled across and knelt opposite. Sweet lay immobile, his eyes wide and unblinking, staring up at the cabin ceiling.

"Sweet?" Doug said, the word lost in the roar of the engines.

Costello knelt next to Bosco as the other operators gathered around. He twisted Sweet's head, and that's when Doug saw the bloody hole above Sweet's right ear. Blood ran down the Marine's neck, soaking his uniform, spreading across the floor plates.

Doug shook his head. He didn't understand. Sweet was alive when he climbed on board. He'd grinned at Doug, a *we made it* grin. How could he be dead?

He heard Costello shouting.

"Round must've caught him just before the ramp closed."

"At that range?" Drake said, hanging onto the grab rail. "Lucky shot."

"Not for him." Bosco cradled the young man's head, his hands covered in blood. He ran his fingers over the Marine's eyes, closing them forever.

It was too much for Doug. He was gripped by an overwhelming confusion of emotions; fear, guilt, loss, relief—a jumble of competing feelings so intense that it squeezed his throat and filled his eyes with tears. They ran freely down his bloodied face and Doug didn't have the strength to wipe them away. He looked at Bosco and saw he was struggling too.

To the east, the sun crept above the horizon as the night retreated to the west. The Chinook thundered low across the countryside, still wrapped beneath the cloak of darkness, ferrying its precious cargo back from the brink of death.

Towards safety.

Towards life.

CHAPTER 17

TERMINAL VELOCITY

HE WAS EXPECTING A VISITOR BUT HE DIDN'T KNOW WHO IT WAS. He heard footsteps out in the hallway, the quiet murmur of voices beyond the door. The words were indecipherable but the tone suggested congeniality.

He'd been quarantined at the Al-Salam airbase in Kuwait for almost a fortnight. He'd accepted the necessity of the incarceration because he understood the nature of the threat only too well, a threat that had led to the loss of over twelve hundred lives. He recognised the need for isolation, the void of information, the twenty-four-hour CCTV surveillance. He accepted the daily blood tests administered by bio-suited military personnel. He accepted the monotony of the interviews, the repetitive testimonies both written and verbal, the intrusive polygraphs. He'd borne the burden gratefully, because he was grateful to be alive.

He'd watched the world outside the barred window of his accommodation, the military planes that thundered overhead, the distant vehicles that shimmered in the blistering heat haze. Not many of them approached the remote cluster of buildings at the far edges of the airbase. He thought he knew why.

He thought about the Delta guys and hoped they'd recovered their fallen comrade from that distant palm grove. He wondered about the Marine, Sweet, and hoped he'd been given the burial he deserved. He felt an incredible urge to write it all down, not in the stunted, dehumanised language of a legal statement but words and phrases conjured from deep within himself. He wanted to record everything from the very beginning, his reactions, emotions, decisions and mistakes. He wanted to record the lives lost, the names of those around him, those he'd known and others he didn't. He felt a duty to them all, to record how he'd interacted with them, the words spoken, how they'd lived and died. He wanted the truth to be known as far as he could tell it.

The murmuring voices ceased. Footsteps receded. The door swung open.

He was grey-haired, mid-forties, light blue shirt, dark blue tie, dark suit. Not just a bureaucrat, something more. He approached the table and held out his hand.

"Mister Bosco, my name is Erik Mulholland. It's a pleasure to meet you finally."

Bosco stood and took the man's hand. A politician's hand. "Likewise," he said, and he meant it. Every day was a gift now.

Mulholland unbuttoned his jacket and took a seat across the table. He smoothed his tie as he looked around the windowless, stuffy room. "Are you being treated well? You have everything you need?"

"Pretty much," Bosco lied. Now was not the time to bare one's soul. He'd let the bureaucrat do all the talking. So he folded his arms and waited.

"Can I call you *Tom*?" Mulholland opened. "If I recall, the last time we spoke we'd dispensed with the formalities."

"Feels like a lifetime ago."

"I can't begin to imagine what you've been through. I hope you're bearing up."

Bosco registered a note in Mulholland's voice, a slight narrowing of the eyes as he spoke, as if he'd felt the pain of the experience himself. Bosco was surprised; maybe Mulholland was genuine.

"I'm fine. How are the others? The other survivors?"

"Traumatised. They're home with their families now but rest assured, the State Department takes care of its own. All of you are going to be given the support you need, for as long as you need it."

"That's good to know," Bosco said.

"I'm sure you have questions," Mulholland said.

Bosco unfolded his arms and leaned forward in his chair. "I have a lot of questions, Erik."

Mulholland nodded gravely. "I'm sure you do, and let me start by saying that your patience in this matter is much appreciated. I know the last week has been tough on all of you, but we've had to take the necessary precautions, the medical workups and so forth. And to record your statements while the events are still fresh in the mind."

"Not sure we'll ever forget them."

"State has your back, Tom. Anything you need."

"A few answers would help."

Mulholland nodded, holding Bosco's steady gaze. "You want to know about the coup, the warnings you were given—"

"You were wrong about Delta. Those guys saved our asses."

"This is true. However, the fact remains that factions in DC tried to circumvent the democratic process. I can't go into specific details but certain individuals are now the subject of a special investigation. People will be going to jail, Tom."

Bosco took that at face value. He knew DC well enough to know that even the most serious crimes could be swept under the carpet if it served the right people to do so.

"That's good to know, but there's so much more we don't know. The comms failures, the destruction of the embassy—"

"All of which is the subject of a separate State Department investigation. That's why your statements are so important. Getting to the truth is crucial."

Bosco could feel his irritation rising. Maybe he was wrong about Mulholland's sincerity because he knew what bullshit sounded like.

"Someone triggered those explosions, and I can tell you this much; it wasn't anyone in that embassy." He stabbed a finger on the table. "There's more to this than we've been told—"

"And you want answers," Mulholland finished. "Of course you do. You want to know why you were kept out of the loop on *Messina,* why you were not briefed about Grand Slam, and why you had no knowledge of the VIP escape facility. You want to know who cut the embassy off from the outside world and why the Northridge contractors were pulled from the perimeter walls. And no doubt you'll want to know why Bill Jacobs and his team were found dead in their bullet-riddled vehicles on the outskirts of Baghdad."

Bosco felt the blood drain from his face. "What?"

"I'm sorry to have to tell you, Tom. It seems they tried to make a run for the consulate at Erbil and were ambushed en route. ISIS, we think. The bodies were stripped and left by the roadside. Everything was taken, weapons, phones, IDs etcetera. A terrible tragedy."

"Jesus Christ," Bosco breathed. He'd assumed that somehow Bill and the others had made it, were in quarantine like himself. More deaths, more good people gone. "What about the virus itself? Is it still a threat?"

"The embassy has been sealed off. USAMRIID and CDC teams are still picking through the rubble, but so far they haven't found any survivors, infected or otherwise." He glanced over his shoulder at the closed door. When he spoke again, he dialled down the volume. "CCTV video has been recovered from the site. Many of us have seen the horror, Tom. A nuclear option is still on the table, should it be needed."

Bosco swallowed. "Nuke Baghdad?"

"If that's what it takes. Hopefully it won't come to that. The unpalatable truth is, Grand Slam might've saved the city."

"Yes, but the question remains; who pulled the trigger?"

"There's a theory that it was an automated process. That the system triggered itself after the Chancery was hit by the helicopter."

"That doesn't explain the flares and claymores," Bosco protested. "They happened long before that crash."

Mulholland shrugged. "It's frustrating, I know. The Baghdad embassy has reeked of controversy since its inception. We're pulling documents from the archives, the original structural designs, Pentagon briefing papers, Appropriations Committee minutes and suchlike, much of it still classified and Top Secret. There's a mountain of work to be done. It could take years to get to the bottom of it all."

Mulholland propped his elbows on the tabled and steepled his fingers.

"It seems that the original concept was to create a fortress in the heart of Baghdad, one that could defend itself and, if necessary, destroy itself. Grand Slam was the bastard-child of some pretty paranoid thinking. A dark period of American history."

"Times have changed," Bosco noted.

"Indeed, yet the system was never decommissioned. In fact its infrastructure was regularly maintained and updated, albeit under a cloak of secrecy. We're going to find out how that was possible and who signed it off."

Mulholland took an envelope from inside his jacket and

placed it on the table in front of him. Bosco glanced at it - *was he getting fired? Or indicted?*

"There's still so much we don't know," Mulholland continued, "but what we do know is that a terrible tragedy has occurred. We also know that a global catastrophe was avoided, thanks to the bravery and actions of the people in that embassy. People like you, Tom. You've shown exemplary courage and leadership throughout this whole crisis."

Bosco opened his mouth to protest but Mulholland silenced him with a raised hand.

"You don't agree. Neither did the other survivors. They struggled with the concept of personal heroism, argued strongly against it in fact, but America is not ready to hear that twelve hundred lives were lost because mistakes were made. They want to believe that twelve hundred Americans who were doing their duty far from home made the ultimate sacrifice to protect others."

Bosco snorted. "We ran for our lives, that's the truth."

Mulholland smoothed the envelope in front of him. "It's not about the truth, Tom. It's about your duty to a wounded Republic that remains adrift on a sea of uncertainty. Soon we'll have a new President, which will go some way to restoring balance. That president is likely to be Secretary Coffman, and I can tell you that this event has troubled her deeply. If the American people decide to put her in the Oval Office, she's going to leave no stone unturned. Justice will be served, but in the meantime the country needs something to cling to. They need to rationalise the loss of so many lives. They need a story of courage and American exceptionalism." Mulholland paused for a dramatic beat, then said, "They need to hear *your* voice, Tom."

He pushed the envelope across the table. Bosco picked it up, felt the weight and quality of its creamy paper, the State Seal embossed on its flap. The name, handwritten with a creative swirl of real ink: *Tom Bosco.*

"It's a personal letter. I can't tell you what's in it but I can tell you that Secretary Coffman wants you to consider her words very carefully."

Bosco waved the letter in his hand. "I will. And please thank her for me."

"I have a better idea." Mulholland stood and buttoned his jacket. "You can thank her yourself. I have a jet waiting to take us back to DC. Secretary Coffman wants to meet you, Tom. She wants to talk to you about your future."

Mulholland walked to the door and held it open.

"I know you don't have any belongings so why don't we get straight on board? We can be wheels up in ten minutes and there's a suite waiting for you at The Hay Adams. What do you think, Tom?"

Bosco stared at the envelope in his hands. He still had so many questions, but being in DC might give him the answers he was still desperately searching for. He also needed to get as far away from Baghdad as possible.

He pushed his chair back and stood.

"I think I'm ready to go home."

Six-thousand-four-hundred-and-twenty-eight miles away, another jet was lifting off the runway at Dulles International Airport, Washington DC.

There were only two passengers onboard the one-hundred-and-twenty-six-seater Kroll Industries Boeing 737-300 and they each occupied window seats on opposite sides of the aisle. They were excited, which was why both men nursed very large twelve-year-old malt whiskeys in crystal-cut glasses. They had much to celebrate, because today was payday. Today they were cashing in.

The plane left the ground at six-thirty-two pm local time and climbed quickly, bumping through low clouds until they broke through into clear blue skies at twenty-two thousand feet above the Delaware countryside. The Boeing continued to climb, soaring through the thin air until it reached its cruising altitude of thirty-six thousand feet. The flight time to Grand Cayman was just over three hours, and when the seatbelt light chimed off, both men snapped their belts loose and stretched out.

"Nice out there," Chuck said, looking out of the window. The clouds were below and behind them now, and the earth consisted of nothing more than blue sky and endless sea. Chuck tipped back the contents of his glass, served to him by a smoking hot redhead just before they'd taken off. He was in the mood for another. He was also in the mood for the stewardess. He pressed the call button above his seat and tried to get Eugene's attention. Eugene was looking out of the window.

"Hey, you want a drink, buddy?"

Eugene shook his head, still staring out of the window. "I'm good. I'm going to wait until we get to the hotel."

"Your choice. You think maybe that stewardess will join us?"

"I doubt it."

Chuck grinned. "You don't think I've got a shot? Five grand says the bitch'll be waking up in my bed tomorrow morning."

Eugene turned to look at him. He was grinning too. "You didn't see? She got off the plane. Looks like you'll have to make do with some local ass."

Chuck frowned. He looked up at the display above his seat, at the call sign that went unanswered. "So who's taking care of us?"

Eugene shrugged and turned back to the window. "Maybe it's a self-service deal. And while you're back there, see if you can find something to eat."

Chuck pulled himself up and headed to the rear of the plane. He dragged back the curtain, saw the empty attendant seat, the small galley to his right. He raided the cupboards for Johnny Walker miniatures and several snack packs. He dropped a couple onto the seat next to Eugene.

"You're right, the bitch *did* get off. Her loss."

"Yeah, she'll be devastated," Eugene chuckled.

Chuck retook his seat. He topped up his drink and tipped some nuts into his mouth, chewing as he watched the world drift by outside. He read a few pages of a magazine. He took a nap. Turbulence shook him awake a little later. Outside the sky had turned from blue to grey. He stretched and yawned. Across the aisle, Eugene was reading a paperback. "How long 'til we get to Cayman?"

"Two hours," Eugene told him, glancing at his watch. Then he looked at Chuck and said, "I hope so at least."

"What do you mean?"

"We've been heading east since we took off."

Chuck laughed. "What are you, a goddam Eagle Scout?"

"The sun's directly behind us, you dumb fuck. Has been since we left DC. We're flying due east. We should be heading south."

Chuck crossed the aisle and slid into the seat behind Eugene. He stared out of the window, trying to see what Eugene was seeing. There was a thin layer of cloud far below them. Beneath that, a grey slab of ocean dotted with tiny white caps.

"So where the fuck are we?"

"Somewhere over the Atlantic."

"Goddamit."

Chuck stood up and marched towards the cockpit. He pulled back the aisle curtain and saw another empty attendant seat. He checked the toilets; also empty, likewise the forward galley. He cleared his throat and tapped on the cockpit door.

"Guys, this is Charles Jackson, one of your passengers. Can I have a word?"

Chuck waited for a response. Nothing. He knocked a little louder. "Guys, can we get an ETA on our arrival?" Still nothing. Eugene appeared behind him.

"What's going on?"

"They're not answering."

"So knock a little louder."

Chuck rapped his knuckles on the cockpit door. "Guys, can you hear me? We need a little information out here."

They waited for an answer but all they heard was the dull roar of the engines as they headed further east.

"Motherfuckers are ignoring me," Chuck snarled. He banged on the door. "What is this, some kind of FAA thing? We're Kroll executives and we've got important company business in Grand Cayman, goddammit."

Eugene put his ear to the cockpit door. "This is bullshit. They can't treat us like this."

"Damn straight," Chuck agreed. He hammered on the door with a big fist. The door shook. "Open this fucking door right now or I'll have your jobs."

The door remained locked. Chuck cursed and marched back down the plane. He returned a moment later with a large screwdriver. "Stand back."

Eugene stepped out of the way. Chuck jammed the screwdriver into a gap above the lock and began to work it.

"Don't be assholes, open the goddamn door," Chuck grunted as he forced the lock. Then something snapped and the door opened a couple of inches. Chuck shouted through the gap.

"This is on you guys. I didn't want to do this."

Chuck barged the door with his shoulder and it swung open, crashing against the bulkhead. He stepped into the cockpit.

"What the fuck?"

Eugene pushed past him.

The cockpit was empty.

All the instruments appeared to be functioning normally, a myriad of displays, lights and digits. There was even a small camera on top of the instrument panel, pointed directly at the door. But no pilots.

"Jesus Christ," Eugene whispered.

"Where the fuck are they?" Chuck said.

"There never were any pilots," Eugene stammered. "The plane's being controlled remotely." He looked at Chuck, his face drained of blood. "They fucked us, man. They really fucked us."

The engines suddenly wound down, the whine fading to nothing. An eerie, unnatural silence filled the aircraft. Then the nose began to dip.

"No, no, no, no!" Chuck jabbered, his eyes widening, his heart racing.

The instrument panel suddenly flickered and died. The cabin lights went out. The nose dipped further and suddenly Chuck could see the whitecaps thousands of feet below.

He lost his footing and fell forward into the cockpit. He braced himself between the pilots' seats and then Eugene cried out and fell into him. Chuck collapsed onto the flight controls, levers and buttons digging painfully into soft flesh, scraping against hard bone. He pummelled Eugene with his fists, cursing in fear and rage as the aircraft plunged into a terminal dive and started to spin out of control.

Chuck felt himself being tossed around the cockpit, his bones breaking against instrument panels and bulkheads, against Eugene who bled like a skewered pig, spraying blood around the cockpit. Chuck prayed his own head would hit something, knock him out, but then he flew sideways and found himself wedged against the cockpit window. He saw the whitecaps spinning wildly below, heard the roar of the air rushing by, and then he heard an earsplitting crack as something broke loose from the airframe.

The plane fell from the sky.

He saw Eugene bleeding and clinging to the seat above him, praying to a God he'd never believed in. Chuck turned his head, his face jammed against the cockpit glass.

The ocean filled the window. The whitecaps had become cold, dark rolling waves. The airframe shuddered and screamed. Eugene screamed.

Chuck closed his eyes.

The plane hit the Atlantic Ocean at seven-fifty-one pm local time and disappeared beneath the waves.

CHAPTER 18
CLICKBAIT

The cell phone rumbled across the nightstand, insistent.

Amy Coffman reached out and snatched at the offending device that had interrupted a particularly thrilling dream. She'd found herself standing behind the lectern inside a packed White House Press Briefing Room, fielding questions from the media. She'd handled each one with courtesy, authority and intelligence, and the smiling, eager faces had responded with fawning respect. As arms were raised and attention sought, Coffman had signalled to the seasoned, sycophantic reporter from CNN who gushed…

Thank you, Madam President.

Coffman turned off the alarm. Her dreams had become reality. Recently she'd started to imagine what else she was capable of.

She lay there a while longer, savouring the luxury of the handmade bed, the thirty-thousand-dollar Kluft mattress, the Braun Shanghai bedding, nestling in the insanely expensive eiderdown duvet. The reality of Camp David was a far cry from her preconceptions.

She'd imagined a collection of musty log cabins, stinking of damp and crawling with bugs. She's imagined filthy boots squelching along muddy paths, the harsh bite of winter drying her skin to parchment, the burning heat of summer giving birth to clouds of insects. She'd wondered why former presidents had sought the sanctuary of the Maryland retreat, but then again, they were boys. Boys liked to squat around smoky wood fires, getting drunk and singing songs, pissing against trees and howling at the moon.

That was the Camp David of her imagination. The reality was far different.

The cabins were state-of-the-art and luxuriously appointed, comparable to anything that Coffman had experienced. Aspen Lodge, the presidential cabin, was huge, with several bedrooms, a magnificently appointed dining room and a climate control system that ensured the wilderness outside the bullet-proof windows would never encroach upon her unless invited. In the three months since President Amelia Coffman had been inaugurated, this was her sixth visit to Camp David.

She was a convert.

Coffman rolled out of bed and padded into the walk-in shower. She dressed in sturdy boots, a pair of tailored outdoor trousers and a thick coat. She'd taken to walking every morning before breakfast, a routine she'd shared with the media on several occasions. Coffman had proven herself to be a forthright and honest presidential candidate, and that had endeared her to the nation. As predicted, it had also ensured her ascension to the Oval Office.

Baghdad had proved to be the vote-winner she'd expected it to be. In the wake of the disaster, Coffman had back-channelled with the Aswad's, ensuring her narrative gained traction. She'd travelled to Iraq several times, and the scale of the destruction had truly shocked her. During her last visit, just before the final presidential debate, she'd delivered the speech that had sealed the fate of the other candidates.

The memorial event was held in the Grand Festival

Square, between the famous Swords of Victory monuments. The audience was huge, and consisted of US, foreign and Iraqi dignitaries, bereaved families and carefully vetted Iraqi citizens. Coffman had milked the opportunity for all its potential. She'd worn a black chiffon Hijab and spoke passionately of American courage and sacrifice. She'd addressed the Iraqi citizens directly and thanked them for their own bravery, their continued tenacity and stoicism in the face of historic adversity, and she did it all in flawless Arabic that earned her an ecstatic ovation that had lasted for several minutes. Her words - and her candidacy - had been further endorsed by President Aswad, praising the bravery of the unknown Americans who'd sacrificed their own lives in order to save Baghdad and its teeming populace.

Coffman's crafted narrative had become fact. The victims had become heroes, their stories, modern-day legends. The Secretary of State had left the country with the roar of a grateful nation ringing in her ears.

Days later, her political stock still rising, Coffman had wiped the floor with her opponents. The media had anointed her. For once, the polls had proved accurate. The presidency was hers.

Yet there was still work to be done, a loose end to be tied. A potential thorn to be removed from her side. Admiral Schultz was aware of that thorn and waited for her in the snug. He was dressed casually in a blue turtleneck and corduroy pants. He greeted her warmly and Coffman smiled. She was no longer *the cunt* because Admiral Charles Schultz was her new Chairman of the Joint Chiefs of Staff. As she'd sensed, they had more in common that they'd both imagined. They had become allies, then friends.

"How are you, Charlie?"

"Good."

She took a seat on the sofa opposite him. Schultz was nursing a coffee.

"How's General Moody?"

Schultz shook his head. "Deteriorating. The family are making preparations for the worst."

They'd found Moody in his den, lying face down on the floor. He'd been that way for several hours. Coffman was pretty sure that she'd put him there because she'd spoken to him on the telephone that very evening. She'd assured him that the lives lost in Baghdad were on his conscience, the blame for the virus to be laid directly at his door. His incompetence and a grave lack of judgement would be exposed for America to see because the people needed a scapegoat. Coffman had ended the call with a smile on her face. The ensuing stroke was a wonderful and unexpected footnote. Without nature's intervention, Coffman thought the general might've eaten a bullet. Either way, Moody was history.

"We should also prepare," she told Schultz.

"I'll make some calls."

"Thanks, Charlie." She got to her feet. "How do I look?"

"Vulnerable," he told her. "You're sure about this?"

"It's the only way."

Schultz stood and took her hands in his, squeezed them. "Good luck, Madame President."

At the door, a white-coated Navy steward handed her a Brazilian roast in a reusable thermo cup and bid her a pleasant walk. That had also become part of her daily Camp David routine.

Outside, beneath grey skies, her Secret Service detail waited. They were dressed in winter clothes and brandished a variety of automatic weapons, and for the fourth day in a row Coffman waved them off. The detail leader complained but Coffman was adamant. Camp David bristled with layers of security. She needed peace and quiet, to think and strategise. The country was relying on her.

Besides, Coffman didn't like guns. They were obscene tools, made readily available to most by a Constitution that was dangerously outdated. She had plans for that troublesome Second Amendment, but they were for the future, once another term was assured.

She left the compound behind and continued into the woods, heading up towards the ridge that offered stunning views across the Catoctin Mountain Park. There she would sit and enjoy her coffee. And wait. She hoped it would be today.

A fine mist crept up from the valley and settled across the hills. Shale crunched beneath her boots. The path ahead meandered up through the trees, the ground to the right falling away towards a steep-sided gorge. Far below, boulders glistened in the shadows. Coffman kept to the steep left bank, unwilling to venture near the edge. She didn't care for heights and the path could often be slippery during inclement weather. With fall fast approaching and the trees starting to shed their leaves, Coffman would have to find other routes on which to take her walks.

A bird screeched overhead, and the sound startled her. Ahead the path wound upwards into the mist. She glanced behind; deserted, the shale ribbon swallowed by the shifting fog. Coffman suddenly felt very alone and vulnerable.

Twigs snapped close by. She turned, searching the trees. A figure descended the bank towards her and Coffman almost screamed. Its head and body were festooned with long, loose strips of green and brown material that matched the surrounding terrain perfectly. It looked like a creature from a horror movie, a faceless monstrosity. It jumped down onto the path in front of her, and Coffman took a couple of frightened steps back.

"Don't fucking move," the creature growled. He pulled off the hood he was wearing and she saw a face that was streaked with green and black camouflage paint. She saw hard eyes and a thick moustache that drooped above the man's top lip. His gloved hands were empty but that didn't make him any less dangerous. Coffman had never been so scared in all her life.

"Who are you?"

"Keep your voice down," he warned, and Coffman complied. She hadn't been spoken to like that for as long as she could remember and it was a wholly unnerving experience.

"How did you get in here? This is private property."

"Technically it's a Naval Support Facility. I wouldn't expect you to know that, given your contempt for the uniform."

"What are you talking about?"

He took a step closer. "I watched all your speeches. The debates, the memorials; the one in Baghdad was a real crowd-pleaser."

"I hoped I—"

"Shut your mouth." He brought his hand up, a hand that held a black, vicious-looking knife. "You spoke of bravery, of sacrifice, and that's all true, but you don't know the half of it, lady."

"You were there," Coffman whispered. It wasn't a question.

The man nodded. "You condemned us all to death."

"What are you talking about? We tried to save you."

He took another step closer. The knife was held low now, and well within striking distance. She had to hold her nerve.

"I know about the lies you spun Ashcroft and Bosco. I know you pulled the contractors—"

"You're wrong," Coffman blurted.

The man slapped her across the mouth. She staggered backwards, spilling her coffee to the ground. He grabbed her by the collar of her coat and dragged her towards the edge of the gorge.

"Wait! Please don't do this!" Her eyes rolled wildly, searching the surrounding woods, the thick grey mist.

"Quiet!" the man hissed, shaking her like a rag doll. The knife came up to her face, brushed against her neck. "Northridge was ordered to kill anyone who left that embassy. Admit it."

"How can you—?"

"You think I ain't connected? That I don't know people? That order came from the top. The Iraqi's, they were in on it too."

"No," Coffman stammered, forcing herself to remain calm. "You're wrong. Whoever's feeding you this information is using you. Let me go, please. I'll tell you everything I know. The truth."

The man spat on the path. "You wouldn't know the truth if it ran you over, you lying sack of shit. I came here to tell you that you didn't get away with it. You murdered twelve hundred Americans and used their memory to steal the White House. You've signed your own death warrant, Coffman. Hell's waiting for—"

The dull thud punched the air from his lungs and he staggered backwards, dropping the knife to the ground. Coffman scrambled away from the edge. The man bent down and picked up the knife. He grunted as the second punch threw him backwards against the bank. He slid down it and dropped on his backside, wheezing, staring at Coffman with hateful eyes.

Coffman stepped forward and picked up the knife. Two men came running out of the mist. Both wore woodland camouflage and carried suppressed marksman rifles on slings across their chests.

"Are you okay, Madame President?"

"I'm fine." She heard a scrape of loose shale and saw Schultz hurrying up the path towards her. "You cut it close."

"We lost you in the fog. The guys had to reset, reacquire. Here."

He handed her a handkerchief and she dabbed at the cut inside her lip. "No harm done."

She waited until her would-be assassin had been thoroughly searched then squatted down in front of him. "It's Nick, right?" She saw his hooded eyes register surprise. "Oh, come on, Mister Costello. Are you really that naive? You and your Delta buddies were put under surveillance the moment you got back from Baghdad. I've heard the tapes, Nick, especially the ones where you tell the others what you'd like to do to me. They didn't seem that interested but you had a real hard-on for me, isn't that right, Nick?"

Costello glared at her like a wounded bear, his chin resting on his chest. Blood leaked between his teeth. "You...won't..." He coughed, spraying blood over his chin.

Coffman smiled and patted his leg. "Don't go yet, Nick. I want you to hear how you failed. You people hate to fail, right?"

Costello wheezed. Coffman smiled.

"We were on you the moment you handed in your papers and walked out of Fort Bragg. We saw your internet searches about Camp David, the articles about my long, lonely walks. We watched you and we let you in here, Nick. We let you set up shop and you swallowed the bait. And now look at you."

Costello spluttered, his throat rattling. "There'll... be...others..."

"And I pray they'll be as incompetent as you. By the way, the guys that killed you? Northridge. Take that to the unmarked hole they're going to bury you in." She got to her feet, slapping her hands clean. She took a look over her shoulder, at the deep gorge behind her. Costello had almost made it. "Walk me back, Charlie."

Schultz spoke briefly to the contractors and escorted Coffman back down the ridge. As the path behind them was swallowed by the mist, Coffman linked her arm through the Admiral's.

"Make sure he disappears. I don't want to see a coyote running through the compound with one of Costello's hands in its mouth."

Schultz smirked. "The hole's already dug. No one will ever find him."

"I hope you are right, because we have a great future ahead of us. There's so much to be accomplished. We can't risk it by being sloppy."

Schultz patted her hand as they walked side-by-side down the misty ribbon of shale. "I'm a details man," he told her. "You have my word that things will be taken care of properly."

"That's good to know. And speaking of trust, Bob Blake and Matt Sorenson are coming to dinner tonight. Erik too. Bob tells me there are some exciting new developments in the UAV field. Breakthrough stuff."

"Sounds interesting," Schultz admitted.

"We'll see. Bob gets wood just thinking about that kind of thing."

Schultz laughed and Coffman unlinked her arm. Ahead the mist had cleared and the compound came into view. Her Secret Service detail looked relieved. *If only you knew,* Coffman waved.

The threat Costello presented had been real, the trap a risky one, but the thought of having a rogue Special Forces operator hunting her down had caused her sleepless nights. The plan had worked although it had scared the piss out of her. Hopefully it would be the last time she was required to dangle herself on a hook.

With each new sunrise, the events in Baghdad retreated further into history. There would always be whispers of course, both here and in Iraq, of nefarious political skullduggery. *Cui Bono?* they will ask, and fingers will indeed point to those who benefitted. Over time those whispers would build into conspiracy theories, some of which would gain serious traction. Erik had a whole team monitoring the internet for them, but right now people were still consumed by the impeachment and incarceration of former President Stein. His demise would keep the keyboard detectives busy for a while longer.

Again, she considered visiting Bob in his Colorado prison. She imagined herself smiling sweetly as she inquired as to the frequency of his ass-raping, then decided against it. It was petty vindictiveness and a waste of her precious time. Bob Stein and his New World Order were old news. That was all behind her now. What lay ahead was a bright world of opportunity.

She saw Erik Mulholland standing outside her lodge, talking on his cell. He saw her and waved.

"Lunch at one-thirty," Coffman told the Admiral as they parted.

"I look forward to it, Madame President."

She watched him peel away towards his own cabin. Bizarrely, her cold brush with death had given her quite the appetite. The violence had excited her, she realised, much like the footage from Baghdad had. Watching it again and again had become a guilty pleasure.

As Erik smiled and kissed her on both cheeks, she wondered where that dark gratification might take her in the months and years ahead.

CHAPTER 19
GONE GIRL

Doug Walker paid for another vodka and orange and took it to a quiet corner of the Hilton's Grill and Bar restaurant. It was his second drink of the evening but Doug wasn't planning on getting loaded. Instead, he needed something to smooth out his mood, and he didn't want the stink of beer on his breath. Not today of all days.

The bar was pretty empty and that suited Doug because now was not the time for small talk. The bartender had tried and failed, and now the kid had turned his attention to a young Hispanic waitress. Doug sipped his drink and tried to relax, but it was proving very difficult. His emotions were like clothes in a tumbler.

He looked at his watch. A whole two minutes had passed since the last time he'd checked. His heart pounded. Holly was on her way. He could sense her getting closer with each passing minute, could feel the bond between them strengthening. It wouldn't be long before she was standing right in front of him. Doug took a deep breath and another sip of vodka.

They were travelling from Ascension to El Paso, which was about a hundred-and-twenty-mile drive, most of it freeway. They'd cross the border at the Paso del Norte International Bridge, hopefully without any problems. After that it was a short twenty-minute hop to the hotel.

The investigator had warned him that the crossing could be a choke point. He also said that because it was late on a Monday evening and a thunderstorm was rolling across the area, they should be able to transit the border reasonably quickly. Doug did the calculation; a half hour, maybe less. He took another sip of vodka. Holly was coming home.

He'd only just made it himself.

He closed his eyes. The roar of the Chinook filled the bar.

He felt the wheels thump down on the Kuwaiti airbase. He heard the whine of the ramp being lowered. Blinding light had filled the chopper. They were ordered out, told to sit on the ground. The Chinook took off again and things got real quiet. Shadows moved behind the floodlights. A voice through a bullhorn told them to strip, every man and woman, soldier and civilian. One by one they passed naked through a decontamination shower. Doug had looked over his shoulder and saw Sweet's body lying on the tarmac, surrounded by abandoned clothes, gear and weapons. It was one of the saddest sights he'd ever seen.

He remembered being handed a set of medical scrubs by a bio-suited soldier and that scared him. Half the infected had worn medical scrubs.

The civilians were led away in one group, Costello and what remained of his Delta team in another. It was the last time Doug saw any of them. He wondered where Costello was now. He made a mental note to look him up once Holly was safe and settled.

Doug stirred a little orange in with his vodka. Thinking about the past was helping pass the time. It also dredged up other emotions.

He remembered the anger he'd felt when they'd refused his demands to make a phone call. He was detained in a cinderblock building that was barred and locked. Bio-suited guards patrolled outside.

He made his first phone call forty-eight hours later. Doug learned that Holly and the Flores kid had already walked out of their Brooklyn hotel and boarded a Greyhound bound for El Paso. With Doug still MIA, Rick Gould was unable to intervene or authorise continued surveillance, but he asked a local contact in El Paso to meet the Greyhound. Holly and Flores were not on board. Doug found out later that they'd crossed into Mexico via Fort Hancock. Holly disappeared after that. The following week in quarantine was the longest of Doug's life.

They'd interviewed him endlessly. They'd even polygraphed him. Doug told them about the power cut but not about the accusations of sabotage. He figured they'd bring that up, but no one ever did so he kept his mouth shut. After ten days they said he could go home.

They gave him clothes and a new passport. He'd left Kuwait in a C-17 Globemaster with a State Department minder for company. The plane refuelled in Germany and then flew onto Langley AFB in Virginia. It took two cabs and a three-hour bus ride before Doug made it home to the trailer park in Gainesville.

He'd met with Rick Gould in Philly the next day. Gould was apologetic and Doug had understood. He told Rick the truth about where he'd been and Gould was staggered that Doug had made it back. He promised to try and reacquire Holly for a reduced fee. Doug thanked him and left.

After a call from his line manager, Doug drove to the DOD Civilian Contracts Office in Rosslyn, Virginia, where he was interviewed by two very concerned HR managers. He was offered a full mental and physical health support package, which Doug had expected. What he didn't expect was the immediate bank deposit of eighty-one thousand dollars and change. Some of it was due but the rest was hazard pay and a bonus. There would be a further compensation payment in the weeks ahead, they'd told him, a significantly higher sum. All Doug had to do was update his confidentiality agreements with the United States government. He did, and he left Rosslyn with his Top-Secret clearance intact and a sizeable chunk in the bank. It was hush money, he knew that, but Doug didn't care. He wanted his life back. That meant finding Holly. Now he had the means to do it.

The call came nine long weeks later. Rick told him there'd been a hit on Holly's Freedom card in the Mexican town of Ascension. Doug had been elated and quietly terrified; the town was pretty lawless, even by Mexican standards, and an American girl would be a prime target.

Rick Gould despatched a local agent across the border. He'd asked around, greased a few palms with Doug's money. Finally, he got word; Holly was staying with a couple of American kids in a house on the edge of town. There was no sign of Flores, and the other kids were hippy backpackers who liked to smoke weed. Rick told him that a physical intervention south of the border was not advisable. They had to get Holly back into the States. Doug was encouraged to write a letter. It was a non-confrontational ice-breaker, and besides, a local guy, Raul, was watching her. If she bolted again, they'd find her. Doug didn't have any choice.

He sent the letter and made the trip south. By the time he got to El Paso, Holly had read the letter. Raul left word with Rick's office. It was good news; Holly had agreed to come home.

Doug had broken down in his room. That was twenty-fours ago. It was the longest night of his life.

He checked his watch; it was almost time. He finished his drink and went outside. He took a seat beneath the covered terrace and watched the wind drive silver sheets of rain across the half-empty parking lot. He took a cigar out of his shirt pocket and lit it, allowing the smoke to roll around his mouth before the wind snatched it away. He wasn't much of a cigar smoker but it helped to countdown the clock.

Rain drummed the awning above him. It bounced off the road as cars hissed by on the strip. Doug watched them all, waiting for one of them to turn into the parking lot. That would be his cue. That's why a large golf umbrella waited on the table next to the ashtray.

Lightning lit up the surrounding mountains as the storm drifted over the city. Thunder rumbled across the night sky. Doug thought about his next move once Holly was home. A move out of the trailer park and into the rented duplex at Spyglass Hill. Doctors, therapists, whatever it took. He had to learn to listen and not to judge. It would take time and lots of love. Doug was in it for the long haul.

Headlights swept across the terrace and a silver Nissan saloon turned into the parking lot. It beeped its horn once and flashed its headlights. Doug ditched the cigar and grabbed the umbrella. He snapped it open and ran out into the lot. The rain soaked his pants but Doug didn't notice. His heart threatened to burst out of his chest.

The Nissan pulled into a parking spot outside the main entrance. The driver killed the lights and Doug caught a glimpse of someone in the passenger seat, long hair, smoking a cigarette. The driver's door swung open and the local investigator, Raul, climbed out. He was overweight and held a newspaper over his short black hair. He trotted towards Doug.

"Señor Walker," he began, but Doug was already pushing past him. He held the umbrella over the passenger door and yanked it open.

Doug's heart was in his mouth.

The man looked up at him. He was about Holly's age, with bloodshot eyes and a smile of crooked teeth. He had long, dirty-blond hair and wore shorts and a Hawaiian shirt. Doug stared at him for several speechless seconds.

"Who are you?"

Raul stood by the hood, rain dripping off his soggy newspaper. "Señor Walker, this is Scott, your daughter's friend. She sent Scott to give you a message."

Scott nodded. "She got your letter. Powerful stuff, dude. Brought a tear to my eye."

"*You* read it?"

"Holly wanted me to. She said I needed to understand."

Doug's mind reeled. "Who the fuck are you?"

The kid bared his crooked teeth again. "Something wrong with your hearing, hombre? Scott. Or Scotty. Whatever."

Doug leaned into the car. The kid smelt of weed. "Where's my daughter?" Thunder rumbled overhead.

"She's gone."

Panic flooded Doug's system. "What d'you mean *gone*?"

Scott shrugged. "She didn't say and I didn't ask. One thing you gotta understand about Holly, she's a free spirit, man. No one can touch her. Especially you—"

Doug flung the umbrella away and grabbed Scott's shirt. He dragged him out of the car and into the rain. Scott fell to the ground, his shirt ripped and flapping open. The rain plastered his hair flat. He looked like he was going to cry.

"What the fuck, man?"

Raul grabbed Doug's arm but he shook the investigator off. He dragged Scott to his feet and slammed him against the car.

"Where is she?" Rain hammered the Nissan's roof.

"I told you, she's gone."

"Why are you here? Why did she send you?" Doug slapped the kid hard around the face. He regretted it the moment his hand made contact. He yanked him back to his feet. Scott's eyes were wide with fear and pain. He shouted over the thunder.

"She said you'd help me! That I could take her place!"

Doug shook him harder. "What the fuck are you talking about?"

"I told you, man, I read the letter. You want to make things right with Holly. You want to help her because of what happened with her mom. It's the guilt, right?"

Doug buried his fist into Scott's ribcage. The kid went down onto his knees, clutching his belly and gasping for air. Both of them were soaked through. Raul had retreated beneath the awning and was talking on a cell. Doug watched the umbrella tumble away across the strip. He was breathing hard. His stomach churned. Scott was babbling something and Doug dropped him back into the passenger seat. The kid was sobbing, trying to talk.

"What?"

"I said, Holly don't need your help, man. She said that if you want to make it up to her, you should help me."

Doug couldn't believe what he was hearing. "Help you? Why?"

Scott's face screwed up in self-pity. "I got problems, man, that's why. Serious issues you know? Booze, smack, whatever. She said you should take care of me."

Doug grabbed Scott by the throat. He pulled his hair back with the other hand and snarled, "Where's Holly? Tell me, now!"

"She's gone," Scott spluttered.

"When did she leave?"

"I don't remember. Couple of days ago."

"Where was she headed?"

"She didn't fucking say, man! Let me go! You're choking me!"

Doug backed away a few paces. His clothes were stuck to his body and the rain ran off his nose and chin. He didn't feel any of it. Right now, he felt nothing. He was running on empty.

Scott was coughing, a deep, wet smokers' hack. "She

didn't tell me where she was going, man. I got trust issues, you know? I get high and I run off at the mouth."

He flinched as Doug leaned into the car. He reached into his pocket and dumped a roll of wet bills in Scott's lap. The kid's eyes widened. As he gathered up the money, Doug grabbed his thin wrist and shoved a business card in his hand.

"You find out where she is, there's more where that came from. A lot more, you understand me?"

"Sure, dude, I can do that." Scott was beaming crooked teeth. He shoved the money into his shorts. "Tell Raul I'll get the bus back over the border."

He climbed out of the Nissan and hurried across the lot towards the main strip. By the time Doug noticed the business card screwed up and lying in a puddle of rainwater, Scott had disappeared around the distant corner.

"How much did you give him?"

Raul appeared at Doug's elbow. It was only then that he noticed that the rain had stopped.

"Five hundred."

"He'll go and get loaded somewhere. I doubt he'll remember any of this in the morning. If he lives that long."

"Do you know where my daughter went?"

Raul shook his head. "I never saw her. The pickup was arranged by phone and I brought the kid here. That was the longest two hundred miles I've ever driven. He never shut up." He flicked his cigarette across the lot. "I'm going to head back to Ascension, see if there's a trail to be found. Might take a while."

"Understood," Doug muttered.

Raul held out his hand. "I'm sorry, Señor Walker."

Doug shook his hand. "Thanks for trying."

"I'll be in touch."

Doug watched the Nissan's brake lights flare as it slowed

for the turn out onto the strip. A few seconds later the car was gone. Doug's hopes and prayers went with it.

Is this it? he wondered. *Is this where the search ends? A hotel parking lot on the Mexico border?* Because that's how it felt. There was no one in sight, no guests coming or going, no cars to be seen, no life. Doug felt like the last man on earth.

If Holly was gone - really gone - then it was pointless surviving Iraq. Better to have died in Baghdad than live a life of pain, uncertainty and regret.

Yet where there was life, there was hope.

Holly was out there somewhere, he knew that much, and he prayed his daughter would be safe on her travels. He prayed that wherever she was going she would be happy, that someday, somehow, she would find it in her heart to forgive him and come home. Until then, he would never stop hoping. And searching.

The storm mustered a parting rumble as it crossed the mountains and faded into the distance.

Doug stood there for a moment longer then headed back to the hotel.

CHAPTER 20
OPEN BORDERS

THE SCHLOSS KUNSTHAUS WAS LOCATED AT THE FAR WESTERN edge of the Sachsenhausen Forest, a mere fifteen miles from the centre of Germany's bustling capital, Berlin.

For much of its life, the country estate had been owned and occupied by a succession of wealthy German families, all of whom had fallen in love with its Gothic architecture and huge interior spaces. When the Nazis expelled its Jewish owners before the war, the Schloss became a country retreat for the hard-working disciples of the Third Reich and in particular the SS, whose senior ranks retreated to the Sachsenhausen Forest when duty permitted.

By day they enjoyed walking the forest trails and riding the numerous bridal paths that surrounded the exclusive country house. By night, hard drinking, wild debauchery and bizarre rituals took place under its roof. Screams of pain and fear were often heard echoing through the forest. Dark rumours abounded, and the locals avoided the area. Evil spirits had been woken and now lurked in the house and surrounding woods.

After the war, the property fell into decline and lay abandoned for several years. The Jewish owners eventually returned and converted the building into a hotel. For a while it turned a profit, but then its fortunes faded and the estate was eventually sold to a series of less visionary speculators who neglected the estate. Recessions and seasons took their toll. Roofs leaked. Timbers rotted. The lawns and flowerbeds ran wild. A few short years ago, Schloss Kunsthaus was sold at auction for two-point-one million euros. Or thereabouts, the passenger told him.

"Who bought it?" asked the driver. His name was Osman, and he was impressed by the passenger's vast well of knowledge. The man had proved to be an entertaining travel companion. He was well-versed in almost any subject, from politics to religion, the economy, history and culture. Osman, on the other hand, was a lorry driver and possessed only a perfunctory grasp of such things. He knew what he knew, that was it.

The passenger's name was Philip, and he explained that every man had a purpose in life. Osman's was to drive his Volvo FH16 truck from Turkey to Berlin or rather to the Schloss that Philip had told him about.

Osman didn't ask Philip what their cargo was and Philip wasn't saying. The container had been lowered onto the back of his Volvo at the port in Istanbul. Philip, who'd been a passenger on the ship, had supervised the loading. Drugs, Osman assumed, or maybe guns. It wasn't people, he knew that much. That was one cargo he avoided. There had been too many deaths and Osman had no intention of transporting dead kids in the back of his truck. Anything else was fair game.

On their long journey to the north-west, Osman had learned that Philip was not only a smart guy, he was also influential. Their papers had been scrutinised on several occasions, at the Bulgarian and Serbian borders, in Hungary and Slovakia, but not once was their cargo inspected. And Philip had money too, a rucksack stuffed with euros and dollars that he palmed off to several border officials. Osman had been promised part of that stash and the Turkish long-distance driver had every intention of making good on his delivery.

South of Berlin he steered his truck onto the A10 and looped around the city before heading north on the E251. Fifteen minutes later, its lights carving through the mist that blanketed the estate, Osman and Philip finally arrived at the Schloss Kunsthaus. They'd travelled fourteen hundred miles in thirty-eight hours.

Osman was ordered to stay in his cab while the vehicle was unloaded. He drew his privacy curtains around the windscreen and sat in the dark, wondering what it was they were unloading. He thought about checking his phone and then remembered that Philip had politely confiscated it before they'd crossed the Czech border into Germany.

He heard the whine of a forklift. He also thought he heard an animal. A dog perhaps? No, something fiercer. Then he remembered the evil spirits and suddenly Osman wanted to get out of there. As soon as the deal was done he would head for the bright lights of Berlin. These days the German capital was more like a Turkish city. It was just like being at home.

The truck shuddered as the container doors slammed closed. Philip tapped on his window. Osman jumped out of the truck and his erstwhile companion handed him the rucksack and his phone. Osman checked the contents and beamed a smile. They shook hands and Osman climbed into his truck and drove off into the night.

He didn't look back.

PHILIP WATCHED HIM GO. A MOMENT LATER, A DARK MERCEDES saloon followed the truck out onto the main road. Osman would be watched until he reached the Czech border but Philip was unconcerned. He understood people and he knew that Osman would give their organisation no trouble. He was a businessman after all, a simple one to be sure, but a man who knew the value of a good trade. A man who knew when to keep his mouth shut about the remote manor house on the outskirts of Berlin.

With the cargo stored safely below ground, Philip and his associates enjoyed a quiet evening meal in the main dining room. The Schloss had been recently renovated to provide the basics of heat and light, a warm room to sleep, and that was all any of them required. They were soldiers and they were used to hardship.

Another vehicle arrived after midnight, a powerful Audi saloon that parked inside one of the larger outbuildings. The driver escorted his passenger into the main house where cheeks were kissed and heads were bowed. Strong, bitter coffee was brewed and next steps discussed. Afterwards, it was agreed. The time for discussion had passed.

It was time for action.

The cellar was huge and could be accessed from several entry points. The cargo had already been lowered through the huge wooden hatches at the back of the building. Philip and his associates took the stairs that led down from the kitchen.

The basement was like any other country cellar, filled with dusty barrels, discarded furniture and chopped wood. One end of the cellar had been completely cleared and in the empty space, a camera had been set up to face an empty chair. Behind the chair a tarpaulin had been draped between two stone pillars. The businessman stood to one side while more tripod-mounted lights were switched on. One of the associates stood behind the camera. Philip stepped into the light and sat on the empty chair. He was wearing a black turtleneck, a ski mask and dark sunglasses.

"Keep it short," the businessman warned. "No grandstanding."

Philip nodded. "Are we ready?" He saw a thumbs up from behind the camera and cleared his throat. He saw the *record* light blink on and began speaking in heavily-accented English.

"President Coffman, for many years I have been a great admirer of your country, especially your armed forces. Your technical supremacy, your devastating firepower, are without compare. Many innocents have died proving this point. And I have always been impressed by the spirit of the individual American soldier, his loyalty to country and comrade. What is it your soldiers say? *Leave no man behind.* An admirable sentiment, no? However, I fear that this spirit had been betrayed. The United States does, in fact, leave its people behind."

Philip raised a hand and the tarpaulin fell to the ground, revealing a large, vertical steel box. It was roughly seven feet high, square, with the facing panel made of impact-resistant, kevlar-composite safety glass. Behind that glass, bathed in the harsh light of the cameras, its uniform shredded and soaked in blood and vomit, was a monster. Its hands clawed at the lights and its eyes rolled wildly as it screamed and sprayed blood across the thick glass.

"His name is - or *was* - Lance Corporal Hector Nunez of the United States Marine Corps. He was declared dead several weeks ago, by you, during one of the many memorial services held in the wake of the Baghdad incident. As you can see, Corporal Nunez is very much alive. And luckily for me, you left him behind."

Philip raised a fist to his mouth, cleared his throat and continued.

"You will learn of my demands in due course, Madame President, as will the rest of the world. If they are not met, Nunez's body fluids will find their way into the human food chain and when the virus spreads, the Corporal himself will be released somewhere in a major western city. Perhaps it will be in America, or Canada, or maybe Europe. You know what will happen after that - chaos, the collapse of western civilisation, the deaths of billions. *The End of Days.* We are prepared for this. The question is, are you, Madame President?"

Philip vacated the chair and the camera zoomed in on the steel container.

Nunez screamed, spraying vomit across the glass.

The container shook violently.

The red light blinked off.

HAVE YOUR SAY

Did you enjoy *Fortress*?
Would you mind leaving a rating or short review?

Your feedback would be very much appreciated.

END ZONE

THE ROGUE STATE SERIES: BOOK 3

Abandon all fossil fuels or face an unstoppable plague...

In the wake of the Baghdad disaster, President Amy Coffman is battling to get her administration back on track when eco-terrorists threaten to unleash a gruesome contagion across the globe, one that transforms ordinary people into blood-thirsty savages.

Unless the world dials the clock back a hundred years...

Visit Amazon to learn more.

NEVER MISS A NEW RELEASE

To learn more about my writing and filmmaking life, and to receive all the latest book news and updates, please sign up for my occasional newsletter.

www.dcalden.com

ALSO BY DC ALDEN

Invasion: Downfall
Invasion: Uprising
Invasion: Frontline
Invasion: Deliverance
Invasion: Chronicles
Invasion: Redux
The Horse at the Gates
The Angola Deception
Fortress
End Zone
The Rogue State Trilogy
UFO Down

Join the conversation on social media: